DEAD MAN FALLING

DEAD MAN
FALLING

Randall Silvis

CARROLL & GRAF PUBLISHERS, INC.

NEW YORK

Copyright © 1996 by Randall Silvis.

First edition 1996.

Carroll & Graf Publishers, Inc.
260 Fifth Avenue
New York, NY 10001

ISBN 0-7867-0313-X

Library of Congress Cataloging-in-Publication Data is available.

Manufactured in the United States of America.

As always . . . for Rita and Bret and Nathan

DEAD MAN FALLING

O N E

━━━━━━━━━━━━━━

The morning of the twenty-first day. Wet red light on a lavender sky, one long, scorching streak against the horizon, alive and fluid. The light seems drier somehow as it bleeds toward me through the trees, the dust and ash of dawn, an afterglow. And the trees themselves look black as burned skeletons.

Black coffee in a blue metal cup. Twenty-one mornings of black coffee in a blue metal cup, and still no wolverine. If I am to see one today, it will be within the next hour, as the animal returns from its forays through the night, belly full. I've seen it a hundred times in my mind already, the way it will look when I finally spot one, at first just a black shape moving from tree to tree, sniffing at the ground. I will think it a bear cub, and as I reach for the binoculars I will try not to jinx myself with too much hope. Then in magnification I will see the bearish head on the dwarfish body, the dense, coarse fur, the agile, loping stride on oversize paws, the massive savage jaw.

If I fail to spot one within the next hour, before the sun loses its bloody sheen, I will write and read and nap and take care of camp chores until nightfall, when the nocturnal creatures come out to feed again. All my allies of the night. I have decided to give this project another nine days; if I don't spot a wolverine by the end of the month, I'll either move farther north, deeper into Canada, or abandon the project altogether. I would hate to have to give up, but if I do I won't be the first person to have been bested by the "demon of the North."

Not that merely spotting one will be any kind of victory. Even if I manage to locate a wolverine, or better yet a mating pair, will I be able to stay with one long enough to get three hundred minutes of tape, and of sufficient drama that it can be rendered into a half-hour-to-hour-long tale? They are such peripatetic creatures, their movements so unpredictable, it is a matter of pure luck whether I even see one or not.

Especially here. This pine forest is a good hundred miles southeast of their normal territory. And I of all people should realize how little credit should be ascribed to reports of random sightings. I know my chances are minuscule here, yet here I sit, twenty-one mornings of black coffee in a metal cup, three weeks lived close to the needle-matted ground. Sometimes I puzzle myself. I realize, for example, that this is my nature, to always pursue the path of most resistance. But I have no inkling as to why this is my nature. I understand that I like the idea of filming a wolverine outside of his normal range, in terri-tory unfamiliar to both of us, where both man and animal, predator and prey, will be forced to rely on instinct rather than habit. But why do I prefer to have the odds so stacked against me?

I understand also that it is the mystery of the wolverine that keeps me sitting here through the chilly October nights. Like all good mys-teries, this one is difficult to unravel and is heavily laced with fear. Apocrypha abound. Do I feel a kinship with this elusive, maligned creature? Possibly. Do I envy his reputation for ferocity, the unde-served terror he inspires? Unfortunately, probably so. Do I covet his freedom of movement, the nonchalance with which he wanders far and wide? Absolutely.

And so I sit and drink black coffee and wait for the sun to rise above the trees. I listen for a scrape of leaves, a rustle, a nonsuspect-ing crunch of footsteps. In another forty minutes I will light the camp stove and have some breakfast. Then I will sleep awhile. Late this afternoon I will make another thermos of coffee to see me through another night. In the meantime, this final hour of my watch suffuses me with something akin to peace, a fatigue beyond caring, an indif-ference to the world back home and all the ways it lies in wait for me.

It is the wolverine this time that has brought me into the woods. But there is always another reason too, the reason I keep coming back, the reason, despite the discomfort of staying here, I am always reluctant to leave. This reason does not change from project to project, from animal to animal. The reason is one aspect of myself that I truly understand. And the reason is this:

Here in the woods, I never dream of fire.

▬▬▬ Mac Parris climbed out on the gray side of sleep and waded toward his door, or, rather, toward the sound of knocking, the three short raps echoing again, but louder, from the vapors of his dream. By the time he reached his front door he was sufficiently awake to realize how dark the room was, so he switched on the living room light and squinted at the door in the sudden brightness, and now it seemed that the knocking had been a part of his dream and that he had been sleepwalking again. He rubbed his face one more time, pulling at his cheeks. It was then he heard the footsteps on his porch, and a moment later it dawned on him that somebody real had been knocking.

He opened the door just in time to see a young woman heading back down his porch steps. She turned at the sound of the wooden door coming open. Parris pushed open the storm door and put one foot onto the porch. "Oh," she said. "I didn't think you were home."

She was wearing a brown leather jacket and carrying a small brown attaché case. Her hair was long and brown and her eyes were brown and she appeared to be standing in relief against the flat background of sidewalk and street and neighborhood. What startled Parris most was that her hair seemed alive with tiny lights, it sparkled and glistened. Then he realized that a fine snow was falling and melting in her hair and that the drops of moisture reflected the sunset, the blazing red of an April afternoon.

"You'll have to give me a minute," Parris told her. "I just now woke up."

"Oh," she said again. "I didn't mean to wake you, I'm sorry."

"Is it really snowing," he asked, "or am I still dreaming?"

"It's really snowing."

"What time is it?"

She glanced at her wristwatch, a slender black leather band on a thin wrist. "It's five twenty-eight."

"Just two hours ago it was sixty degrees," he said, "and now it's snowing. This is still April twenty-seventh, isn't it?"

"It still is." She smiled and shifted the attaché case to her other hand. "You *are* Mac Parris, aren't you?"

She looked too young to be a federal agent, as well as too guileless. Her smile seemed sincere and almost hopeful, and there was no trace of the feral in it. Even so, he waited, giving her an opportunity to continue with "otherwise known as." But she said nothing more. She stood very straight and made steady eye contact with him. The leather jacket and dark blue skirt—stylish but inexpensive—made him think she might be a sales rep of some kind, except that salespeople these days usually made their pitches via phone and fax lines, and this young woman lacked the nervous aggression of somebody who worked on commission.

"What can I do for you?" he asked.

"My name's Diana Westover. I came to talk to you about this." She balanced her attaché case on one knee and popped it open and took out a folded newspaper. Then she closed the case again and when she came onto the porch to hand the newspaper to Parris he saw that she was taller than he had thought, maybe five six or seven. Her legs were slender but strong and she moved with the natural grace of a woman too preoccupied to be conscious of how she moved.

"Maybe you've seen it already," she said, and held the newspaper out to him. "This piece here." She pointed to a short article on page two slugged *Human Leg Bone Found in Trash*.

A portion of the left leg of an adolescent male Caucasian, Parris read, neatly sawed off at the knee joint and with the muscle and flesh in the initial stages of decomposition, had been found two days earlier in a Dumpster near a playground in the center of town. The limb had sustained a compound fracture, but authorities could not yet speculate as to whether the fracture had preceded dismemberment or was a result of it. The condition of the tissue was consistent with tissue that had previously been frozen.

"Yesterday afternoon part of an arm was found in a landfill about ninety miles from here," she told him.

Parris lowered the paper. So she wasn't a sales rep after all. Her eyes were clear and bright and her gaze was made steady not by hardness but resolve. She smelled of sandalwood. "This is somebody you know?" he asked.

"Oh," she said. "I should have told you. I suspect that they belonged to . . ." She blinked once, a languid, heart-steadying blink. "I think it's my brother."

Parris drew in a slow deep breath and looked past her into his yard. The sunset had painted the opposite side of the street in a wash of pink, and the green of his yard was darkened to a shadow under a powder of snow. Beyond the edge of his porch everything was a watercolor, a Turneresque impression. But here beneath his porch roof the first smirking characters of a Bosch panorama were peeking around the corners. He had the dizzying sense of having only dreamed that he had awakened to answer the door to this young woman.

"I don't understand why you're showing this to me," he said.

"I'm looking for somebody to help me find out if this really is my brother. And if so, who did this to him."

"But why . . ." If this was a dream it was a new kind for him, not like the others, from which he awakened seared from the heat of imagined flames. "Look, I'm a filmmaker," he told her. "What you want is a private investigator."

"And as far as I can tell, there's not a single one living within a fifty-mile radius of here."

"Even so, I don't understand why you came to me."

"I was told I should speak with you."

"Told by whom?"

"Henry Carlyle." Her smile broadened just a bit now, and he thought he detected on her cheeks the delicate suffusion of a blush. "I'm studying piano with him."

Parris chuckled softly and shook his head. "The longer I talk with you, the more confused I become."

"Henry said that you might be available to help me. That you have the right instincts and the right equipment to do the job. He said that you're used to working odd hours, that you enjoy a challenge, and that you don't frighten easily. He also said that you're the only person young and angry and sober enough to get this job done for what little I'm able to pay."

"You and Henry must do a lot of talking. When do you have time for the piano?"

"He thinks very highly of you," she said.

"His opinion is hardly reliable."

"Just because a man has a drinking problem doesn't mean that he's a liar. Some men are more trustworthy when they drink."

"You've had a lot of experience with drinking men?" he asked.

"I've had my share."

So, Parris thought, and with unfocused eyes he regarded a point just above her left ear, her brown hair blurring nicely, softening, filling the frame of his vision. So. Early this morning he had completed the rough cut on his wolverine film and he had intended to deliver the video to Henry Carlyle that evening. During the next two weeks or so, while Henry extemporized a piano sound track for the film, Parris would consider himself on hiatus, at large, on holiday. He would sleep late and watch old movies on TV and read a few books and maybe give a thought or two to his next project. It was a kind of pupal stage for him, this respite before the final edit and then the circus of distribution and promotion. He rarely went about in public during these two weeks, he explored no new territories of the mind or the soul, he lay low, he courted a kind of emotional dormancy in which the past had never happened and the future was worth little more than a passing glance. He had always considered these periods a necessary time of recharging, of gathering the strength to see the current project through to its end and to prepare to tackle another one, another self-imposed purpose to his life, another temporary reason to keep on living.

But now there was a vague, high-pitched whistling in his right ear and his heart was racing. The scent of sandalwood sharpened the air and the snow was pink and an image flashed through his mind of a boy reaching out for him through a curtain of fire. When he looked again at Diana Westover she had not moved but stood there waiting, waiting, neither smiling nor frowning now, her brown eyes steady with resolve but also warm and soft and he knew that one firm no from him and she would say Oh. Oh . . . well . . . in that case thank you for your time, I'm sorry if I dis-

turbed you, and she would walk away to that car parked at the curb, that car he had just now noticed, a Chevette, powder blue, five, maybe six years old, the rusted dent in the front fender not much younger. The car was battered but waxed and clean—a condition, he guessed, equally indicative of the owner.

He could tell her no and she would not argue or make him feel bad about it. She was a sturdy girl, this sister in search of her dismembered brother; not emotionless but practical. She would regroup, consider her problem from another angle, attack it from some other direction. So this one would be easy.

Yet he stood there for what seemed to him a long time, trying to find the proper words of refusal. And in the end he merely turned and stepped back to the door and held it open for her, because it was April after all, and his house was empty, and in just-spring, when the goat-footed balloonman is whistling far and wee, and when a dreamboy has smiled back at you from within a womb of fire, reminding you, among other things, of old tragedies and errors . . . it is physically impossible at a time like that to say no to a girl with snowlights in her hair.

▪ ▪ ▪

The details of Tony Jakowski's life and times, sketchy as they were, had an unsettling effect on Parris, an effect exacerbated by their delivery. Diana Westover was calm and methodical—a cynic might even have called her cold. She sat very straight in the center of his sofa, sipping tea, her knees pressed tightly together, right foot hooked behind her left ankle. She took her Earl Grey straight, without lemon or sugar or cream—just as, by all appearances, she took her life: undiluted.

A few days days earlier Diana had been reading the local newspaper over breakfast when she came across the two-inch article about a human leg bone found in a Dumpster. She paused, lowered her spoon into the cereal bowl, and exhaled slowly, filled with a certitude that the brother she had not heard from in two months was dead. She sat there at the table for a half hour, breathing shallowly, hoping with the force of reason to dissuade herself. But the feeling could not be shaken loose, the knowledge would not be denied. Tony was dead.

She telephoned the state police and identified the leg bone as that of her brother. They were interested and kind and spoke to her at length, but in the end there was no proof that this body part belonged to Tony. There was no proof that Tony was dead. Nobody else had reported anyone by the name of Tony Jakowski missing, and since it was typical for Diana herself not to hear from him for weeks or even months at a time, he could not legitimately be listed as a missing person. Nor could the police check on his whereabouts, because there was no known address for him. Diana could only suggest that he probably lived somewhere between Pittsburgh and Buffalo. So it was impossible for the police to conduct a search. They agreed to keep her advised if other body parts turned up, but they were not encouraging as to an eventual identification.

All of this she had talked about with Henry Carlyle the next evening. Henry had sipped his bourbon in semidarkness and then asked her to play the Berlioz piece for him. Afterward, as she sat with fingertips still poised lightly on the piano keys, she felt the lightest of kisses graze the top of her head. She had not even heard the old man pad up behind her. But he kissed her once and laid a warm but gnarled hand on her shoulder and that was when he said, "I have a friend whom you should meet."

Parris was both amused and puzzled that Henry had thrown him together with Diana. Was the old man attempting a bit of matchmaking, some romantic palliative for the dark aches he sensed inside both Parris and Diana? Or did he truly think that Parris might be of some help to her?

"Well," Parris said to her now, "I have to agree with the police. Two months isn't such a long time to be out of touch with somebody."

"In truth it was more like three years," she answered. "The last time I heard from him directly was two months ago, yes; but he left home not long before his twelfth birthday. It was less than a month after I had . . . after I had moved out of the house myself."

That glitch in her statement drew his attention. She had tried to cover the pause with a sip of tea. "And how old were you at the time?"

"Eighteen. I left the morning after my last day of school."

"And you moved out to go where? Off to college?"

"No," she said. She did not look away as she considered her response. "I moved to Pittsburgh for a while."

"On your own?"

"Yes."

"Because of a job?"

"Not at first, no. But after I'd been there a few months, working as a waitress, I got a better job . . . as a receptionist. For a brokerage firm downtown. I worked there until just last September, when I enrolled in college."

"What are you studying?"

"Architectural design."

He smiled. "You like to build things?"

And she smiled in return. It was not a cold smile, but guarded. The pale imitation of a smile, slightly chilled. So she was not a glacier after all, but more like an ermine using a glacier for camouflage.

"I think it might be interesting, yes," she said. "To look at something real—whether it's a house, an apartment building, a church—and to know that you, in a sense, created it." She seemed slightly embarrassed by her disclosure. "As a filmmaker, I'm sure you know what I mean."

He knew too well. He knew for example that the profession she had chosen represented something more to her than mere career. He knew from the things she avoided telling him about herself, the explanations left unfinished, that her life thus far had not been a creative one, had probably been, from her perspective, the antithesis of creation. And so now she sought redemption. She had turned herself around in her early twenties and had seized on a metaphor that might in the future allow her to sleep more soundly at night, to quiet whatever rumblings disturbed her dreams.

And yes, he knew about the pride of creation from his own experience too. He knew that it could be temporarily fulfilling, that the attention and concentration needed to do the job well could create an aura of significance to the work, could make you think you were doing something that might captivate others as it was captivating you, might make them, too, feel closer to some ancient mystery, some secret to the nature of things. But he also knew how ethereal such an aura was. When the project ended, so would the sense of accomplishment. It would be as if he had done nothing, there was no redemptive power to the past. The real value of the project, of any project, was in how long it distracted you from this knowledge.

And that was why he now had to admit to himself his dissatisfaction with the vacuum of his life, a vacuum he had sought and cultivated and until two minutes ago had believed he enjoyed. But which he now recognized as sterile and useless. Or at best a resting place; an interlude.

It has to do with balance, he heard, the residue of a too-familiar dream.

Hearing that, he felt a sudden heaviness in his chest, a vague anxiety.

"Since you don't want to talk about yourself," he told her, hoping to turn his own attention aside, "tell me about your brother. How does a boy Tony's age provide for himself?"

She took another sip of tea. She considered the rim of her cup. And then she answered softly, "As you might imagine."

"He lived on the streets?"

"He would never tell me much, but yes, that's what I always believed. Occasionally he might mention that he had hooked up with some friends, or that he was staying with some kids he'd met, something like that."

Parris nodded. "But still you kept in touch? Up until two months ago?"

"As much as he would permit." She set the teacup on the coffee table, then leaned slightly forward, hands pressed together in the shallow valley between her knees. "You might say that I raised Tony—until I left home, that is. So there's always been a bond between us. Our mother was never what you would call maternal, especially not after my father died."

"And how old were you when that happened?"

"Two. He drove his car off a bridge one night."

"But then . . . So Tony is your half brother."

"I didn't tell you that?"

He smiled and shook his head no.

"Yes, well . . . Tony's father was just another man in a long succession of . . . companions for our mother."

With each additional fact her ostensible detachment from them became more revealing. A woman determined to build and create was a woman determined to survive, and survival sometimes depended on detachment. Parris had a sense that he was meeting someone familiar.

"Our mother never married Tony's father, though he would live with us, off and on, from before Tony was born until I was eighteen." She picked up her teacup again. "By that time I had found it necessary to leave home."

Parris speculated on the unspoken connection between her last two statements. But he would save further inquiries for later. "And so you moved to Pittsburgh."

"Yes."

"And apparently, with you out of the house, Tony also found it necessary to leave."

"Apparently," she said. In the shadow that flickered across her eyes, Parris finally knew her clinical demeanor for what it was.

"You can't blame yourself for anything that happened to him after that," he said.

She was gazing into her teacup now, staring into the shallow puddle of brown. He watched her as she breathed, as her chest rose and fell, rose and fell. He imagined he could read her thoughts, though they were very much his own. Her guilt was powerful and she was using it now, she had used it to bring her here, she would use it to see her through to whatever waited at the opposite end of now.

It was a negative emotion, true, but Parris knew that there is great power in the negative. He knew that a negative charge is more powerful than a positive charge of equal number because it must work against the grain of hope, the physics of human nature. The danger lies in letting yourself slide too far into the negative, where the tug of hope is so diminished as to be negligible. Then the slide into negativity becomes frictionless, a free fall. There you will find the Richard Specks and Gary Gilmores and Jeffrey Dahmers. So the trick is to work the scale between minus and plus without lingering too long in neutrality, without succumbing to the lure of either blind faith or utter despair. The trick is in drawing energy from the higher numbers without being thrown out to the edges, where energy destroys itself. The trick is to withstand the battering without complaint and to take your strength from it.

Diana Westover was strong and battered and she had steeled herself to absorb even more. She had embarked finally upon a path of creation, but then the half brother she had raised through a life she did not care to talk about was found in pieces, and now the tension between guilt and love and the tension between past and future had temporarily altered her course. Parris could only hope that with his assistance it would not be a permanent derailment.

And he found to his sudden surprise that this was something he actually wanted to do. He could not resurrect Tony or anybody else but maybe he could help keep Diana from being consumed by her own fires of guilt. Maybe *that* would make his nights pass easier.

"So," she said, and set her cup on the table again. She brushed an imaginary something from the palm of each hand. "I'm going to take a semester off and get a job, so I'll be able to pay you in installments, if that's all right. And I'm perfectly willing to sign a contract, if that's the way you work. I don't want to leave any doubt in your mind that I will fulfill my financial obligations, no matter how this eventually works out."

Parris could feel his heart hammering inside his chest, swollen and sore. He warned himself Just stop it, man. She doesn't want your pity and she damn well doesn't need your admiration or anything else you're feeling. And you don't need it either. What you need is to remember that this is what life is, a scratch in the eye, a mouthful of dirt, a song like a bee in your ear. Some dancing, some stumbling, some bloody knees and prayer.

Parris pushed himself to his feet. "I'm going to wash up," he told her. "How about taking some Lean Cuisines out of the freezer and popping them into the microwave. I'll be ready in fifteen minutes or so."

He smiled briefly and then headed for the bathroom. Just as he crossed the threshold he heard a tinkling of piano keys, five high notes of a familiar melody whose name he could not recall. He turned in her direction and was about to ask if she had heard it too, but at that moment she put her face in her hands and doubled over and so he turned away and left her to herself as quietly as he could.

▪ ▪ ▪

It was 1964, the September of changes. A cool, clear night, fragrant with leafsmoke. The moon was high and white and full. Around the two-acre cemetery that had once been part of the Seneca Allegheny Reservation stood a wall made of plywood sheeting, eight feet high. Outside the eastern wall, not far from what had been the entrance to these burial grounds, fifty or so Seneca Indians stood huddled around campfires, their voices low and mournful, chanting, praying, speaking to the spirits of their dead. Not far away, the remains of their bulldozed homes, their longhouse, their community of five hundred and seventy residents, continued to smolder.

Outside the southern wall were maybe a dozen college students from Buffalo, a loose assemblage of strangers who had gathered at the student union earlier that night in response to a poster tacked up outside the door:

> Another Treaty Broken!
> 10,000 Acres Stolen from Seneca Indians
> in Pork-Barrel Scheme
> to Build Kinzua Dam for Wealthy Industrialists
> Another Culture Decimated
> DO YOU CARE?
> Discussion Meeting Here Tonight, 8 PM

The students, after a half hour of disorganized debate, had piled into three cars and drove forty miles south to the Pennsylvania–New York border to have a look at the situation firsthand. What they saw behind the plywood wall immediately silenced their rhetoric and made their vague, amorphous disgruntlement taste sour and small.

Illuminated by the moonlight and the dirty yellow glare of machine lights were numerous open graves, mounds of steaming dirt, wooden caskets stacked lopsidedly on a flatbed truck, some of the caskets cracked and splintered by the backhoes that had excavated them. Once, when a casket was being moved by forklift, as it was being lifted toward the bed of the overloaded truck, the coffin disintegrated. The boards fell to the soft dirt with a sound more like a sigh than the creak of desiccated wood. And at the moment of its collapse there arose from inside the box a puff of dust, saffron-colored in the forklift's light. It hung in the air for just a moment, then drifted to the ground, a handful of fine ash.

One of the college students who observed this incident was reminded of the dusty exhalation of the papery spherical fungi that grow in the woods, and which young children delight in hopping on. And he wondered if he had just witnessed the failed ascent of a tired soul. And, if so, whether that exhausted dust was now consigned to mingle forever with the dirt because of its prolonged captivity, or by virtue of the debilitating disrespect with which it had been treated.

Near one grave site a man in brown coveralls gathered bones from a shattered coffin and shoved them into a black plastic bag. Another man wrote in a pocket-size notebook. Occasionally a flashbulb popped, its brief, sudden light as startling as a gunshot. The air smelled of wood smoke and wet earth and ashes. The machinery growled and rumbled and beeped.

Inside the fence a pair of Seneca shamans were permitted to walk from black hole to black hole, chanting, now and then reaching into their leather pouches, anointing the darkness with a sifting of herbs and prayer. Outside the eastern wall of the fence a hundred or more Senecas huddled around a dozen small campfires, and their soft voices, too, wafted through the darkness in a monotone that was somehow lyrical. Old men and old women passed their hands through the smoke, fanned at it with eagle feathers, spoke to it, murmured and importuned, and rubbed it over their faces.

The college students took turns watching through gaps in the fence. They watched, for the most part, in a silence of uncertainty, their abstract resolve quickly faltering in the face of real machines and real men and real corpses. Some of the students watched for only a few seconds before turning away to find a quiet place to sit, roll a joint, crack open a beer. Others, as if mesmerized, had to be reminded to give somebody else a turn. By midnight all of the students had straggled back to their cars and headed north again. The Indians, the machinery, and the darkness worked on.

Riding in the passenger side of one of the cars was a twenty-one-year-old sophomore, a journalism major, a tall and lanky young man who said almost nothing during the entire ride back to Buffalo. In later years, after he had assumed the name of Mac Parris, he would wear his sandy-blond hair cut short and brushed back hard, the military severity of this look tempered by a thick mustache and eyeglasses with thin metal frames. For now, however, his hair was several inches longer and parted on the side, swept back along the ears, shiny with a dab of hair cream. He wore blue jeans, a khaki shirt, and white Converse basketball shoes, the same basic uniform he would wear in middle age, when, still at six feet one and 174 pounds, he hoped the universality of his wardrobe would help him pass unnoticed through all the stores and streets and cafés he found it necessary to frequent.

But in 1964 he had no thoughts about the virtues of obscurity. Until that night he had remained fairly single-minded in his desire to make a name for himself, to become another Jimmy Breslin or Norman Mailer, another chronicler of all the songs and screams and impossible desires in the tessellated carnival of America. On this September night he had no idea that he would soon abandon the exercise of words altogether, that he would live by images alone, those he courted and those impossible to push aside.

This night he rode back to Buffalo in silence, writing in his head, painting anger and despair in phrases repeated over and over to himself in the rhythm of a prayer while an amorous couple in the rear seat grappled and panted. In the middle of the front seat, between him and the tight-jawed driver, sat his wife, Jennifer, also tall and blond and attractive, also silenced by what they had seen within the plywood enclosure. She held his hand the entire way home, sometimes taking it into her lap, sometimes holding it on the seat between them, but always holding it, her fingers rubbing lightly over his, or gently squeezing, never still.

They were both sophomores that year, friendly and popular. They looked so much alike that were they not always in physical contact with each other when together, holding hands or arm in arm or with one's hand fingering the hair at the back of the other's neck, they could have been mistaken for brother and sister. They were two years older than most of their classmates, having waited, after the birth of their son, Michael, to begin their college educations.

The boy, who was called Mackey by his family, had been born midway through Jennifer's senior year of high school, conceived the previous May in a hotel room in Paris with a view of the Champs-Élysées. His father and mother had been dating since the ninth grade, and since the beginning of their junior year had planned and anticipated the consummation of their romance. A month before the French Club's trip to Paris, Jennifer visited a health clinic in downtown Buffalo and came home with a clock-shaped container of birth control pills.

On their first evening in Paris, the French Club split into two groups, each dining at a different restaurant. Fifteen minutes into the meal, Michael's parents, in different parties, each claimed a sudden attack of nausea and returned to the hotel. Michael's father brought to Jennifer's room a bottle of Dom Pérignon, a box of Godiva chocolates, and a bouquet of daylilies. Jennifer brought a white silk camisole.

The birth control pills didn't work.

▪ ▪ ▪

Parris slipped into his bedroom and closed the door and left Diana alone in the living room, bent over her knees. He did not know if she was crying softly over her lost brother or merely summoning strength for the rest of the ordeal. He knew only that something about her had set his heart to beating fiercely and made his lungs heavy. He felt as if he had run a one-mile sprint, and lost. He sat on the edge of his bed and put his hand to his chest and felt the thudding of his heart, an organ he had thought all but shut down, or at least in a kind of dormancy, immune to such illogical excitement.

A few other things had long ago shut down too, not least of which was whatever organ is responsible for ambition and contention, that desire to compete and excel, to breast the tide of the second law of what Parris called humanynamics, a theoretical science he had invented to explain the perversities of human existence.

Parris had worked harder devising a name for his science than in positing its laws, spending an entire July afternoon last year to come up with a word that evoked both thermodynamics and dianetics. His favorite name had been diuretics, but this choice had eventually been abandoned as too fluid. Humanynamics, on the other hand, was not only hard to pronounce, but it epitomized his favorite assertion from the renowned philosophical team of Gilbert and Sullivan: "If this young man expresses himself in terms too deep for me—Why, what a very singularly deep young man this deep young man must be."

In the universe according to Mac Parris, the organ responsible for a man's desire to grapple with the angel of decay was either the pineal gland or the hypothalamus. The evidence he had accumulated thus far pointed toward the pineal gland as most likely culprit, because even his still managed to function sporadically, to throw off a spark or two of defiance now and then, whereas the mutterings of his hypothalamus had been so effectively suppressed as to be utterly silenced—at least in their ability to overwhelm as he had been overwhelmed by Jennifer, from those earliest stirrings of need in the ninth grade to that first magical night in Paris to that final explosive night in September 1964. There had been no one like her before or since; no desire or satisfaction that went so deep. And until this night he had thought the scars impenetrable, a belief that both plagued and comforted him.

But now here was a young woman in his living room, a young woman he saw as a kind of mirror of himself, her need a reflection of his own, unrecognized until she had revealed it for him. He had cocooned himself so completely all these years that until she came seeking help he had not even realized that he wanted his freedom. Freedom from what he had become.

He sat on the bed and looked at the photo on the nightstand, his wife and son smiling back at him. Consciously he regulated the flow of his breath, slowly in through his nose, slowly out through his mouth. He closed his eyes. Eventually he felt his heart calming, muscles relaxing. He envisioned himself in a gelid darkness and watched his body sinking slowly down, deeper and deeper, until finally invisible.

It was a sometimes calming exercise, this imagined descent into annihilation. He practiced it nightly and not infrequently during the day. On occasion the ooze of blackness would envelop him completely and he would drift off into sleep, only to awaken minutes or hours later grateful for that eradication of time, that por-

tion of consciousness he would not now have to endure. But sometimes the tar pit would explode into flames and he would lie there
wide-eyed with his soul ablaze, smelling of cordite and charred
wood, his hatred so scalding that it threatened to boil over into
random violence, self-destruction, if he did not hold hard and fast
to the image of one particular man and the prospect of someday
subjecting him to his own everlasting pain.

But this time Parris found neither sleep nor fire at the bottom of
his darkness. This time his brain would not stop clamoring. Remember the second law of humanynamics, it told him. A consum-
ing passion can not consume itself but will consume the host if the
host does not actively pursue a more satisfying meal; i.e., a hungry
heart will eat itself if it has nothing else to eat; i.e., if God won't
climb into the ring you will have to jump him in the alley; i.e.,
despite seasonal fluctuations and the scent of a pretty girl a man's
body heat rises in inverse proportion to his willingness to expend
that heat; i.e., if you can't do the mambo don't turn up the music,
cha-cha-cha.

And on and on his mind chattered. He found it easier to let it
run at the mouth than to silence it or try to force it into sensible
thought. Besides, there was always the chance that it might come
up with something practical. It had never happened yet, but he
was still willing to believe in the possibility.

Ten minutes later Parris opened his eyes. He looked at the
photo again. "You see how I've become?" he said. He smiled and
pushed himself to his feet.

He smelled the sandalwood incense even before he reached the
kitchen. But the moment he crossed the threshold into the
kitchen, the incense had to compete with the scent of spaghetti
sauce and the steam of boiling water. Diana Westover stood at the
sink, her back to him as she expertly carved a radish into a rosette.
The kitchen table was set for two.

"What's all this?" he said.

"Oh." She turned at the waist, her face delicately flushed. "You
didn't really want to eat frozen dinners, did you?"

"I hadn't planned to eat mine frozen," he joked. He crossed to
the stove and, using the wooden spoon beside the saucepan, tasted
the spaghetti sauce. "This is delicious. What's in it?"

"Family secret."

"In this house there are no secrets."

"Really?" she asked, and regarded him with upraised eyebrows.

It made him uneasy, and yet strangely pleased, to realize that she had been reading him just as he had read her. What was it Melville had called his reaction upon first reading Hawthorne— "the shock of recognition"?

"I just threw together a few things from your cupboards," she told him. "I hope you don't mind."

"Not as long as you let me help. What else needs done?"

"You can put the pasta in the water now."

As he did so he looked around for the source of the sandalwood aroma. The scent was too strong for his tastes, and, he felt, anomalous here in the kitchen. In the living room he had thought it was Diana Westover's perfume, pleasantly vague, but now he discovered that it emanated from a chunk of incense smoldering on a saucer on his windowsill. Apparently she had been carrying the incense in her pocket or purse.

He stood beside her and placed his fingertips on the edge of the saucer. "Would you mind very much if we doused this for now? I'd much rather smell your secret family recipe."

A flicker of apprehension showed in her eyes. "It's, uh . . . considered bad luck to not let it burn out on its own." Her eyes, brown and bright and momentarily wild, reminded him of the eyes of a cornered animal.

"Then how about if I take it into the living room?"

She smiled. Her relief was obvious. "That would be fine."

In the living room he resisted the urge to rifle the pockets of her leather jacket, which she had draped over the sofa. He knew one thing for certain, however; while Diana Westover might be as wary as an ermine concealed against the white of snow, it was no glacier on which she hid herself, it was an iceberg, a jagged spear of rudderless cold that had broken off from the pack and was drifting rapidly to sea.

▪ ▪ ▪

"So where do we begin?" she asked.

It struck him as a funny question, funny because she knew as well as he did that it had begun the moment he opened his door to her three hours earlier. With instincts and intuition he had fingered her every gesture as closely as a blind sculptor fondles his model's face. All through dinner he had asked questions designed to sound casual, almost indifferent. And as a consequence the insights he gained were not from what she revealed as much as from what she worked so hard to keep hidden.

And now she was scraping the remainder of her secret sauce—Parris thought he could detect just a touch of cinnamon, and, on one occasion, he was certain he had tasted chocolate—into a mason jar. He remained at the table, watching her lovely back as she worked, the slender shoulders and graceful neck.

"A good place to begin is to tell me something more about yourself," he suggested. "I don't think I've ever met anyone as adept at invisibility."

She smiled; his observation pleased her. "It's not me we need to find, is it?"

"If you trusted me enough to hire me, you'll have to trust me enough to let your guard down a little."

She wiped the jar clean, then screwed on the metal cap. As she placed it in the refrigerator she said, "You can heat this up in the microwave if you want, but it's better if you let it simmer for thirty minutes or so."

"I'm not giving up," Parris said.

She turned to him and smiled. "From what I've heard, that's one of your most admirable qualities."

"Maybe my only one."

"Time will tell." She collected the silverware off the table. Parris stacked up the plates and salad bowls and carried them to the sink. "My kitchen, I wash," he said as he turned the hot water on. "No arguments."

"Bully."

She cleaned off the table then and straightened the counter. Afterward she pulled out a kitchen chair and watched as he scrubbed each dish, then rinsed and stacked it in the drying tray. "You like to keep your hands busy, don't you?" she said.

"I'm a Puritan through and through."

"It's how you hide from yourself."

He said nothing until he finished the last dish, pulled the plug from the drain, wiped his hands dry, and turned to her. "Enough fencing," he told her. "We can thrust and parry all night, and it isn't going to find your brother's murderer. But if I'm going to help you do that, I've got to know about you and I've got to know about him. Every fact that you think is relevant, and some you might not."

"Fine," she said. She stood and pushed in her chair. Her smile was deliberate. "But that came dangerously close to a lecture. And I want it known from the start that I will not be lectured to."

"Noted," he said.

The air seemed to buzz between them. She stared at him for another five seconds, her jaw set. She breathed through her nose like a boxer who answers the second-round bell after being knocked flat in the first—not winded but angry.

To Parris, she had changed in the course of a few hours from attractive to painfully beautiful. "Look," he said, "I apologize if I offended you. I'm just trying to get to know you, that's all. But I'm old, and I'm not very smart, and I think I ate too much spaghetti."

Her eyes softened almost immediately. She looked down at the table for a moment. "You did eat too much spaghetti," she told him. Then she looked up. "But that's the only part you got right."

Without explanation she turned and walked away. He heard the front door open and close, her footsteps crunch lightly over the porch and fade away. With his confusion came a sudden pang of loss, not for the job, because he had not accepted the offer just to have something to do, he had plenty to do, damn it, he had a video to deliver and a project to plan and a quarter-century of the past to keep at bay. He had too much to do, goddamm it. Who the hell did she think she was to come and use up his night and then walk off and throw it away without so much as a—

The front door opened again. He went to the kitchen threshold and looked into the living room and there she was standing just inside the door, shaking the snow out of her hair, her coat and purse precisely where she had placed them earlier. In her hand now was a manuscript of some kind, maybe twenty-five pages neatly combbound in a plain white cardboard cover. She crossed the room and handed it to him.

"Everything is in here," she said. "Everything that seemed important anyway. If, after reading it, you still have questions . . . relevant questions . . . then I suppose I'll have to answer them."

He opened the manuscript at random. He had hoped to see her handwriting, whether cramped or expansive, the letters leaning backward or seeming to dive headfirst off the page, but the information was typed instead, perfectly transcribed on a laser printer, probably not a single typo from beginning to end.

"Are you always this efficient?" he asked.

"Only about things that matter."

Then only, he thought, about everything.

She asked, "So when should I get in touch with you again?"

"How's Sunday for you? After church?"

"Why not tomorrow?"

"I have some things to attend to tomorrow."

She nodded. "In that case, Sunday's fine. And since you asked, no, I don't go to church." A smile played at the corners of her mouth. "Though I hardly see why that's relevant."

"We are going to be friends, aren't we?" he teased.

She walked to where her coat lay, picked it up, and pulled it on. "Oh, I think we've crossed that line already." She collected her purse and, holding it under one arm, buttoned her coat. Parris wondered in which direction they had been headed when they crossed that line.

"So then, I'll see you the day after tomorrow," she said, "and we can proceed from there. How early do you get up on Sundays?"

"Earlier than you, I'll bet."

She looked at him only briefly as she turned up her collar. "Thank you for doing this," she said.

"It's way too early to thank me for anything."

She started to turn away but then stopped herself. She regarded the floor. "I'll try to be a . . . friendlier person next time," she told him. "I know it's a problem I have. But I'm working on it."

"There's nothing wrong with being cautious, Diana. It's not the friendliest of worlds out there."

"I've noticed," she said.

He walked her to the door that night and then he walked her to her car. As she climbed in he told her, "I know it's a little late for this, but just so you understand, I have one very important ground rule before we go any further."

She turned the key in the ignition, listened to the engine rumble and then smooth out. Only then did she turn to look up at him.

"No matter what happens," he told her, "nobody is to know that I'm working with you. Not now, not when it's over, not ever."

"What about Henry?"

"You just tell Henry that I've asked you not to discuss it. He'll respect that."

She eyed him critically, half smiling, her head cocked to the side.

"And something else," he said.

"You said one ground rule."

"I just thought of another one. It's called 'Leave no footprints.' "

"Care to explain what that means?"

"There's an approach to camping, hiking, exploring the wilderness that aims to leave nothing behind that wasn't already there, except for one's footprints. Where we're going, we can't leave even those."

"Will we be walking on air, then?"

"It means no credit cards, no personal checks, no paper trail of any kind. We pay with cash and we use phony names. Whoever did this to Tony is an animal, and a lot of animals are very good trackers. We don't want this one finding us before we find it."

"Fine," she said. "I can live with that."

"And one last thing."

She rolled her eyes. "I hope you're not going to make a habit of this."

Parris smiled, and was surprised to do so. It had been a long time since he had engaged in this kind of conversation, this give-and-take of good-natured teasing, this kind of interaction that went beyond the merely practical to hint at the intimate. He liked it and he liked the way it made his brain work, the snap of quick decisions, the tension of wit parrying wit. He liked her and he liked the cool, sweet fragrance of the night.

On the other hand, he did not want to be enjoying himself. Not with her or with anyone else. He did not want to like Diana or to feel good in her presence. God damn the sweet fragrance of the night. His time for enjoying things had been short-lived and was gone. Now was the time for calculated action with as little feeling as possible.

"The last thing is this," he finally told her. "You don't ask personal questions."

"About what?"

"About me."

"Why not?"

"Because that's one of my rules."

"But why is it?"

"Because I don't like personal questions."

"Why don't you?"

"I mean it," he said, and he looked away, fighting the tug of another smile. She was as innocent as a child, as seductive as a memory, as dangerous as a jade-green snake.

"You some kind of desperado?" she asked.

"Let's just say that under certain circumstances I'm not a very nice man."

She nodded. "Well," she said, "under my circumstances, I guess you're exactly what I need."

And as she drove away with her windshield still frosted but for the half moon scraped clean by the faulty wipers, he stood in the street and shivered without his coat and watched until the car turned the corner and then he listened to its engine awhile longer. The light from the streetlamps lay in shallow pools of golden ice on the sidewalk. Silvery flakes of snow seemed to hang weightless in the light or were perhaps buoyed by it, like phosphorescent cosmic algae in an ocean of heavenly black.

Parris could see his breath in the light and his breath was dimly illuminated too. Everywhere he looked he saw a light of some kind—the quaking stars and frozen moon, the flickering ghost-blues of TV sets in windows up and down the street, the globular glares of headlights and porch lights and even the winking wing-lights of a jet high overhead.

It was a pleasant and reassuring spectacle, this illusion of ubiquitous illumination. But Parris watched the vapors of his breath and hugged himself and could not help wandering instead about the rest of the universe, that ninety percent still invisible and unknown, that vast nonluminous glue of dark matter that holds the illusion together and keeps it all from flying apart in scalding pieces like a distant exploding star.

▪ ▪ ▪

On Saturday morning Parris arose early after a restless night. A little before eight he set off on foot toward the center of town, a videotape copy of the rough cut of his wolverine film in hand. He was pleased to find that it was spring again and the only evidence of last night's winter was a damp shine on cars parked along the street and in the particularly clean scent of the air.

Over a breakfast of tea and apple juice and a Glorious Morning muffin at the Whiffenpoof—a bed and breakfast on a back-street bluff overlooking the river valley—he tried to collect his jangled thoughts and to make some decisions.

When he first entered the Whiffenpoof he was glad to see that the table beside the bay window was empty. In fact there was only one other table occupied and this in a dim corner, where a middle-aged man with a bad toupee was whispering to a woman who in good light would probably not look, as she did now, less than half his age.

Parris served himself from the tea trolley and before assuming his seat he had already sized them up. He did this not deliberately but as a kind of reflex left over from a previous life. This couple, he guessed, had checked in late last night and after lingering over breakfast would remain in their room until checkout time. Then, instead of spending the day wandering through the Cathedral Forest at the nearby state park or shopping or seeing a movie, they would get into separate cars and without so much as a peck on the cheek in the parking lot they would drive away.

Although Parris would not have cared to admit as much, one of the reasons he came to the Whiffenpoof for breakfast was to indulge in these observations. More than any other hostelry in the area, this stately turreted and gambreled building encouraged illicit liaisons, much to the resigned dismay of its owner.

As one of the town's many Victorian mansions built in the sudden wealth of America's first oil boom in the mid-1860s, the Whiffenpoof had deteriorated more graciously than the rest, most eventually converted into cramped apartments for college students or into boutiques that changed products and owners every six or seven months. The Whiffenpoof had survived as a family home until eight years ago, when Caroline Paglia lost her husband, a local politician, to a myocardial infarction. At forty-seven she had already lost three sons to ambition—one to Silicon Valley, another to the musty backstages of off-off-Broadway, and the youngest chasing disaster around the globe with a zoom lens pressed to his eye. Faced with the choice of flinging herself toward one of her distant children or discovering some means of self-support, Caroline chose the latter. Unfortunately, given the appeal of a town that has nothing to offer in the way of divertissement but for the sporting and other events at the local college, the Whif-fenpoof—almost, at one point, renamed the House of Seven Gables and converted into a kind of nightclub *délabrement*—was either overbooked or virtually empty. As a way of smoothing over some of the rougher periods, Caroline had opened her house to the public for breakfast. She had a no smoking policy and attracted a much quieter clientele than the local diners and truck stops did—customers who preferred a lighter and healthier bill of fare as well as a more discreet ambiance.

Parris breakfasted here on weekends for three reasons, only one of which he would admit to himself. First, he felt certain that he was addicted to the Glorious Morning muffins—a combination of whole wheat flour, oatmeal, raisins, apples, walnuts, and brown sugar. Had his diet allowed, he would enjoy one every morning. The second reason he came here was to indulge himself in speculations about the other customers, how these private moments dissected with their public lives. The third reason, and the one he would most readily deny, approached his table just as he, with a deliberateness akin to reverence, began to peel the paper from the bottom of his Glorious Morning.

"I hope you know that I make those just for you," Caroline Paglia said. She stood across the table from him, her left shoulder to the wide bay window. The morning sun, just a handspan above the lush hardwood hills of the river valley, painted her auburn hair with a wash of soft rose.

"And I hope you know that I eat them just for you," Parris replied.

"I was hoping that was the case."

Parris smiled warmly and motioned toward the empty chair. "Please, join me."

She sat across from him, her knees bumping his as she slid the chair in. She leaned forward and took his right hand in both of hers. "And how's my favorite auteur this morning?"

She was a tall woman and not quite slender but she moved with a grace and assuredness uncommon in a town like Ormsby. Her mouth was thin but kind and her eyes were emeralds and she reminded him of a girl he had known when he was young and brave and lucky.

And why is it that everybody I like reminds me of somebody I used to know? he wondered.

"Auteur?" he answered, turning his hand so as to give hers a squeeze before drawing away. "The animals do all the work. I'm just a court reporter."

She smiled. It was obvious even to him, who did not care to acknowledge such things, that she believed otherwise. He noticed that the corners of her eyes turned up slightly when she smiled. And he wondered why women were always looking at him like that—as if they knew more about him than he did.

"You're not eating," she said, and nodded at the paper muffin cup he was meticulously folding like a Japanese fan.

"I'd hate to drool in front of you."

"Somehow you don't strike me as a drooler, Mac."

"You might be surprised."

"Try me sometime." It had come out more explicitly than she intended, and both she and Mac looked away, he out the window and she toward the couple in the corner. Half a minute later Parris looked at her again. Now that she wasn't facing him directly, masking her deeper emotions with the glint of playfulness which at that angle seemed always evident in her eyes, he thought he detected a sadness in her gaze, a quality which to his thinking made her even more attractive and complete.

She turned to him, found him studying her, and smiled again. They held each other's gaze for a few moments. Then she said almost shyly, "So what do you make of those two?"

"He's a sales rep," Parris said without looking toward the corner, "and she's—" Now he glanced over his shoulder at the woman. Five seconds later he faced his breakfast plate again and delicately broke the muffin in half. "She's his boss."

"Really?"

"Look at the way they're sitting. She's very erect, not rigid but . . . her posture very clearly says 'Listen, I make the decisions around here, and I will damn well do as I please.' He, on the other hand, looks like a little boy whose mother just caught him with his hand in his pants. And then there's that rug he's wearing. He thinks it actually looks good."

She studied the couple out of the corner of her eye. "Why in the world would she be with him?"

"Why indeed," he said.

Caroline smiled and looked at Mac and found him looking at her. She regarded her place setting. She moved the butter knife an inch to the left, then returned it to its original position. During each of their conversations there came a time when, as happened now, she felt uncomfortable being looked at, or being caught in the act of looking at him. "What if that was us over there?" she asked quictly. "What would our postures suggest to the discerning Mr. Parris?"

Mac held up his spoon and looked at his reflection. "He's a potato farmer," he said. "Thinking of switching over to soybeans. But he's worried that he's too old to adapt. Wishes people would go back to their old eating habits instead."

"And that woman he's with?" Caroline asked with a smile.

"She's heiress to a fortune; her grandfather invented macaroons. She flies helicopters in her spare time and has a fondness for antiques. Statuary, mainly. Rubenesque nudes."

"And what are these two so different people doing here together?"

"Why does everyone come here?" Mac said, and held up half of his broken muffin. "In search of a Glorious Morning."

She blushed and lowered her eyes a moment and then pushed back her chair. "Well, if you refuse to eat in front of me, I suppose I'll just have to leave." When she stood and pushed in the chair, she finally looked at him again. "They're showing *Key Largo* on cable tonight. Know any potato farmers who would care to watch it with me?"

"I can't tonight," he told her.

"I don't have anybody coming in. No reservations. Just the two of us."

"A woman like you should always have reservations about being alone with a man like me."

She nodded and smiled and looked down at her hands. "Some other time, then."

"It's an old movie," he told her. "We'll catch it one of these nights."

Now she raised her eyes to meet his. "I hope so, Mac." He saw the glint come back to her eyes then, and he knew suddenly that it was deliberate, a trick, a pose as self-supporting as that of the woman's in the corner. "In the meantime, enjoy your muffin. It's got soybeans in it."

She crossed to the other customers and chatted with them briefly. Parris waited until she returned to the kitchen to refill their coffeepot, then he laid some money on the table and picked up his muffin and, wishing that he too had a talent for the graceful exit, hurried for the door.

▪ ▪ ▪

It was a clear, bright morning and Parris's head was thick with fog. He walked the six blocks to Henry Carlyle's apartment and all along the way he continued the argument he had been having with himself since the previous night. In truth he had been having this same argument for the past thirty years, every time he met or glimpsed or even thought about a woman to whom he felt attracted, a woman who, with a smile bold or shy, a word, a nod, a touch, insinuated that she shared the attraction and that he would not be out of line to consider acting upon the attraction, essaying the warm ground of mutual need.

The question was always the same: *Why not?* And the answer, too, never varied, it was the same answer as always, the only answer. Because of Jennifer, he told himself. And then the argument would begin anew. Only the numbers changed.

Jennifer is gone, Parris.

But not forgotten, never forgotten. Impossible to forget.

It's been more than thirty years, man. When are you going to stop being such a masochist?

When I'm twenty-one again and carrying little Mac on my shoulders.

You like depressing yourself this way, don't you? You enjoy playing the role of the martyr. The reluctant survivor.

Fuck you.

That's the only person you fuck.

And the only one I ever will.

What's wrong with Caroline?

Not a thing. Not a goddamn thing.

She's very interested.

De gustibus non est disputandum.

And whose questionable taste are you referring to—yours or hers?

It would have been easier for Parris to question Caroline's taste if in every other particular she didn't conduct herself so tastefully. In business matters she was precise but never penurious. Socially she was the perfect hostess, capable of making everyone feel pampered and well attended without ever becoming harried herself. And in appearance . . .

In appearance Caroline reminded him of a gracefully aging Jennifer. There was no getting around that fact, no denying it to himself, not if he wished to maintain any integrity at all. And integrity, he reminded himself ad nauseam, was the only thing of importance he had left.

So there it was. He liked being around Caroline because Caroline reminded him of Jennifer. Dozens of women since Jennifer had reminded him of Jennifer. Any woman he looked at with any affection or desire brought the image of Jennifer to mind, the way she had been on that last day, sitting at the piano. "Ole buttermilk sky," she had been singing, her last words, just before Mackey said "Mommy, look," and came walking out of Spangler's bedroom, and Jennifer turned to look, and Spangler beside Parris in the kitchen muttered, "Jesus Christ . . ."

Stop it! Parris told himself. A familiar exclamation by now, repeated thousands of times over the years.

This time he looked up and blinked and when the grayness lifted from his eyes he saw that he was standing at the Laundromat. Above it, on the second floor, was Henry Carlyle's apartment. Parris had no recollection of the five side streets he had crossed to get there. But he was used to this phenomenon by now, of losing time and distance to the deep gray embrace of Mnemosyne. By his calculation he had lost a quarter of his life to her. His truest and only lover.

And now he needed a few moments to pull his thoughts together again before going up the dark staircase to Henry's dim apartment. He went into the Laundromat and sat in a green plastic chair facing a washer full of spinning clothes. He did not even notice the young woman sitting two chairs down until the washer shut off a few minutes later and she stood to pull the limp and twisted clothing into a cart.

He tried not to stare at her, but she was young and nicely built and he was still dopey with nostalgia and he could not convince his eyes to look away. Finally he forced himself to lean forward, elbows on his knees, head bowed. He stared at the dirty linoleum.

"Are you all right?" the young woman asked.

He looked up at her. "Excuse me?"

"You just . . . I don't know, you looked like . . . you might be sick or something."

He nodded and smiled weakly. "Nausea," he told her. "It comes and goes."

"It must be the flu."

He smiled. "I've had it a long time."

"Then it's probably an ulcer," she told him. "You should have it checked."

He thanked her with a smile. She pushed her cart to the line of dryers and started tossing the clothes into one of them. "My dad has an ulcer," she told him. "His doctor wants to operate, but he won't let him."

Parris nodded again. It was time to leave.

"What kind of work do you do?" she asked, and flashed him a long smile, the standard opening, the come-hither question.

Parris pushed himself to his feet. "I'm afraid I'm late for an appointment," he told her. "Take care." And he headed for the doorway, the sunshine, someplace that did not smell of laundry detergent. Even the narrow stairway leading to Henry's place, redolent of spilled beer and cat shit, would be a welcome change.

Am I wearing a sign? he wondered as he mounted the worn steps. Is it tattooed on my forehead: *Pathetic single male in need of mothering?* Why was it that women took such an interest in him? Could they smell his celibacy? Did all that unspent sperm send out a radio wave of some kind, a Morse code of invitation?

He laughed softly to himself and shook his head. And then he answered, "It's not funny, Parris." And to stop the argument from beginning again, he rapped loudly on Henry's door.

▪ ▪ ▪

Henry Carlyle moved with the unintentional stealth of a blind man. And indeed, people who met Henry for the first time often asumed that he was blind, a judgment engendered by the economy of his movements as well as the gray tint of his eyeglasses. Somewhere between sixty-five and eighty years old—Parris had never inquired—Henry had lived in Ormsby since a relatively young man, having come from Los Angeles. Among his battered baggage was a colorful if sketchy history, a plethora of secrets, and a quiet addiction to alcohol.

Every time Parris visited Henry's dim apartment, every time he watched the deliberateness with which Henry mixed a couple of eleven A.M. bourbon and waters, Parris could not help but wonder about all the stories he had heard. About how Henry, the stories went, had been a rising star on the West Coast music scene in the fifties and sixties, resident composer not only for the Los Angeles Philharmonic but also with several movie sound tracks to his credit. Only, unfortunately, to fall in with a dangerous crowd, with Steve McQueen and William Burroughs and John Huston. With whom there were excursions into Mexico, shopping trips for peyote and mushrooms, the wild parties, the sex and booze and yachts and starlets and . . . and, finally, the end of it all, the beginning of the downward slide into Ormsby, the love affair, the broken heart.

Parris had heard that the woman was Kim Novak, but he had also heard that it was Howard Hughes's teenage paramour, Terry Moore. Even Montgomery Clift had been mentioned. Whomever she or he was, Henry never recovered. It was an old story and certainly not limited to Henry Carlyle and it was one of the reasons Parris felt somehow close to the man—another poor sap done in by the heart; clubbed, as it were, into submission.

There was also something strangely feral about Henry Carlyle, and it was that quality—not in the sense of being ferocious or brutal, but in his apparent reversion from domesticity to a primal, elemental state of being—that allowed Parris to believe that

Henry's involvement in the films was not a compromise. Parris's wildlife films were distinctive for their lack of narration, the absence of human voice. Parris spoke only through the camera, through images rather than words. On occasion he would be forced to rely on a title card to indicate time or place, and in editing he would cut and splice so as to fashion a tighter three-act structure of introduction, conflict, and resolution, then layer in ambient sounds of wind, stream, birdsong, the voices and movement noises of his subjects, but the story was always told by the animals themselves. It was after all their story, condensed but nonetheless truthful. And it was a story that more often than not ended in death.

The only concession Parris was willing to make to a less austere form of storytelling was the inclusion of a musical sound track. And here was where Henry Carlyle's instinctual methods came into play. He would take whatever videotape Parris delivered to him, he would watch it in silence and in solitude, as many times as necessary—though the process never required more than two weeks. When he felt ready, Carlyle would place his bourbon and water on a coaster on the piano, turn on the tape recorder setting on an end table, and begin to play. He did not tinker with melody lines, repeating and polishing, searching for musical themes. He closed his eyes and watched the videotape replaying in his head and like those masters of the spontaneous who used to bring silent films to life with their in-theater organ accompaniments, he would submerge himself in images remembered and imagined and in the music itself. He would follow the music wherever it led, sometimes along a simple and straightforward path, sometimes convoluted, through underbrush and tangled growth, through thick, sticky cobwebs of memory and into sunless forests of damp and fecund pain, playing the hunger, the loneliness, the drive for dominance and companionship and sex, playing the sadness of wind and the cool, distant wistfulness of the moon, playing sometimes for an hour without pause, two hours, the old man's life-callused fingers as red as blood, joints throbbing, the music rising and falling in emotion all along the way, soaring into hope, plummeting to despair.

When finished, Henry would shut off the tape recorder and reach for his drink. The ice would be melted by now, the bourbon warm. Henry would drink long and slowly. In time he would get up from the bench, hit rewind on the tape recorder, cross to the telephone, and call Mac Parris. "It's finished," Henry would say. Parris would pick up the tape that same day, listen to the extemporaneous composition with something akin to awe, and then bit by bit, bar by bar, work it into his film.

Parris had never seen Henry Carlyle dressed in anything but a shiny black suit and white shirt grayed by time and a skinny black tie, the very picture of attentuated gentility, but the music revealed the old man in a far clearer light, the youthful spirit within, enamored of both the light and the dark, impetuous, full of longing, and wild, wild, impossible to restrain. It was only in the music that Parris saw him like this, but it was sufficient to an understanding, an empathy deeper than words.

These recordings, and then the film soundtracks, were the only records of Henry's creations. The original tapes, along with copies of Parris's films, were preserved in a large air-conditioned closet in Parris's house. Henry claimed to have no interest in them himself. He seemed, in fact, disdainful of what he had created, so much so that he would not even look at one of Parris's finished films. The act of creation he could not resist, but the thing created was, to Henry's way of thinking, repugnant.

Why? Parris could only speculate. Perhaps for the same reason he refused to use a voice in any of his films. The same reason he would not make love to another woman. The same reason he dreamed of fire.

Because he was striving for a purity he knew he did not deserve. And, no matter the effort, could never attain.

Now the old man came slowly across the room and handed Parris a bourbon and water. Under normal circumstances Parris refused to allow himself a drink until five or six in the evening, when the day's work was completed. At those times when he most wanted a drink he would deny himself altogether—just another desire to be subjugated.

But circumstances were never normal in Henry Carlyle's apartment. There was Henry's funereal wardrobe, the stale, dry air, the single green-shaded light always burning atop the piano. It could be eleven P.M. as easily as eleven A.M. In fact it was always the same hour in Henry's apartment, the hour of twilight. Parris supposed that time must speed up or play in reverse when Henry was at the piano, and he would have liked to sit and watch it happen, but Henry never played for anybody these days. Not even when he was teaching did he touch a key. As far as Parris could tell, the old man avoided the instrument except when composing for one of Parris's films. At those times the music could be heard on the street, and people sometimes stood outside the Laundromat door, smiling, heads cocked, while their laundry sloshed and tumbled in the noisy machines. Most times, though, the piano stood like a coffin, dimly lit, untouched.

"I had a visit from an attractive young lady last night," Parris said after a sip of his bourbon.

Henry settled into a thickly padded chair near the darkened window. "Count yourself a lucky man."

"One of your students, coincidentally."

The old man sipped delicately, smiling to his drink.

"I can't help but wonder why you sent her to me," Parris said.

"If you can't help it, you can't be blamed for it."

"Henry."

"You're too young to adopt my lifestyle. You need to get out more."

"I get out all the time."

"Among people."

"I see no reason for that. Besides, look who's talking."

"Appearances can be deceiving," the old man said. "What you don't know is that I'm a lycanthrope by night. I prowl the streets for fresh blood."

"I see you more as a vampire. Black velvet cape, Romanian accent, a fetish for virgins . . ."

"That's how I spend my weekends."

Parris smiled. The bourbon was as warm as friendship in his throat and belly. It was a friendship he could have succumbed to easily, surrendered to with his morning coffee the way Henry did, if only his balance of anger and grief were, like Henry's, tipped a bit further toward the cooler emotion.

"In any case," Parris said, "your timing is impeccable. It just so happens that I'll be free for a while."

"I have a metronome for a heart."

"Somehow I doubt that." Parris swirled the ice in his drink, watched the reflected green light dance atop the liquid. "So what can you tell me about her?"

"She doesn't play as well as you. Blame it on the teacher."

At this, Parris flinched. His teacher had been his wife, Jennifer. From their first date until their last day together. During that time everything of any importance he had learned about himself or the world had been taught to him, a gift from Jennifer.

"What do you know about her family?" Parris asked.

"We don't talk about family. We talk about hand positions and chord signatures and matters of technique."

"She must have confided in you about her brother."

"She asked my advice concerning private investigators."

"Your shady past, no doubt."

"Not to mention my shady present. So . . . are you going to come to her rescue?"

"Well, my lance is a bit rusty—"

"No need to get phallic, Mac. You'll make me nostalgic."

Parris chuckled softly. "I guess it won't hurt to ask a few questions, snoop around a bit. Though I really don't see how I'll be able to find out anything the police can't find out quicker."

"Your biggest asset is that your mind doesn't work like a police mind. You're more instinctual. You won't let yourself be swayed by reality."

"Is that supposed to be a compliment?"

"Will you keep me apprised of how things are going?"

"If I don't, I'm sure Miss Westover will. Don't tell me you've taken a personal interest in her."

"Let's just say that she reminds me of somebody I used to know."

"It's going around."

"Would you like another drink?"

"I would love another drink. And that's why I'd better go now."

Parris set his empty glass on the end table and stood. His body felt warm and somehow lighter. The room itself seemed better illuminated now, and he could make out certain details not apparent earlier. The faded floral wallpaper, slender vines of tiny roses twisting to the ceiling. The dried flowers in a funnel-shaped brass holder mounted on the wall.

It's simply a matter of getting accustomed to the dark, he told himself. Henry must have the eyes of a cat by now.

"I'll do my best for the wolverines," Henry told him.

"I'm sure you will."

"What kind of music do you suppose a wolverine would like?"

"You'll know it when you hear it," Parris said.

T W O

——————————

Another morning, and this one brings the heaviness. The recognition of defeat. Long past first light I lie curled in my sleeping bag, long after my black-domed roof has lightened to gray. Jays chatter, squirrels and chipmunks skitter over the ground and across branches, pinecones drop to the earth, crows scold the morning. And I lie here thinking it is time to move on, farther north maybe. There are no wolverines here, not in these woods. I should postpone this project until the snows come, when a wolverine would be easier to track. Or choose a less elusive animal. Choose another livelihood. Another life.

It must be at least seven o'clock before I drag myself out of the sleeping bag. The fecund scent of forest dampness is already lifting, rising with the mist, giving way to a drier fragrance. The ash of last night's campfire. The ash of ambition.

And the first thing I see when I unzip the tent flap and poke my head outside is a black frown in a graceful glide across the distant sky. A turkey vulture, maybe a quarter mile away through the trees. Something is dead somewhere. It's not a startling revelation, because something is always dead somewhere, something is always dying. Yet the sight of that bird engaged in its slow survey of the skies gives me a vague kind of hope, because just like me it is north of its normal range here. And instead of crawling back inside the tent to roll and pack my sleeping bag and call it quits, I stir the ashes with a stick, I find an ember, lay on some dead twigs, coax up another fire, and stumble down to the stream to rinse out my coffeepot.

I have always liked the turkey vulture. Of the family Cathartidae, *from the Greek* cathartes, *"a cleanser." The earth's sanitation engineer.*

There are certainly more attractive birds than this ungainly buffoon with its boiled red head, the crooked beak, and almost sloppy-looking six-foot wings. It is not sleek and trim like the redtailed hawk, not as elegant as the eagle nor as aerodynamic as the bullet-shaped falcon. But it's a necessary bird nonetheless, and maligned for the very fact that it does its job so well. The trash man of the natural world, devourer of refuse, gourmand of what the rest of us would prefer to ignore.

I watch the solitary bird while I wait for the coffee to boil, and by the time I pour my first cup, there are two birds in the distant sky, cutting interlocking spirals on the coral blue. I wonder if one has been attracted by the other, by the buzzard equivalent to loyalty and love, or if they are strangers drawn to the same spot by their keen sense of smell and by what they see below with those scavenging eyes, those eyes that occupy more skull space than do their brains.

I watch awhile longer, a second cup of coffee, a handful of Fig Newtons for my breakfast. "Till the air is dark with pinions," Longfellow said in his Song of Hiawatha, *describing the way vultures will congregate over a sizable meal. But only these two come, only these two tourists. Must be a raccoon or skunk or possum out there, I tell myself. A small carcass rotting in the wild.*

Whatever the source, if sufficient to attract this small audience of buzzards . . . I dash the last of the coffee into the fire, watch the tiny geyser of steam. It's worth a look, I tell myself. Or would you rather just sit here all day and feel sorry for yourself?

Then into the tent for notebook and pencil, 35mm Nikon, binoculars. I gaze long and hard at the Sonycam; it weighs forty pounds; do I really want to lug it around on what will probably be a wild-goose chase? On the other hand, do I want to miss what might be my only opportunity?

I shoulder the little beast and head off into the woods.

Just for fun, I try for a while to follow my nose to the carcass, but it's an exercise in futility. I can smell the needles and leaves I kick up, I smell the leaf mold and the rotting bark, I smell the coolness of a dew-studded cobweb hanging empty in the shade, I smell the warmth of exertion beginning to rise off my own body. But as for that carcass out there somewhere, I am ill equipped to sniff it out. Every hundred yards or so I have to search for a break in the canopy and relocate myself in relation to the vultures.

It's suspected that in addition to their acute sense of sight and smell, the birds are drawn to carrion by the buzzing of insects. I cock my head to listen, but all external noises are drowned out by the thrumming of blood in my ears. How limited I am in comparison to those birds. None of my senses is as sharp as those of the world's scavengers, the feathered and furred garbage cans of the earth and sky.

Is there a continent on the planet where the buzzard or his equivalent is not found? Wherever there is death there is a carrion eater.

I hike quickly through the woods, already sweating, trying to make as little noise as possible but churning up leaves all the same, stirring up the thick scent of humus, mother earth's funky perfume. I am vaguely aroused by it all—an adolescent on his way to a date: Will she or won't she? Through shafts of dusty sunlight, into and out of deep pools of cooling shade, the pine bark red, the pine bark black. Light and dark, acceptance and rejection, desire and repulsion, fire and ice, life and death. The balance is everywhere, as ubiquitous as the birds.

Thank goodness we humans do not see as keenly as vultures. Do not smell as acutely as jackals and dingoes and hyenas. Thank goodness we cannot hear every death yap or feel every life flickering out. Thank goodness we have been blessed with the ability to turn our senses away from all this to concentrate instead on a patch of scalded blue glimpsed through the needles, the way the branches lay black against the sky, the flutter of sunlight, the trill of a wood sparrow.

Everything dies. Muscles rot and cartilage disintegrates and bones bleach and fall apart. Not that there is any comfort in this knowledge that the same end comes to us all, some sooner, some later. There is only resentment over having to stand by and watch the carnage transpire.

And then . . . a quick rustling of dry needles, the scrape of something being dragged across the ground. I lean against a thick-trunked tree, become still, focus my limited senses. Forty yards to the west, cutting across my intended path—something moving. A low-slung shadow the size of a bear cub. And in its mouth, forelegs dragging—I lift the binoculars to my eyes—the head and torso of a spotted fawn. There is nothing left of the fawn from the rib cage back. Downed by a wolf, no doubt. Half eaten, the remainder buried for later. Only to be dug up by the resourceful wolverine. Who is now hightailing it to the safety of her den, bringing home the bacon.

The hair on my arms and neck is standing up through the sweat. I can't help myself, I'm tingling. How I love this rush of exhilaration.

I test the wind; it's in my favor. The wolverine is heading into the breeze. I let her get so far ahead that she becomes a mere silhouette strobing in and out of the shattered light. Even so, her scent trails thick and foul behind her, as staggering as a skunk's. I hit the power switch on the Sony, finger the zoom, narrow in. I'm wasting expensive film, I know, but I don't care, I will do whatever it takes. A morsel here, a morsel there. I can be as relentless as a buzzard.

══════ Chronicled in Diana's manuscript were eighteen months of telephone conversations and correspondence from her brother. She had not begun keeping track of their communication, she explained, until a phone call late one summer's night raised the gooseflesh on her arms. It became the first call transcribed in her journal, and it marked the onset of a suspicion that her dissembling brother was doomed:

"So how's things in Pittsburgh these days?" he had asked.

"Come see for yourself, why don't you?"

"As a matter of fact, I was in Pittsburgh not too long ago."

"You were? My God, what . . . why didn't you let me know?"

"I was down on the southside. Across the river from you."

"Tony . . . ?"

"I even took a little cruise past your apartment. Looks like a nice building. Nice neighborhood anyway."

"What were you doing in Pittsburgh?"

"Just riding around with some friends."

"What friends?"

"Just friends, okay? Don't ask me things like that."

"Tony, you were so close! Why didn't you stop? What would it have hurt to just let me see you for a minute? After all this time . . ."

"You probably wouldn't have recognized me anymore. Or wanted to."

"What's that supposed to mean?"

"Look, I . . . I don't know if I'll be calling you again."

"Don't even say that."

"I'm into some things now that you wouldn't even want to know about."

"It doesn't matter what—"

"I don't even want to know about them myself. I don't even like to think about them."

"If it's that bad, then maybe you should just stop. You can come live with me, you know that. It doesn't matter what—"

"Sis, don't. Let's not get into this again, okay? You just don't understand."

"How can I when you won't tell me anything?"

"It's because I love you that I won't tell you anything."

"And I love you too."

"I know. In fact . . . do you realize that you're the only person in the entire world who has ever really loved me?"

"Tony, that's not true."

"Sure it is. And that's okay. Well, I guess I don't mean it's okay, I mean I've accepted it as the truth. The way life is for me."

"Stop it, please."

"I hate it that you cry every time I call. Why do you have to do that?"

"Why do you think?"

"Okay, I know. And I wish I could be different, I do. I've tried. But lately I've, I don't know, I guess I've just come to terms with the fact that this is the way it's going to be for me. We work different sides of the river, that's the way it is. You work the day shift, I work the night. You live on the fifth floor, I live in the gutter."

"Tony . . ."

"What's that song Mom used to sing all the time? 'Que Sera, Sera'?"

"You tell me right now where you're living, Tony. I mean it. No more fooling around. We're not children anymore."

"You have a good life, sweetie. Do it for both of us."

"Tony."

"I love you forever."

"Tony!"

And he hung up.

It was the last time she spoke to him. Contrary to his declaration, there were more phone calls, but only during her working hours—short messages left on her answering machine. They were sometimes manic, his voice sounding giddy with optimism, alcohol, or drugs. Sometimes black with despair. Most times he telephoned with a memory: "Hey, you remember that time you and your boyfriend picked me up hitchhiking out on the road to Presque Isle? What was his name anyway—Jack somebody, wasn't it? Big, beefy guy. Nice though. I mean hey, any guy who'd spend his date time driving a hundred miles to look for his date's little brother . . . You should have married that guy, you know that? Jesus Christ, Dynie. Why the hell didn't you marry him?"

There were postcards and letters too. A few with Pittsburgh postmarks. The last two, however, had been sent from New York. The next to the last was a postcard from Jamestown, just across the Pennsylvania line: "News flash! Little Tony has a girlfriend! Can you believe it? She's a long tall drink of water, just like her honey. We fit together like a couple of praying mantises. She even got me a job where she works—low wages, long hours, and all the books we can eat. Told her all about you, sis. She wants to meet you. Who knows? Am I turning respectable, or what? Time will tell. Love you forever. T."

It was the happiest message in a long time, a communication of hope. As if he had proven something to himself—a capacity for love, maybe; an ability to engender love in another. The very implication of renewal was enough to warm Diana's soul. For three months. Until the final postcard arrived, this one of the Panama Rocks in southwestern New York; it had been mailed from Bemus Point, a tiny resort town on Lake Chautauqua: "Ever seen these rocks, sis? Ancient and mysterious. With caves and crevices the sun never reaches. I feel right at home here. The first time ever. Makes me wish I could hole up in the Devil's Den and never come out. Turn into granite myself. Ironic, huh? Or maybe not. Maybe just destiny. I mean, what else would you expect from dirt? Love you forever. T."

And now, two months after the arrival of the last postcard, he was dead. So far, a leg bone and the upper portion of an arm had been found in different places in northcentral Pennsylvania. Neither had been positively identified as belonging to Tony, but Diana had no doubts. She knew in her heart that her brother had been murdered. And Mac Parris suspected that she was right.

So now they were driving through the sun-dappled chill of a Sunday morning, in search of a beginning to the puzzle of Tony's life, a place to start. They rode in Mac's red Jeep, the faded canvas top fluttering. The seats were not as comfortable as those of his Ford F250, but the truck, with its aluminum bed cap sealed and outfitted for camping, was reserved for filmmaking trips. In the camper he had constructed shelves and a short wall of cabinets to secure not only his camping gear but all the filmmaking equipment he would need for a prolonged shoot. There was even a foam-lined compartment for his battery-operated computer, with which, late at night in his tent, he could do a rough edit of the day's film. When in the field the camper became his office, his kitchen, and his studio. On rare occasion, when he arrived too late or tired to pitch a tent, it was also a snug little bedroom.

He also owned a Cessna 172, a single-engine highwing he used for more distant shoots, for flying into remote areas. He used it mainly for scouting and could equip it to land on skids, floats, or wheels, whatever the situation called for. On a few occasions, such as when chasing the Arctic caribou herd across Alaska's Brooks Range, he had rigged up a camera on the wing strut and operated it by remote control for aerial shots—fifty thousand caribou racing like one massive animal over the tundra, one gargantuan throbbing dust-raising mosquito-feeding rippling muscle of life.

The Cessna was also his favorite nonprescription drug. He used it in lieu of Thorazine, instead of Valium or Lithium. He used it on those afternoons when the shadows grew too long and there seemed to be somebody behind every shadow, somebody watching his every move, preparing to close in on him—afternoons when he all but trembled with paranoia, taut with anticipation of that tap on his shoulder, that knock at his door.

And he used the Cessna on those mornings when he awoke with the scent of smoke in his nostrils, smoke burning his lungs, inflaming his eyes. He used it to hold on to life a little longer, to keep from causing just yet the damage he knew he would someday cause.

The Cessna was housed at the local airport, a private low-budget operation with an airstrip too short for any craft larger than a ten-passenger commuter. The plane had cost him thirty thousand dollars used and the pickup truck another twenty. His filmmaking equipment cost as much as the truck and he was mortgaged to the hilt. Only in the past couple of years had the combined royalties from his nine films begun to outstrip his interest payments. But he was a good credit risk and he regularly received preapproved credit cards in the mail with the name Mac Parris embossed on them in gold letters, and he no longer had to think twice when introducing himself as Mac Parris and sometimes when he dreamed he saw Mac Parris in the background curiously watching that desperate firelit man he had been before the identities separated.

The presence of Diana Westover on his doorstep last Friday made him want to take to the air again on Sunday morning. But he had promised her they would get started today and he was a man of his word whether he liked it or not. It was a two-hour drive to Jamestown and they would need the mobility of a ground vehicle after they arrived.

Still, he would have much preferred flying into Jamestown and missing all this lovely countryside. It was familiar territory to Mac Parris. He knew the area too well—north to Buffalo, and beyond to misery. Once past Kane, Pennsylvania, every tree and road sign seemed to spark another painful memory. He did not like being here. His palms were damp on the steering wheel, his hands clenched tight.

Diana did not notice. She gazed out the side window or stared at the horizon through the bug-spotted windshield. Every fifteen minutes or so she would look down at the 3-by-5 photo in her lap. It was a faded Polaroid of a tall, thin young man, a man not yet twenty, leaning against the wide, curved fender of a 1979 Chevy Monte Carlo. He was dressed in khaki trousers and a white shirt with the sleeves rolled above the elbows, and the Marine Corps cap pulled low over his forehead cast his dark eyes in shadow. The photo's colors had paled and yellowed over time, softening all definition, but the angularity of the subject's face was still discernible, the aquiline nose and chin, the thin-lipped smile that could appear either melancholy or wolfish, depending on how one chose to regard it.

It was a photo of Tony's father and the closest thing to a likeness of the adolescent Tony that Diana could come up with. She also had a photo of Tony as a boy of nine, a gangly stem in swim trunks, grinning and pointing an air rifle at the camera. Diana herself had taken that photo. But she considered this photograph—and Mac agreed—misleading of the teenager Tony had apparently become. If anybody at the hotel had seen Tony, fourteen going on forty, the memory of him was more likely to be sparked by the older photo than by the more recent one.

"Pretty country up here," Mac said for no reason but that they had been riding in silence too long. And it was pretty country, the lush, rounded hills and deep valleys, the myriad of green. Unfortunately the word beauty had long ago assumed a connotation of irony for him, so that he could not experience a moment of appreciation for the beauty of nature without being reminded of the brutality that lay just beneath the surface.

"A little to the east is the Kinzua Dam," he told her. "Ever see it?"

She shook her head no. "There's a guy where I used to work who's mentioned it though. He goes fishing up here or something."

Mac nodded. "Walleye and pike probably. Some of the pike up around the dam can grow to be monsters."

It all seemed so artificial to him, this talk of attractions and icthyology. They were not tourists, after all.

"I wish I knew of a better way to get this started," he told her. "Other than just walking around and showing that photo to everybody."

"That's how they do it in the movies," she said with a small smile.

"I guess what bothers me is that I don't feel very useful. I can't think of anything I might do for you that you can't do just as well yourself."

"I'm counting on your eye for detail."

"You're counting on a lot," he told her.

In Jamestown he left her out in front of the Holiday Inn while he looked for a parking garage. He found one two blocks away, and by the time he walked back she had already taken the bags upstairs and was waiting for him in the lobby.

"We're all checked in," she told him, and held out the key. "Room 407."

He looked at the key briefly but did not take it from her. "I'll see if I can get a room on the same floor."

She put a hand on his arm as he turned toward the front desk. "Let's not be childish about this," she said.

He glanced at the desk clerk, a young black woman who smiled at him before looking away. He spoke to Diana in a soft but firm voice. "I just think it's best if we avoid any complications right from the start."

"So do I. And the way to do that is to let me pay for everything up front. I brought cash, just as you suggested, but since I'm not a rich woman I need to keep our expenses to a minimum. So let's not be extravagant here, okay? We need two beds, not two rooms. And I'll assume that you know how to keep your hands to yourself."

It wasn't his hands he was worried about. But he smiled nonetheless. "What are our names?"

"Mr. and Mrs. Jacques Holmes."

"Jacques?" he said.

"For Jacques Clouseau. The Holmes is for Sherlock."

"You have a strange sense of humor," he told her. "Am I the Mr. at least?"

"We'll flip a coin later," she said. "So . . . do you need to go to the room first, or can we get started?"

"Why don't we start with the desk clerk?"

"I talked to her already. No luck."

"Then let's hit the street," he said.

■ ■ ■

Jamestown was gray and faceless, all broken concrete and dusty glass. Maybe back in the days when it had been first named for King James it had had a personality, but no longer. Or maybe it had had some other namesake, a founding father, a wealthy industrialist. Maybe it had been named after the country's first Jamestown, where according to the history books Pocahontas had saved the brave Captain John Smith with a love that transcended and united opposing cultures, and where Pocahontas and John Rolfe later married to become ancestors to some fifty thousand proud Virginians out of whom America grew strong and bold and good.

Except that Pocahontas was eleven years old at the time, and Captain John Smith was a liar and braggart who probably stole his story from the Greek myth of Theseus, and Pocahontas later married John Rolfe only after having been kidnapped and held captive for a year and that at the age of twenty-one she died in a foreign land, and the incompetent Jamestown colonists who were repeatedly saved from starvation by Pocahontas's people eventually attained a unification of cultures by wiping the opposing culture out.

So much for the history books, Parris thought. He knew from personal experience how easily history could be fabricated. And something about this small gray city made him uneasy. But then, all cities made him uneasy. The crowds and the noise, the stink of carbon monoxide. Just the sight of an apartment building made him nervous. He wondered how people could live like that, off the ground, falling asleep to noises heard through the walls, sirens screaming outside.

My, aren't you a barrel of laughs, he told himself. You're going to be a lot of help to Diana like this, aren't you?

He warned himself then to keep his own feelings and his fears in check and to attend to Diana's needs. But he had not attended to any needs other than his own for a long time now and he was more than a little rusty. This altruism thing was going to take some practice.

They worked one side of the main street and then the other. They skipped the art gallery and the expensive French restaurant and the women's clothing boutiques and any of several establishments that Diana dismissed with a glance and a quick shake of her head. It was Sunday after all and several of the shops were dark. Parris fully expected them to strike out and that was what they did. It took nearly two hours for them to work their way back to the Holiday Inn, returning with not a single lead. Parris felt like a stray dog tagging along behind his master.

"How about some lunch?" he suggested. "It's nearly one-thirty."

"Let's do a couple of side streets first."

"You're going to deplete your energy. We don't have to question the entire town in one afternoon."

She nodded absently. Then, "Let's go this way," she said. She crossed the street against the light and he hurried after her, one

stride behind as she entered a dim little A-frame squeezed between two concrete office buildings. The sign over the A-frame's
door said HOTDOG HAUS. At the counter she ordered three hot dogs
and two vanilla milkshakes and Parris told himself that now was
not the time to say anything. He stood back and kept quiet and
watched an old man gumming a hot dog at a yellow wooden table.

A minute later Diana handed him a cardboard tray holding the
hot dogs and milkshakes. "The condiments are over there," she
said, and nodded toward the far wall. "Just a little mustard on
mine, please. The other two are yours." Without waiting for his
reply she turned back to the cashier, her money in one hand, the
photo of her father in the other.

At the condiment counter Parris covered his boiled weiners with
cold sauerkraut and brown mustard. Calm down, he kept telling
himself, even though he was breathing rapidly and everything
around the edges of his vision had gone dark. He carried the food
outside and sat at a small yellow table two feet from the sidewalk
and kept telling himself to relax. He punched his milkshake straw
down through the plastic lid.

A couple of minutes later Diana came outside, walked over to
him, picked up a hot dog and a milkshake and said, "Are you
ready to go?"

He looked up at her calmly. "Sit down, please."

"We can eat while we're walking."

"I would like you to sit down a moment. There's something we
need to talk about."

She sat across from him and ripped the paper off her straw.
"What is it?"

He watched her shove the straw into the milkshake and take a
long sip. Not until she looked up at him again did he speak. "I
prefer chocolate," he told her.

She blinked once and cocked her head, as if he had cursed at
her in Sanskrit.

Now that he had her attention, he felt better. He smiled.
"That's not true, actually. I do prefer vanilla. As long as I'm the
one who chooses it."

For the next several seconds she continued to stare at him, puzzled, her cheeks concave as she sucked milkshake through the

straw. Then her eyes widened slightly. She slipped the straw out of her mouth. "Ah!" she said, a soft gasp of understanding.

"You need to slow down, Diana. This isn't a marathon."

"I'm just so anxious," she said.

"Well, you're driving me crazy."

She blushed and looked away.

"Look," he told her. "It's not a matter of covering as much territory as we can. We have to cover the right territory. And how are we going to know what's right and what isn't if we're moving so fast that everything is a blur?"

She nodded, still looking at the table.

"You're dragging me around like a chihuahua on a short leash," he said. "I've got sidewalk burns on my butt."

Now she smiled too. She looked up at him. "I'm sorry, I—"

"You don't have to apologize. I know what it means to be so caught up in something that nothing else seems to matter."

"Nothing else does," she said.

"I understand. But we need to slow down."

She nodded again, then took a bite of her hot dog. She chewed thoughtfully, swallowed hard, and washed down her thoughts with a long draw from the milkshake. Her eyes were glistening with tears.

"How did you know I like vanilla?" he asked.

"The three gallons of vanilla ice cream in your freezer."

"And you hired me to keep an eye out for details?"

She blinked, grateful for the compliment. "Is this all a wild-goose chase?" she asked a moment later. "An exercise in futility?"

He shrugged. "It's a long shot, there's no question about that. To be honest with you, I think our best hope is back at the hotel. We need to find out who was working there a couple days before you received that postcard."

"Do you think they'll let us take a look at the guest register?"

"Nope."

"Then . . . even if somebody does remember Tony, what good will it do us?"

"Maybe a little, maybe none."

"I still have to look for him," she said. "For some information about where he lived, what happened to him. Even if it's hopeless, I have to try."

"That's what we're here for," he told her. "I'm ready to continue if you are."

"You haven't finished your lunch yet."

"If you promise to keep it under twenty miles an hour, I think I can eat and walk at the same time."

She nodded. "Can I make just one last suggestion, though?"

"As long as it's a suggestion and not an order."

She handed him a napkin. "Wipe the mustard off your face." Quickly she added, "But only if you feel like it. It's entirely up to you."

■ ■ ■

September 1964. Nearly two A.M., a cool, clear night. Pin-prick stars dimmed by the glow of mercury vapor lights overhead. The moon a pale flat wafer, small and opaque.

Spangler dropped the backseat passengers off in the middle of a parking lot on the south end of the campus. Then he turned to Jennifer and smiled. "Where to?" he asked.

Parris, on the other side of Jennifer, told him, "We can walk from here."

"No problem," Spangler said. "You guys live in town, right?"

"How did you know that?" Jennifer asked.

"Because you're wearing a wedding ring, and neither one of you seemed to know anybody else who went down to Pennsy with us. Besides, I'm a townie too. I know the look."

"We live in Mayfield Heights," Parris told him.

"Nice neighborhood." Spangler started driving again. "I live with my old man on the East Side. Three blocks from the brewery. That's why the car smells the way it does. I've got air fresheners hanging from the mirror and the gearshift and in the glove box and even under the seat, but I still can't get rid of that smell."

"I never even noticed it," Jennifer said, and squeezed Parris's hand to tell him she was lying.

Spangler had said very little on the long drive home, commenting mainly with grunts and nods. Suddenly, with the evening over, the ride nearly at its end, he became garrulous. He smiled to himself in the dark. "So what'd you think about that cemetery business?"

"It's sad," Jennifer said.

Spangler drove for a moment, then cut a quick look at Parris. "That what you think too?"

Parris did not answer.

"I'll tell you what I think," Spangler said. "I think it's criminal. Not to mention unconstitutional. Just another goddamn example of how white America thinks it can push us Indians around."

"You're Indian?" Jennifer said.

"Half Osceola Sioux. On my old lady's side. She died when I was a baby. Tuberculosis. Another gift from the white man."

Again Jennifer squeezed Parris's hand, a long, lingering squeeze, meant this time to convey or perhaps release some of the feeling she felt for Spangler now. She would not live long enough to realize that it was all a fabrication, that Spangler was no more Indian than an Indian-head nickel, his mother a former greasy-spoon waitress who had raised Spangler to the age of nine before she tired of the weekly slapfests from her husband and disappeared in her housecoat and slippers in the middle of a wintry night, her footprints coming to an end half a block from the house, as if she had levitated out of their lives forever. This was what Parris would learn years later from talking with Spangler's former neighbors, by pretending to be a journalist researching a story. But on this September night in 1964 he was not yet Mac Parris and not yet sufficiently informed to doubt anything Spangler told him.

"You know how many treaties the government has broken with the Indians?" Spangler asked as he drove. His long, thin fingers were curled like stiff roots around the steering wheel. "Every goddamn one of them. How does *that* make you feel?"

Parris had answered, "I don't feel responsible for it, if that's what you're saying."

"You better feel responsible. Everybody should. Because by not doing anything to stop it, you're just perpetuating it."

"As a matter of fact," Parris said, speaking more to Jennifer than to Spangler, "I've been thinking about doing something."

"Such as?"

"I don't know yet. Maybe write a piece for the newspaper, something like that."

"Shit," Spangler said, his thin mouth a hard, derisive curve.

They rode in silence then until Jennifer spoke. "Turn here. It's the yellow brick house on the left."

Spangler pulled up to the curb and held his foot on the brake. "Nice place," he said. "You rent it or what?"

Jennifer answered as Parris popped open the door. "It's my parents' house. We have an apartment in the basement."

"How cozy," Spangler said.

"Thanks for the ride," Jennifer told him.

Parris stood on the curb until Jennifer had climbed out, then he closed the door, and taking her hand, turned toward the house.

Spangler opened the driver's door and stood on the running board. "Hey," he said. Parris looked over his shoulder. "You really want to do something, come on over to my place tomorrow night around seven. I'm having a meeting. Six-nineteen Glendora."

Jennifer whispered to Parris, "Mom and Dad have their club meeting tomorrow night. They won't be able to babysit."

Parris told him, "I don't think we can make it."

Spangler grinned contemptuously. "That's what I figured you'd say." He climbed into his car and slammed the door and sped away, tires squealing.

Parris felt a chill of anger rattle down his spine. "What a jerk," he muttered.

"I don't know," Jennifer answered. "I guess maybe he has a right to be."

■ ■ ■

For another ninety minutes Parris and Diana canvassed the shop-owners of Jamestown. Sometimes the merchant would take a quick glance at the photo of Tony's father, sometimes a long, lingering gaze. But inevitably the response was the same: a shake of the head, an apology.

On a street corner facing a railroad overpass, with the sluggish Chadakoin River beyond, they paused. They watched the traffic for a moment, as if hoping that a passing motorist might toss a map out the window, their itinerary well-marked. Finally Parris said what they were both thinking.

"We're in the wrong place."

She turned slightly to look up at him. "There are still a lot of places to look."

"It's just a feeling I have," he told her. He looked down at her and smiled. "Sometimes when I'm out on a shoot, a feeling will come over me that I'm in the wrong place, and it's time to move on. Sometimes it takes weeks to get that feeling, sometimes only minutes. The thing is, I've learned to trust it. And I think we should trust it now."

"So where do we go?" she asked.

"I've been thinking about that last postcard he sent. From the Panama Rocks, wasn't it? Where is this place?"

"I think it's about twenty-five miles from here. A tourist attraction of some kind."

"Maybe we should have a look."

"I don't know," she said. "I hate to give up here too soon. You never know . . . I mean the very next person I talk to might be the one to remember him."

And the very next corner we turn might be the one leading to El Dorado, Parris thought. Never mind that humanity has been searching for paradise for thousands of years, always hoping to find it beyond the next hill, around the next turn, behind the next door.

But he said none of this aloud. "Tell you what," he suggested. "We're just keeping each other company here, which is nice but . . . not especially productive. So how about if I go check out these Rocks while you keep working the streets."

She pursed her lips for a moment, then nodded. "Should we get a copy made of this photo?"

"Honestly? I think that picture might be hurting us more than it's helping. People take one look at it and it's Tony's father they're trying to remember seeing. No matter how often you say, 'This isn't Tony but he might resemble this person,' this is the image imprinted in their brains. A picture doesn't allow any room for imagination, for speculation. I think you might be better off just giving people a general description of Tony. Tall, thin, brown hair, green eyes—something like that."

He could tell by the look on her face that she was not eager to put the photo away; it had become her connection with Tony. The man in the photo had transmogrified and split, so that she despised him as her stepfather, a cruel and malicious man, but she also clung to him as the embodiment of her brother, the personification of a love forged in pain.

"I guess I'll walk back to the hotel and get the Jeep," he told her. "You want to meet for dinner?"

She nodded. "Okay." Her eyes looked frightened, and he felt a flush of shame for abandoning her.

"Meet me in the lobby at six," he said. "If I come across anything and can't make it back in time, I'll call the front desk." He touched her briefly on the shoulder, lightly, the communication of an emotion he had not yet categorized. And when he walked away and left her standing there on the corner, trying to decide her next direction, he felt a curious ambivalence of freedom and entrapment.

▪ ▪ ▪

Driving west on Highway 394 with the sun in his eyes and a sixty-mile-an-hour wind in his face, the Jeep's canvas top stored in the trunk, Parris could not shake the delicious but disturbing sense that he was escaping something confining. He did not know what that something was or whether this temporary escape was noble or cowardly, but the tightness of his grip on the steering wheel suggested the latter.

It was good finally to pull into the hamlet of Panama, to give his consternation a rest. He could focus a critical eye on something other than himself for a while. And there was a lot in Panama to be critical of. The streets were empty but for a scrawny yellow dog standing in the middle of the street half a block away. There was no traffic to disturb it. Not even wind, it seemed, had blown through here in a good long while, nothing to scatter the layers of dirt that had accumulated against each curb. The buildings were dingy and gray, the windows filmed with age. A few dim yellow lights burned here and there, but these seemed more like afterthoughts than indications of life.

One of the lights burned dully behind a wide gray window, and above the window was a dented metal sign, the lettering chipped and faded. The sign read PANAMA DINER. Parris parked across the street from it and climbed out. He looked up and down the street before crossing—a needless gesture.

The entrance to the diner was through a general store, a rambling building that smelled of dust and hard times. Then along a short hallway crammed with soft drink coolers, past a door marked REST ROOM, KNOCK FIRST, and into a diner with three booths against one wall, a short counter with four stools against the other. One customer sat alone at the counter, but every booth was empty. Parris took the middle one, dead center behind the gray-filmed window. He half expected to glance out and see his Jeep being picked apart by Clockwork Orange delinquents, but it was as solitary as ever, with not even a meter maid to enliven the view.

"Bam!" somebody said, and Parris looked quickly to his left, just in time to see the waitress set a plate of eggs and ham in front of the only other customer. "Deer guts all over the place," she continued. "New headlight, new grille, new left front fender. Let me warm up that coffee for you, Bill."

Bill was a small, white-haired man wearing glasses and cowboy boots, blue jeans and a flannel shirt. A huge turquoise ring on his index finger, silver tips on his snakeskin boots. He could have been Tennessee Williams masquerading as Gene Autry, still waiting for that elusive streetcar. He forked the fried egg into his mouth with his left hand, held a cigarette in his right. He sat very erect on the counter stool, only the silver tips of his boots touching the floor as he swiveled an inch to one side, an inch to the other, constantly in silent and subtle motion.

The waitress came to Parris's table then and turned his cracked coffee cup rightside up. "What'll it be, hon?" she said as she filled the cup. She was a well-worn woman in her thirties, probably attractive for a couple of fleeting years in her teens, years that were half-believed memories now, occasional refuge from the teenage children of her own.

"Got any burgers?" Parris asked with a smile.

"There might be one back there somewhere. I'll dust it off and see how it looks. You want fries with that?"

"Sure, why not."

"That's what I like," she said, "a man who lives dangerously."

There was a burger after all, a half-pound of juicy red meat accompanied by a huge platter of french fries, greasy and crisp.

Parris ate slowly, enjoying the solitude and anonymity. He had gotten used to living like this, an unknown man, nameless, here and then gone, barely even noticed. The problem with Diana was that she was always looking at him, waiting for him to say something. She had expectations of him, and he was not comfortable with that. He knew he would disappoint her in the end. What, after all, did he have to offer? A small talent for spectatorship; a proficiency in uninvolvement; a flair for the peripatetic.

Belly full, his platter empty, he felt suddenly sleepy and depressed. He wished he could slink away somewhere and sleep the rest of his life away. Sleep without dreams. Wake up without promises to keep.

The waitress was there at his table then, check in hand. "Anything else, hon? Got a slice of pie left I can chase the flies off if you're interested."

"Maybe next time," Parris told her. "Which way to the Rocks?"

She nodded over one shoulder. "Just up that way a half mile, first left at the top of the hill." She laid the check on his table. "You have a good day now."

She picked up his empty plate and turned to leave. "By the way," Parris said. "Any chance you might remember seeing a young man in here a few weeks ago? He's only fourteen but tall for his age, probably doesn't weigh much more than that burger you made me. Brown hair, green eyes, kind of a somber personality."

"Somber?" she said. "Look, if they're not somber when they come in here, they sure as heck are by the time they leave."

"So you don't remember him, then?"

"Sorry, hon," she said. "Is he your boy?"

Parris flinched, surprised at how sharply a mere word, a thought, could sting. "No. No, he's a friend of a friend."

"Sorry," she said again. "But if a kid who looks like that shows up here, I'll tell him to get his ass back home."

"Thanks," he told her.

Five minutes later Parris was standing at the door of the Panama Rocks lodge and ticket office. A converted barn with snack counter and four scarred picnic tables. Old cross-country skis crisscrossed and hung on the wall for decoration, plus a sampling of antique farming implements: a scythe and square-bladed shovel, a wooden wagon wheel, a long-handled rake. Just inside the door was a rack of tourist brochures and postcards. Behind the ticket counter/concession window a middle-aged man wearing a starched white shirt and an easy smile.

"Afternoon," Parris said.

The man laid a pen in the center of the guest registry. "Four dollars even," he said. "Stay as long as you like, just so you're out by nightfall."

Parris signed his name as Thomas Ghent, his address as Brockport, New York. It was an old habit, this obfuscation. Never leave tracks. Always pay cash.

He handed the man a five. "You mind if I glance through your register a bit?" Before the man could answer, Parris flipped several pages, back to a date eight weeks previous. Quickly he scanned the entries for anybody with a name similar to Tony, with an address in northern Pennsylvania.

"I'm actually more interested in this kind of thing," Parris explained, "than in the Rocks themselves. It's a kind of anthropology, the dynamics of tourism. Who visits what attractions, how far people will go to visit certain kinds of amusements, considerations like that."

The man nodded. "Interesting," he said. "Though we're more of a secondary attraction, if you know what I mean. People come up here mainly from Chautauqua and Bemus Point, after they've gotten too bored to sit still any longer."

Parris's finger stopped moving down the page. "Son of a gun," he said. "Somebody I know."

The man leaned over to read the entry. "Tony Jacobs, Pittsburgh."

"Friend of the family," Parris said. "Been years since I've seen him. He must be, what, thirteen, fourteen years old by now? Tall, thin, a quiet boy as I recall."

"*Very* quiet," the man said, nodding. "But are you sure about his age? He seemed older."

"You remember him?"

"I remember having to go out looking for him at closing time. He'd been out there for five, six hours, all by himself. I finally found him down in . . . Fat Man's Misery, I think it was—which is this long, narrow passage that opens up into a good-size cave."

"Was he okay?"

"Sure. A little embarrassed maybe. He apologized about a dozen times, said he wasn't aware of the time in there. A very nice boy actually. I felt sorry that I had to make him come out."

"That sure sounds like Tony," Parris said. "Always thinking his thoughts."

"This is a good place for it. You ought to go have a look for yourself. It's the longest outcrop of ocean quartz conglomerate in the world. The Eriez Indians hid out in there when they were attacked by the Senecas. Back in the 1800s some outlaws stashed their gold there after robbing the Clymer Bank. There's a lot of history down in those caves and crevices."

"I'll bet there is," Parris said. Though in truth he did not relish the idea of having more history pressing down upon him, more layers of blood, dream, and bone closing him in. The grunts and groans of other people's history he could live without.

So now he had confirmation that Tony had actually come here not long before his death. Had come here to be alone, to hide out for an afternoon, to think his thoughts. But to hide from what or whom? To think what thoughts? It was an interesting bit of knowledge to possess, but what did it reveal?

"So . . . Tony lives in Pittsburgh now," Parris said, his fingertip tapping the register. "I wish I knew his address."

"He doesn't live with his folks?"

"I'm afraid not. Tony's pretty much on his own, which is one of the reasons I'd sure like to check up on him. Maybe take him out to lunch or something."

"He looked to me as if he could use it," the man said.

"Oh?"

"Not just that he was so thin, which he was, but I mean . . . weak, I guess. He looked awfully weak and drained. To be honest with you, I was worried about him. I offered to make him a sandwich and a coffee before he started home, no charge, but he said he was just going down the road a couple of miles. Staying with some friends, he said."

"He didn't mention where he was staying, by any chance?"

The man stared at the wall for a moment. "Brazelton, I think it was."

"And that's near here?"

"Not quite twenty miles, west on 474."

Parris smiled. "I sure would like to track him down, see how he's getting along."

"Too bad I don't have his license number anymore. That might have been of some help."

"You took down his license number?"

"Sure, when he didn't come back from the Rocks, I went out and looked in his car to make sure he wasn't sleeping in the back-seat or something, and then I took down his license number, just in case, you know. I mean, we've never had anything worse than a twisted ankle so far, but there are some thirty-foot drop-offs in there if you're not careful."

"You don't happen to remember what kind of car it was, do you?"

"Honda, I think. Something small. Was it red? I seem to re-member it was, yes. Anyway, it must have belonged to the people he was staying with, because it had New York tags. You sure about him only being fourteen?"

"I could be wrong, I guess."

The man produced a small folded map and handed it to Parris. "In any case," he said. "There are two trails to choose from, de-pending on how long you want to stay. The green trail has nine stations and will take you about forty minutes. The yellow has twenty and will take a couple of hours. And just to be safe, even though it's still early for them to be out, don't put your hand on top of a rock without checking for snakes first."

"I never do," Parris told him, and shoved the trail map into his pocket. "Thanks a lot."

Parris did not venture down into the rock formation that after-noon. Instead, he returned to his Jeep and with his heartbeat quickening he fished around under the seat for his key ring. He felt certain that the boy's few hours of solitude down in Fat Man's Misery had been a temporary escape from something. It might have been an external menace or it might have been the sneering bully of his own dark soul. Parris certainly understood how either threat could drive a person underground.

It was an exciting lead, but like every rush of optimism he had experienced in the past thirty years it was short-lived, quickly dampened by its opposite. Just as he was separating the ignition key from the others, a heavy fatigue swept through him. Suddenly his heart slowed, as abruptly as a sprinter stumbling. He smelled wood smoke in the air, and newly mown grass, and as if he had wiped a veil from his eyes the trees and sky and buildings all around him grew more vivid and real. He sat there for another ten minutes, gently squeezing the key ring in his hand, feeling the jagged metal edges biting into his skin. What's the point of all this? he asked himself, the same nagging question that had popped into his mind a thousand times in the last thirty years, the same nihilistic voice, What's the point of anything?

He was reluctant to continue on to Brazelton now, to discover a dead boy who by all appearances had never wanted to be found. But he was in no hurry to see Diana again either, to be faced by that glisten of hope that was always shining in her eyes.

I'm not very good at this kind of thing, he told himself.

And then he wondered if in his own reluctance he was feeling what Tony must have felt as he hunkered down against the cool wall of Fat Man's Misery. He felt the hushed trepidation of the Cat People, the Eriez Indians, as they listened to the fierce Senecas padding through the woods, thirsty for blood. Yet he understood the Senecas too and their need to wipe out the enemy and it was the sudden recognition of this empathy that enervated him. The same imperative had kept him alive through all these years of wanting to die and it was likely what compelled him to agree to help Diana, this urge of his to track down a certain man, a man he hardly knew.

A man for whom Tony's killer might serve as proxy? he wondered now.

He looked up at the oak leaves fluttering against the faded blue of the sky, the broken flutter of sunlight, and he felt the fluttering of his heart, his breath quick and shallow in his lungs. Is that what you're doing here? he asked himself. Not to help Diana but to find a surrogate for Spangler, somebody equally entitled to a very unpleasant death?

Parris chewed on the inside of his cheek until blood mixed with saliva. The taste both thrilled and appalled him.

▪ ▪ ▪

They had talked about it long into the night, he lying hard against Jennifer's back, his hand pressed to her naked stomach. Out in the living room little Mackey lay curled up on the pull-out sofa, his white stuffed elephant Peanuts clutched to his chest. The sound of Mackey's breathing reminded him of feathers, as soothing a sound as ever he had heard.

In the end it was Jennifer who decided the issue. "I never realized until tonight how lucky we are," she said. "I mean, we don't have a lot of stuff, it's true. And we're living in my parents' basement, which isn't my idea of heaven. But even so . . . we've always had a fairly comfortable life. Everything has always gone pretty smoothly for us. But those poor people on the reservation," she said. "They lose their land, they lose their homes, they lose all sense of who they are. And now they have to give up their families' graves. I just can't get that horrible image of the bulldozers out of my mind."

He did not tell her that the machines had been backhoes, not bulldozers. He smelled the apricot scent of her hair and he held her tighter, shuddering at the thought that it could all be taken from him somehow. He wondered how many men in Salamanca were holding their wives tonight and shuddering too.

"Then we'll go," he told her. "I don't care much for Spangler, he seems pretty odd. But maybe there'll be somebody at the meeting with a couple of good ideas."

She turned in his arms and slipped her hands around his back. "Maybe you'll be that somebody."

"The only good idea I ever had was to marry you."

"And don't you ever forget it," she said.

▪ ▪ ▪

On its surface the town of Brazelton seemed a lovely place, its streets wide and clean, unhurried, content. There were no parking meters along Main Street and not a single Going out of Business or Space for Rent sign in the windows of the brick and stone shop fronts. Parris drove slowly from one end of town to the other, then turned and drove through again. What he saw reminded him of the small towns of his youth, the air of leisure he remembered from his teens, the languid flow of time. Couples strolling hand in hand, eating ice cream cones. Kids riding bikes on the sidewalk. A wide green park with a fountain and bandstand. Behind the two-story businesses, terracing up the gentle slope toward the wooded hills on both sides of town, belltowers and spires, another one every five or six blocks. Parris imagined how sweetly these streets must echo on Sunday mornings with the dulcet chime of carrilons and church bells, and by his third pass of the park he would not have been surprised to see Norman Rockwell sitting there with easel and brush, actually creating Brazelton from the oils of nostalgia.

It seemed a wholly idyllic and anomalous place. Where were the unwashed homeless people, the litter and filth, the apathy and rudeness that were as endemic now to America as optimism once had been? Where were the gun shops, the kids wearing shaved heads and pierced noses, tattooed with swastikas and costumed in camouflage pants and combat boots? Where the pinched faces of hate and paranoia? Didn't these people watch television? Didn't they read the news?

There was a national forest to the southeast of Brazelton, a ski resort to the north, Lake Erie to the west. Hence the town's art galleries and craft stores, its Mom and Pop boutiques, quiche and cappuccino shops, the Victorian bed-and-breakfasts on every block. On sultry summer nights there were probably free concerts in the park, barbershop quartets on Saturday evenings, chamber music on Sunday afternoons.

Parris was having a hard time picturing Tony Jakowski's place in all this. Where did despair and self-loathing fit in?

Tony had mentioned in one of his postcards that he and his girlfriend had jobs in the same place, jobs that entitled them to "long hours, low wages, and all the books we can eat." Bookstore, library, publishing house, or college, Parris told himself. He parked in the center of town and walked to The Bookery, a tiny bookstore crammed floor to ceiling with "gently read" discount books. But the owner, an amiable, bearded bear of man, was the manager and sole employee and he knew no one who matched Parris's description of Tony.

Parris had similar luck at the two other bookstores in town. At the last, a pleasant young woman informed him that the nearest college, which she attended, a sophomore majoring in communications, was in fact back in Jamestown. The public library was on Third Avenue, just two blocks behind the Civic Theater.

Parris bought a pistachio ice cream cone at the shop next to the bookstore, looked up and down the street for the Civic Theater, found it—YESTERDAY, the marquee read, A BEATLES REVIEW—and strolled across the street. He wondered what kind of solace Fat Man's Misery might have offered Tony that the blissful town of Brazelton could not.

■ ■ ■

The Brazelton Public Library was a huge stone building guarded by a pair of bronze lions, their manes and backs worn shiny by the stroke of a million hands, the slide of a million children. The building itself was the largest Parris had yet seen in Brazelton, a relic of a time when books and what they contained were valued, back in that pre-electrified time before television and computers and shopping malls.

He thought it unusual that a public library should be open on a Sunday afternoon, but exceedingly practical. The lobby was cool and dim, tiled with brown terrazzo; the ceiling high, of white molded plaster with spiderweb cracks. Fiction and nonfiction to his right, reference room and periodicals to his left. Children's literature downstairs. A small sign at the bottom of the wide curving staircase read SECOND FLOOR: ADMINISTRATIVE OFFICES, AUTHORIZED PERSONNEL ONLY.

The front desk stood empty. Two patrons in the periodicals section, reading newspapers. Silence and stillness; the air of a museum; contemplative as a church.

Parris looked around for a clock. There was a small one on the wall behind the front desk—4:46. He should allow a half hour for the drive back to Jamestown, where he was to meet Diana at six. That left just enough time to do what he did best: sit and wait and watch.

In the periodicals room he lifted a copy of the *Buffalo News* from the rack, smiled at the older gentleman, who glanced at him briefly, then settled into a brown leather chair so soft and enveloping that had he wanted to, he might have drifted off to sleep.

It must cost a fortune to maintain this place, he thought. Even for a thriving little town like Brazelton. Probably supported by an endowment from some wealthy citizen who died without realizing how useless books were destined to become. Maybe old Doc Brazelton himself; or Judge Brazelton; or Herr Burgher Brazelton.

Remember to look for a historical marker on the way out of town, Parris thought, for no other reason than that he was curious. He could have researched the history right there in the library, of course, but his chair was very comfortable and well positioned and he could see the front desk and the nonfiction section, and if he turned slightly he could gaze up the stairway to the balcony of the high second floor. He had been moving in one manner or other all day and it felt good to be stationary for a while. Besides, he was here to uncover a history more recent than the founding of the town.

Fifteen minutes passed before there was any sign of activity other than the lugubrious page-flipping of his two colleagues in periodicals. Then he heard the echo of a distant click, a sticky door coming open and falling shut again. Footsteps, brisk and long-strided. And now a man crossing behind the second-floor railing, coming toward the stairs and then down, a man maybe Parris's age or a few years younger, silver-haired, wearing pressed gabardine slacks, shiny loafers, a white knit shirt, a heavy gold wristwatch.

He strode confidently through the lobby and outside without so much as a glance in either direction. Parris pegged him as a pharmacist or owner of the French bakery maybe. Returning to his job after an hour stolen in the company of Proust, Thomas Mann, Mickey Spillane. For aging recidivists like himself, Parris knew, there was still something salutary to be gained from an hour spent in the company of books, something almost—though Parris would not go as far to call it such himself—healing.

He was still gazing after the patron, still staring in fact at the closed front door, when the sound of footsteps again caught his attention. He looked upstairs and this time saw a young woman coming toward the stairs—a very tall and thin young woman in sandals and an ankle-length dress, a floppy shoulder bag hanging underneath one arm.

She crossed directly to the front desk and set her bag on the floor. She pulled a stool close to the desk, slid a computer keyboard toward her, and set to work. Her dark brown hair fell straight over her shoulders, not exactly lifeless but without sufficient spirit to muster a single curl or wave. Her eyes were dark too and the angularity of her features bordered on hawkish, though her carriage was straight and elegant, that attractive aloofness that is often borne of a sense of oneself as gawky. She was very thin and nearly six feet tall and when Parris heard in his head a line from one of Tony's postcards—"She's a long tall drink of water"— he sucked in a slow, smiling breath and felt a pleasant warmth flare up in his chest.

Carrying the newspaper at his side, its leaves fluttering, he crossed to the front desk. The young woman looked up at him, thin eyebrows arched just slightly. Parris smiled.

"Hi," he said. "I'm not familiar with your library and I was wondering where I might find a book called *The Old Way of Seeing*?"

She faced the computer screen again and began to type, her thin fingers flying. "Fiction or nonfiction?"

"Non," he said. "It's about architecture. Author's name is Hale. Beautiful building you have here, by the way."

Her head moved in what might have generously been called a nod. She typed, then watched the screen.

From a distance Parris had first mistaken her for a woman in her twenties, but now, up close, he saw the girl behind the stoic expression. It was the grim turn of her mouth that had fooled him, that aging, saturnine frown. He guessed her age at sixteen, but a hard sixteen, heavy with gloom.

"Yes, we have it," she told him. "You can find it right over there, about midway down the second stack, call number 710.9."

"Wonderful," Parris said. "Thanks very much."

He smiled at her a moment longer. "No school today?" he asked.

Her eyes darted his way just once, then back to the monitor. "I don't go anymore. I dropped out last year."

"You should think about going back," he told her, "a bright girl like you."

He stood motionless for another ten seconds, long enough for her to ask herself Who is this man? What does he know about me? Then Parris turned and faced the nonfiction books, but he did not walk away, he gave her just a moment to regather her lost sense of solitude, to feel a moment of relief. Then he faced the desk once more. "By the way," he said, "is Tony here today?"

Her fingers paused on the computer keyboard, froze for just an instant. Then a flurry of typing. Five seconds later she lifted her fingers off the keyboard, stretched and then clenched them, opened her hands again, looked up at Parris, and smiled. Had it not been the first time she had blessed him with a smile, he would have ascribed no importance to it. But it was, and he did.

"Excuse me?" she said.

"Tony, Tony Jakowski. I was told that he works here."

She continued to smile at him, but blinked twice before answering. "No, I'm afraid not," she said. "There's only the director and myself. Plus a couple of elderly ladies who volunteer now and then."

"Really?" said Parris. "Now, that's strange." He allowed her a few moments to ponder just how strange it was. "Tony was a student of mine back in elementary school. We've kept in touch through the years, and a couple of months ago I wrote to him that I was planning to visit some friends in this part of New York. That's when he wrote and said that he worked here, and that I should drop in and say hello."

"I'm sorry," she said. "Are you sure it was Brazelton?"

"Positive."

"The name's not at all familiar. And if he did work here, I would certainly know about it."

"In fact," Parris said, and he studied her critically, holding his gaze so long that a roseate splotch of color appeared in each of her pale cheeks, "I think he even mentioned you. Your name is . . . ?"

She did not part with it easily. "Miranda," she said at last.

"Right, Miranda. And according to Tony, you two were . . . seeing each other."

She looked away, breaking eye contact. She squinted at the green glare of her computer. "I'm sorry, but . . . I really don't know what you're talking about."

"My mistake," he said. He continued to stare at her, waiting to see if she would bolt or charge. In the animal kingdom you could tell a lot about the threat of an animal by its initial reaction to you.

A sow bear, for example, would generally bluff-charge, because a bear's eyesight is poor and only by charging can it get close enough to determine if you resemble prey or enemy. A female deer, on the other hand, will run a bit and then pause to look back, hoping to draw you away from its young. But Miranda assumed neither posture. She chose the reaction of the more timid animals, the herbivores mostly, who think that remaining utterly still will somehow endow them with invisibility. The field mouse, for example, when face-to-face with a thick black coil of rat snake, often wills itself into a state of paralytic suspension. But what it does not realize is that the rat snake locates prey less with its eyes than its tongue, those heat sensors that can zero in on the radiant glow of a rodent quivering against the cool, invisible grass.

Parris, too, often pursued his prey by the heat it gave off. The heat that registered on his intuition, that subtle incandescence of nondeductive perception. But in this case he merely smiled to the field mouse and walked away, back to the newspaper rack. He put his newspaper in its holder and then crossed back to the lobby, glancing over his shoulder to see if anybody was interested in his departure. A normal reaction from Miranda would be to look up as he exited, just a curious glance, a last quizzical glimpse. But Miranda's eyes never wavered from her computer screen. Even for a librarian, a self-conscious, gloomy-eyed high school dropout, her disinterest was extraordinary.

▪ ▪ ▪

On his drive back to Jamestown, Parris posited another variation on the third law of humanynamics: It is impossible to reduce hope to absolute zero unless the vessel of hope is first reduced to absolute zero.

Unfortunately Parris did not like to allow himself too many optimistic thoughts, and so he added a corollary: But since hope is in all probability little more than an annoying subterfuge, it follows that the human condition is one of unabating delusion.

He smiled to himself, pleased with the maliciousness of his premise, pleased too that he had not liked Miranda the librarian and had probably caused her a great deal of consternation, that she was probably even now slowly stewing in the juices of her lies.

Yes, he had to admit it—he liked what he had done today, he liked taking the lid off the slop pot, letting the fumes fill the air. He liked causing trouble for those most entitled to trouble. Even if the individual troubled was not, for now at least, named Spangler.

He continued to smile for another fifteen seconds, until he caught a glimpse of himself in the rearview mirror. The eyes were dark, the mouth cruel. The face looking back at him was not a friendly face, not the face of anyone he would care to know. And certainly not the face of the man Jennifer had married.

On the other hand, Jennifer had married not a man but a boy. A boy with another name, another future. No, Parris was not him. Parris was not the father of a joyous little son. All three of those people were gone, and in the hole made by their absence there was only Mac Parris, a grim-faced man driving east toward Jamestown, a troublemaker, a man with the sun at his back and the wind in his face, a man turning his radio up loud, hoping just to drown himself out.

▪ ▪ ▪

He arrived back at the Holiday Inn a few minutes after six. Diana was waiting in the lobby, and when he came through the glass doors and smiled at her his face felt wind-seared and tight, his smile phony. She did not say anything, but only looked up from her chair with eyebrows arched.

"Maybe, maybe not," he told her. "How about you?"

She stood, her body so close to his that he reflexively moved back half a step. "A little," she said. "But nothing good."

He nodded. "Shall we fill each other in over dinner?"

"Anywhere special?"

"We could eat here if you'd like."

She wrinkled up her nose. "There's a little Italian place not far from here. It's only a few minutes walk."

"I love little Italian places," he told her. "And the closer the better. Just let me step into the washroom and splash some water on my face."

He turned away, but she lay a hand on his arm and stopped him. Her touch, as light as it was, sent a mild shock through him.

"While you're at it, you might want to comb the bugs out of your hair," she said.

He tried not to smile, but her hand was motionless on his arm and her fingers were long and thin and lovely and he felt suddenly weak inside, as if he had remembered something he hadn't known he'd forgotten. "But this is my look," he told her. "I spent an hour in a beauty salon getting each and every one of those bugs strategically placed."

"Oh?" she said. Her fingers slipped off his arm and she looked truly embarrassed by the fleeting feeling they had shared. "Well . . . you might want to think about asking for your money back."

He was surprised at the lightness in his step as he walked away from her. Surprised too at the smile still on his face when he looked at himself in the washroom mirror. Surprised at the flush of anger he felt when he saw his silly smile, the strange unfamiliarity of his windburned face.

In the past forty-eight hours he had engaged in more human interaction than he normally did in a month, and because of it he felt off balance, unfamiliar to himself. He had worked hard at keeping himself uninvolved with the rest of humanity and had structured his life around a single point, a single objective. Everything else was simply a way of marking time. He liked the animals and the film work and the solitude of camping but it was all just marking time until he could come across Spangler somewhere, that serendipitous meeting he was sure would someday occur, helped along by his own observations and alertness and the occasional well-directed inquiry. Spangler was the end of the road and the journey there was of no consequence except as a means to an end. But now here was Diana Westover and her lost half brother and here were new feelings for Parris or at least old feelings he did not want to feel again, and here was the guilt that came with them and the uncertainty and the suffocating longing of remembering what he used to have, and no matter how much cold water he splashed over his face he could not soothe the fire in his face or wash those traces of unbidden memory away.

▪ ▪ ▪

The Italian restaurant was nicely dim and hushed, illuminated only with soft yellow lights in sconces open to the cracked plaster ceiling. There were only two empty tables when Diana and Parris arrived, and they were shown to the smaller of the two, in the darkest and quietest corner. The young man who seated them was dressed simply in black slacks and a white shirt, as were all the servers; he held Diana's chair for her, then stepped back crisply and smiled at Parris.

"Would you care to see a wine list, sir?"

"Thank you, no," Parris said as he settled in, sliding the back of his chair against the wall, his favorite position in a public place. He always felt more comfortable when fitted into a corner, as if protecting himself from a rear attack, though by whom he did not know. "Bring us a bottle of your best Chianti, please."

The server nodded, still smiling, and turned away. Parris looked across the small table at Diana and said, "Just so there's no argument. Dinner is on me tonight."

"Now, wait," she started to say, but he held up a hand.

"Just tonight," he said. "Because I'm starved and I want to overindulge myself without feeling guilty about it. *Capische?*"

A smile crinkled the corners of her mouth. "Don't tell me that you're Italian."

"Just my gastrointestinal tract. I was weaned on prosciutto."

The server returned then with the wine, which Parris sampled and pronounced excellent. Then came the litany of dishes available. Finished, the server turned to Parris.

"May I?" Parris asked Diana, and she said, "I'm in your hands."

To the server Parris said, "We'll start with calamari and an antipasto salad. Then the lady will have the langostinos and linguine, I will have the filet marsala and tortellinis with pesto."

"Very good," the server said, and quietly disappeared again.

"How'd I do?" Parris asked.

"Perfect," she said. She sipped from her wine, leaned back in her chair, and released a feathery sigh. "I am so tired."

"You must have walked ten miles today."

"It's nice here though, isn't it? If I let myself, I could almost forget why we came to this town."

"Go ahead and let yourself. Everybody else thinks we're here for an illicit liaison, so relax and enjoy the service."

"Do they really?" she asked.

"I'm twice your age, you're young and pretty. They seat us in the darkest corner of the restaurant, they look at us with veiled eyes and knowing smiles. They're very big on romance here."

"What a nice thought," she said, and gazed dreamily across the room. A moment later she lifted her eyes abruptly and turned to him. "I meant that they're big on romance here, not that you and I are having . . . not the illicit part, I meant just the thought of . . . I meant the idea that there are people whose lives revolve around the notion of romance."

"Isn't it pretty to think so," he told her, and smiled, and held her gaze so long that she finally averted her eyes. It was a line from *The Sun Also Rises*, the last line in the novel, delivered by the impotent Jake Barnes as he and the lusty Lady Brett go riding off in a taxi together, riding off, the reader must assume, toward that wistful eternity of unrequited desire. If Diana recognized the line, she gave no indication, and Parris wondered why he had teased her with it. He was beginning to realize that he had a malicious streak that surfaced in varying degree whenever he was with another person, and he did not enjoy this perception of himself. It occurred to him that he frequently teased Henry and Caroline, that little of their time together was straightforward and direct but rather filled with misdirections on his part, small deceptions, jokes, lighthearted ridicule of whatever was being discussed. Was this mean-spiritedness? he wondered. An overflow of bitterness? And what of those people he did not like—how might his anger manifest itself with them? What damage was he capable of if he ever let himself go?

"You certainly don't look it," he heard Diana saying.

"Hmm?" He was surprised to see that the calamari had arrived.

"Are you really twice my age?" she asked.

"More than that. Old enough to be your father."

"Would you like me to call you Daddy?"

"I'd like you to be a good little girl and behave yourself."

She sipped her wine and smiled at him over the rim of the glass. "Do I really look like a little girl to you?"

"You look wonderful," he said, and then immediately told himself, Don't. He speared a ring of calamari on his fork and dipped it in the cocktail sauce and tried not to look up at her because he knew that she would be grinning.

"What were you like when you were younger?" she asked.

"Exactly the same as now. Except not quite as old."

"Seriously."

"How much younger?" The calamari was crisp and firm, the sauce tangy with horseradish.

"I don't know, pick an era. High school. The glory days."

"Typical all-American boy," he told her. "One-hundred-eighty-pound running back, all-conference junior and senior years. Point guard on the basketball team, fourteen point average per game, thirty-three point single game high. That one was a school record for a couple of weeks. Never had two beers in a row until the day I graduated. Within a year I had sniffed and smoked and ingested every pharmaceutical available in the tristate area."

He heard his own voice then, and its arrogance, and even though much of what he said was a lie he was ashamed of it, ashamed of this unfamiliar volubility.

"No more sports after that?" she asked.

"Nothing they give a letter sweater for."

"College major?"

"Pinochle mainly. Plus the other liberal arts."

"Did you graduate?"

"By the skin of my teeth."

She nodded, smiling. He watched her nod. She was good to watch. Despite the mix of emotions she aroused in him, the desire to run away and hide from himself, he had to admit that she was very good to watch.

"Now you," he said.

"Now me what?"

"Personal history. Quid pro quo."

"There were no glory days, if that's what you mean. I wanted to try out for the cheerleading squad, and I wanted to sing in the choir, and I wanted to audition for the school plays. I wanted to do all the normal stuff. But I had other responsibilities."

She finished her wine and held the empty glass toward him and smiled. You're a lot better at this than I am, he thought as he refilled her glass.

"Maybe we'd better get started," he told her. "What did you find out today?"

She paused for a moment, and when she looked at him again he could see in her eyes that she had shifted gears, was refocused, single-minded, out of that soft yellow wishful place he thought of as the sloppiness of an undisciplined mind. But she was anything but undisciplined.

"I couldn't find a single person who recognized Tony from the photo," she said. "Later this afternoon I phoned the police department back home; they're keeping track of the forensic analysis of the . . . the body parts, just in case I'm right about it being Tony. Which I am."

"They've conceded that point?"

"Not entirely, no. But everything so far comes from the same individual, according to blood type. But here's the interesting part. You remember I told you that the leg bone was fractured in a couple of places? Well, according to the forensic people, those fractures were the result of what they're calling 'blunt force trauma.' "

"As from a beating?"

"Something like that. The thing is, because of the condition of the blood in the tissues and the way the flesh was bruised, they're saying that Tony was already dead before any of this happened."

"He was beaten *after* he was killed?"

"In any case, the fractures occurred after he was already dead."

"That doesn't make much sense, does it?"

"I asked if the bruises and fracturing could have been caused by the process of dismemberment, but they said no, not in their opinion."

She was being very clinical and matter-of-fact and Parris knew that this was her way of dealing with the enormity of the information, the gut-twisting images it might produce if she allowed herself to envision it.

"Well," Parris said.

He sat there, staring at the tablecloth, feeling her gaze on his face, waiting, waiting for him to provide all the answers, explain the universe. Fortunately their dinners arrived and he did not have to admit his ignorance.

"Will there be anything else right now?" their server asked.

Parris looked up at him and thought, You're damn right there is. Tell God to get his ass down here and explain all this. "Thank you, no," he answered.

The server smiled at Parris and then at Diana. Ah, love! he seemed to be thinking. *"Mangi con gusto,"* he said.

▪ ▪ ▪

He waited until she had finished her spumoni before he told her about Miranda. Diana had tried throughout dinner to discover the results of his day, but he kept putting her off. Now, as she dabbed at her mouth with the red linen napkin, he smiled.

"I visited the Panama Rocks today," he said. "The man there remembers Tony."

Her eyes grew wider. Parris knew what she would want to know next.

"He described Tony just as you picture him. So I'd say that your mental image of him is an accurate one."

And now her eyes softened; the tears pooling in her eyes reflected the candlelight. Parris knew that the flat photographic image of her brother had now become three-dimensional in her mind; a living, verifiable person, not just words on a postcard or a voice on an answering machine, not just a visual speculation. It was a wondrous transition to take place in one's mind, a kind of birth. At the least, a validation of one's desires.

Parris felt good that he was able to give her this, and envious too. How many thousands of times had he tried to conjure up the image of Jennifer as a middle-aged woman, Mac as a young man? Would Jennifer's hair be streaked with glimmers of gray? How tall would Mac be? Would he be nearsighted, like his old man, or would he be blessed with the vision of his blue-eyed mother? Parris would have given twenty years of his life—gladly, without a second's hesitation—for just a glimpse of Jennifer and Mac today, as they would be now, untouched, unstolen by Spangler. He would concede every remaining hour of his life if he could substitute that picture of them for the one he now possessed.

To forestall his own thoughts as well as Diana's predictable questions, he continued quickly. "Unfortunately, he provided no real help in tracking Tony down. But somebody else did."

He paused for a sip of coffee, dark and rich and with just enough bitterness that the flavor lingered on his tongue. Diana waited, her gaze never moving from his face. *"Who?"* she finally asked.

"I think I found Tony's girlfriend."

Diana sucked in a long, slow breath, inhaling through her nose. Her posture was always straight, her carriage just short of stiff, but at this moment she seemed made of marble, smooth and cool and exquisitely carved.

"She works at the public library in a town called Brazelton," Parris told her. At times like these he found himself feigning nonchalance as a defense against the mounting urge to make physical contact with a woman, to take her in his arms, embrace her, to comfort and soothe whatever terrors were taking shape in the recesses of her heart. "We'll go have a look at her tomorrow, and you can decide for yourself."

Another ten seconds passed before she nodded. Her gaze drifted away from him, it flitted toward a wall, a patron, a candle flickering low inside its sconce. Her knew the moment well. It was the moment of coming up hard against the thing you thought you wanted but never really expected to find. The moment of decision, of choosing between the relative quiet of retreat and the inevitable battle of advance. Let sleeping dogs lie . . . or rattle the chain?

"Good," she finally answered, her voice as soft as a sigh, her eyes no longer searching his. "All right."

She did not seem to notice when the check came, and he paid it, and the server held her chair so that she could stand. She walked with Parris outside and did not seem to know which way to go until he touched her lightly on the arm. She turned then and walked beside him, not speaking, and if she felt his arm slip around her back and his hand lie softly on the curve of her hip, if she heard his breath catch or felt his heart quicken, she gave no indication of it, she offered no recognition of either him or the night or the stars.

▪ ▪ ▪

It was a dangerous night; he knew it the moment she unlocked the door to their hotel room and stepped inside and he stood there on the threshold, watching as she turned on a floor light in the corner. She sat on the corner of the farthest bed and took off her shoes and he did not come forward to let the door close behind him. He heard the ice machine down the hall and he heard a woman's laughter. Diana took off both shoes and fell backward onto the bed. With his back to the door he could see her now only from the thighs down, the hem of her skirt and then her legs hanging off the end of the bed, her toes not touching the floor.

There was something calming about the sight of her legs and the way the skirt rode up along her thighs, something calming to the image that came unbidden of him easing down between her legs and her knees rising slightly almost like wings to enfold him and his arms wrapping around her back and the hard, fragile delicacy of her spine and of his head on the mattress and his eyes closing and of him falling into the deepest safest sleep of some ten thousand nights.

But it was a troubling image too, because she was not Jennifer and if two billion Christians were right, Jennifer and maybe even Mackey were watching. But if four hundred million Buddhists were right, nobody was watching, except for maybe the mites in the carpet and a fly buzzing like static behind the curtain.

On the other hand, he wasn't there to entertain himself with pleasurable notions. And what if things progressed beyond the stage of notioning? Is notioning a word? he wondered. Or are you just a very sick man whose only health is in the woods, where there are no beds or female legs and no Italian restaurants to seduce you with the aphrodisiacs of pesto and spumoni?

"Aren't you coming in?" she asked.

He waited a moment before answering. "I'm considering my options."

"Which are?"

"Christianity or Buddhism."

She laughed softly. "Maybe I'm just tired, but that doesn't make any sense to me." She sat up and leaned forward to look at him from the foot of the bed. "I don't bite," she told him.

He smiled. "But I do."

"Promises, promises." A moment later she stood and reached for her bag against the wall. She pulled it toward her and sat on the bed again and zipped open the bag.

"I'm going to get dressed for bed now," she told him. "Would you mind closing the door?"

"Maybe I should get another room."

"Maybe you should grow up and act like a big boy."

"That's exactly what I'm trying not to do."

She leaned forward to see him better. "There are two things at issue here. First, this investigation, if that's what it's called, is at my expense. We agreed on that. And I can't afford two motel rooms every night. Second—" She paused now and looked away, and searched for something in her suitcase.

"Second?" he asked.

She found the bottom half of a pair of silk pajamas, as pale as the blush that suffused her cheeks, and pulled them forth. She shook them once to remove the myriad wrinkles, which refused to go, and laid them on the bed. Then she searched for the pajama shirt. Only after she had found it did she speak again. She stood and turned her back to him and began to unbutton her blouse.

"Close the door, please," she said.

Parris closed and locked the door and without looking at her again he came inside to recover his own bag from atop the bed. He turned quickly and went into the bathroom. He changed into his own pajamas, neither silk nor pink but a faded hospital blue. He looked at himself in the mirror. The light was very bright and his eyes were like an animal's, an animal so hungry that it has overcome its own fear of a peculiar scent and presence to approach a campfire and the shadows that wait behind it. He did not know what he would do or what he should do. It did not seem right to abandon a thirty-year-old discipline. But he wanted both extremes. He wanted her to be Jennifer and he wanted her not to be and he wanted to be alone with his work in the woods. Life was much simpler in the woods. Hotels and silk pajamas were complications he did not want to have to deal with.

He waited in the bathroom for what seemed a long time. He felt silly in his cotton pajamas and bare feet. Finally he looked at himself in the mirror and said You've picked up rattlesnakes and you've looked wolves in the eye and here you are quivering like a schoolboy.

And then he smiled, because it was all right now. He had

shamed himself into submission. Now he could go climb into bed and turn his back to her and say good night.

He opened the door quietly, in case she was already sleeping. But even before he stepped fully out of the bathroom he saw her. Her image was reflected from her bed to the wall mirror he faced, illuminated by the yellow light of the floor lamp in the corner. She was wearing both halves of her pajamas but the shirt hung open as she wound a loose thread around one of the buttons. Her breasts were small and lovely and there were three horizontal striations just above the waistband of her trousers, three thin pink scars nearly as pale as her pajamas.

She looked up and into the mirror and she saw him standing there watching her. She did not say anything and did not smile and did not cover herself. A moment later she turned her attention to the loose thread again.

Parris went to the nearest bed and pulled back the covers and turned his back to her and crawled in. He stared at the empty wall. She was motionless for what seemed a long time, and he wondered what she was doing, and he tried not to envision certain things.

After a while she crossed to the space between their beds and he could feel her standing there. "Should I kiss you good night?" she asked softly, her voice too tremulous, he thought, for her own good.

He considered saying nothing, pretending he was already asleep. Then he decided that silence would not be playing fair. And he had always striven to play fair, no matter who the opponent. "You'd better not," he finally told her. "I'd probably like it."

A moment later he heard her covers being drawn back, and then the creak of the bed as she lay down. He lay there a long time, listening to her soft breathing, and when he thought she was asleep he rolled onto his back and stared at the small red eye of the smoke alarm overhead.

THREE

===

A storm in the woods is a joyous thing. Especially a dry storm, which seems to me a synchrony of opposites: negative ions, the scent of ozone, the freshening wind and the darkening sky, the deepening of shadows and the fulminations of shattering light, a quickening of the air, a settling, a peculiar dichotomy of animal behavior, the deer and foxes lying low, flattening themselves in the grass, the chittering birds, the chipmunks rushing madly to and fro. . . .

In this ambiance I follow the lone wolverine for another mile and a half, maybe two. She maintains a goofy loping stride, even with all that meat in her mouth. I can call her a female with certainty now because when once she paused to give those massive jaws a rest I inched my way closer, zooming in, and saw the teats dangling from her low-slung belly. She's got a couple of pups somewhere, weaned by now, insatiable clamorers, and she's on her way back to them with the booty from somebody's butcher shop.

The wind gusts harder now, the ferns and other flora come alive. I wonder if the animals find the wind as exhilarating as I do. I have always been enamored of the wind, have always believed that if only I could tune my ear to its frequency it would have some wonderful secrets to tell. And if only I could raise my arms and spread my soul out like a sail I could rise forever on those secrets, insentient to everything but the humming music of the air.

Unfortunately this wind is not strong enough to spirit me away. It keeps my scent from the wolverine though, and for that I'm grateful. And more grateful yet when the wind whirls through the trees to bring me a muted yelp, a single short cry that is almost a cough. It came not from the wolverine, who has stopped now too, ears peaked, head cocked. Not from her pups. It's a vocalization I've heard before, in the crenellated Davis Mountains of southwest Texas; in the Canadian Rockies; in the cornfields and woods of upstate New York, when as a boy my father and I chased after our beagles Lady and Tramp, and Lady, acting always as forward scout, always a few yards ahead of her brother—who had a tendency to want to go in two directions at once—would pull him back on course with a little snarl of instruction. And the one just heard is reminiscent of Lady's, but deeper, more resonant. It was a canine voice, no question. And in these woods that can mean only one thing: Canis lupus.

I do not have to wait long for confirmation. The pack first appears like one long shadow moving from tree to tree. Then, backlit by a lightning flash, they stand out clearly for just an instant, seven animals not quite slinking but maintaining a low attitude even in their soft-footed trot, heads slightly tucked. Most of them walk with tail curled between hind legs, to greater or lesser degree depending on the animal's rank in the pack. The alpha male, third one back, carries his tail high, as does the alpha female. The pack's pursuit of the wolverine is roughly perpendicular to mine, they are closing in at an angle.

I look toward the wolverine, but she is gone, her instincts are better and quicker than my own. Me, I cut another look at the wolves and calculate where our paths will cross; if I am lucky their route will bisect mine some twenty yards ahead of me, and they will miss my scent, and I won't have to scamper up this tree.

With my glance up the tree, scouting for the lowest branch, I catch a glimpse of a vulture. The vulture is black and the clouds are black and the sky is a charcoal gray. I hear myself wondering if birds ever get struck with lightning, then quickly remind myself to save that question for later, when and if I make it back to camp without getting my carcass perforated by canine teeth.

It is unlikely that the wolf pack would actually attack me, but nothing is for certain out here. Wolves are intelligent and cautious animals, far less aggressive toward humans than Hollywood would have us believe, but there have been enough documented attacks on humans that I know better than to offer myself up as their next statistic. Or to interfere with their obvious objective here—to recover their stolen cache, and, no doubt, to insure that the bandit doesn't similarly threaten their survival again.

I brace the camera against the trunk of the tree and make sure the audio is cranked up as high as it will go. I focus in on the wolves, I watch through the viewfinder as they close in, I weld myself to the trunk of the tree.

They cross in front of me, and I am holding my breath. The gap between their path and mine is fewer than ten yards. I can see the burrs in their hair, the short, stiff patches of gray-mottled fur. Their eyes are as yellow as fire. They trot with mouths open in what seems a hopeful grin.

It is small wonder that wolves inspire such strong emotion in humans, such extremes of terror or admiration. Like all wild animals, they speak to something suppressed in our own nature, I think. Something traduced by society. Maybe that's why I have never owned a dog. The domesticated dog, in comparison to these animals, is a pathetic creature. All of his natural cunning and instincts have been bred out, replaced with a servile stupidity. I hate to see the spirit squashed in any creature, whether man or beast. That, in the end, is as good a yardstick as any for the morality of an action. If individual dignity is enhanced or at least respected, the action is moral. Otherwise it is not.

The mission of these wolves is to kill, there is no question about that. Their mission is one of revenge. Still, I find them easier to admire than their less dangerous cousins, content to lap table scraps out of dirty plastic bowls.

These wolves will follow the wolverine as long as necessary. Whether they are spurred on by reason or by instinct is not important. The mission must be fulfilled, that is the imperative.

And within minutes they are past me, moving ahead. I release a whispery breath as I swing the camera around to shoot them from the rear. The camera's motor whirrs, my ear against the thin metal housing. And one animal stops. He stops dead in his path while the others continue on. He is the second male, I think, his tail not high like the alpha's but not tucked between his legs like the trailblazer's either. He stands stock-still for just a moment, assimilating whatever it is he has heard or smelled or sensed, processing it with his experience.

A moment later he turns and looks at me, knowing exactly where I am even before he has turned. Does he know what I am? I wonder. That openmouthed grin seems to suggest that he does. And when he approaches, there is not a hint of fear in his glimmerous golden eyes. Even his tail is still; not a single twitch or staccato wag, those semaphores of aggression. He moves toward me like the family dog come to sniff the Fuller Brush man. He smells my boots, the cuff of my trousers. I stand paralyzed and breathless, which is good, because now is no time to move. And after satisfying himself, it seems, that I am as innocuous as he first surmised, he gives me a last look with those yellow-fired eyes, turns, and trots away.

It takes my heart half a minute to remember to start beating again, but when it does it makes up for lost rhythm by pounding out a wild tattoo worthy of Buddy Miles's best hopped-up riff. The wolf is nearly out of sight before I become cognizant of the camera still on my shoulder, my ear glued by sweat to the metal skin, the motor humming inside. I suck in a few meager breaths. They taste of clouds and humus. I smell the sweat soaking through my shirt, I smell the wolverine, the rotting fawn, the strange wolfscent that seems a combination of sulphur and ash.

Eventually I discover my feet again, and set them to moving, unsteadily at first, my legs as weak as broom straws. But before long I am running behind the wolves, panting, lungs already burning and eyes stinging, every sudden crack of thunder an explosion in my ears, every lightning flash momentarily blinding, my senses suddenly on overdrive, my veins coursing with adrenaline. I am running hard now, oblivious of the clamor of my boots. I am in pursuit of death itself, because only there, in that cool, dark dooryard now and then lit by Heaven's jagged fire, will I get my fullest glimpse of life.

▆▆▆▆▆ The morning came clear and cool and bright. Parris awoke thinking he had been awakened by the call of crows in his backyard, the trilling lovetalk of the phoebes that had nested last summer over the light fixture on his patio. But when he opened his eyes he saw that the room was still gray, and not his bedroom at all. The fan on the air conditioner, set on low to drown out the predictable hotel clamor, had been running all night and had chilled the room so that it was nearly as cool as the false dawn outside.

He reached for his glasses on the bedside table and put them on. Not three feet away, a young woman slept facing him on the very edge of her bed, her knees pulled up and hanging over the edge, fingers curled tight around a fold of the pillowcase as if holding the pillow in place. Her breath was susurrous and slow, as rhythmic as a monk's chant. Her hair lay across the valley of her neck and over her throat and an image came to him suddenly of his hand lifting the hair away so that he, lying curled behind her, could lean forward and kiss the soft slope of her throat and she would murmur and smile and turn sliding into his arms and—

He flinched and kept still for a moment. Then he rolled onto his back. He opened his eyes. Ah, there was his old friend the smoke alarm, right where he had left it the night before. The round white shell, the hot red eye. No desire there, no sirree. Thank God for inanimate objects. Thank God for plastic.

He rolled the other way and climbed out of bed as quietly as he could. Best not to look at her again, he told himself as he tiptoed to the bathroom. Best not to watch her sleeping. He eased the door shut and turned the lock and switched on the overhead light.

The small room was cold and hard and glaring, just what he needed. Best not to imagine the scent of her hair or the taste and warmth and softness of certain parts of her anatomy. He flipped up the toilet seat, then looked to his left. A sad-eyed middleaged man was watching him from the mirror. Best to stick with the requisite bodily functions, the man told him, and disregard the rest.

▪ ▪ ▪

Parris wondered if anyone between the ages of thirty and eighty was ever truly happy. He was sitting alone at a table in the hotel coffee shop, looking out the window at the gray Jamestown morning, halfway through his second cup of coffee, still waiting for Diana to appear. He had showered and shaved and dressed without waking her—although he had wondered if she was really asleep or merely avoiding the awkwardness of conversation under those conditions—then had scrawled a note and left it on the dresser for her. He had bought the morning paper but could not concentrate on the news. It was all death and destruction and misery anyway—that and the baseball stats. He had small interest in either.

But at least the coffee was good. Dark and strong and with a slightly bitter aftertaste, just the way he liked it. From the bottom of the pot, no doubt. Smoky and black, his favorite blend.

He wondered if happiness was possible after the age of thirty or so. Only if one did not have children, he decided. Because the moment an individual becomes a parent he begins to accumulate, in addition to his own mounting fears and pains, those of the child. Accumulates them in fact even long before the child becomes aware of them. And at the same time, the parent's parents are aging and changing and you accumulate *their* pains and fears as well. There is no usefulness in doing so because by taking on another party's burden you do nothing to lessen their load, but if you are a caring individual there is no way to avoid it either.

It's the fourth law of humanynamics, Parris told himself. The assumption of another's misery does not reduce the sum total of that misery but in fact doubles it. Even when the original amount is not quantifiable or known.

Take your own parents, for example, he thought. What do they think about on a daily basis? What do they worry about? What keeps them pacing the hallway at night or sitting sleepless in front of the ghostly blue flicker of late-night TV? He had no idea. No, not true. He had a vague idea. A vague idea that bore a startling resemblance to the young man he used to be and who went by another name, a son who had disappeared, a daughter-in-law and grandson gone in the blink of an eye.

Okay, the fifth law. There is no such thing as a truly isolated system. Allegedly isolated systems gain their illusion of order only by shifting the disorder elsewhere. Or by ignoring their own disorder. Comme ci, comme ça.

But his parents were in their seventies now and maybe eventually they would reach that age wherein a kind of peacefulness blooms, that Buddha-like calm he encountered on occasion from old-timers who had survived the raging battles of life. Henry Carlyle had a glimmer of that serenity, but maybe his was more liquid than real. Still, it was possible, Parris thought; that bottoming-out of despair, that point where misery collapses in on itself. He hoped his parents would reach that event horizon soon. Maybe they were precocious and already had. But then where did their pain and sorrow go, that was the enigma. No energy can be created or destroyed, merely displaced.

"You look terrible," Diana said. She pulled out a chair and sat across from him. He hadn't even noticed that she had come into the coffee shop.

Parris blinked once, then smiled. "Thank you. It's the coffee, I think. It really perks me up."

"You didn't sleep last night?"

"As a matter of fact, I slept fairly well." No dreams of fire, in any case. No screams in the night.

"There's something about your eyes this morning. They look tired."

"I just need a little breakfast, is all. The French toast sounds good."

But she continued to look at him, her eyes steady, soft with compassion. "I'm sorry about last night," she said.

He pretended not to understand. "What about it?"

"About trying to seduce you."

His breath caught in his chest for a moment. "Is that what you were doing?"

"I find myself caring about you in a way that . . . isn't typical for me."

"Are you always this straightforward?"

"When I want the same in return, yes."

"All right," he said a moment later. He laid his menu aside and looked at the plastic cover. "I don't think it's me that makes you feel this way. I think it's the situation."

"What if I disagree?"

He waited twenty seconds before answering. "Whatever you feel . . . whatever this feeling is between us . . . now isn't the time for it. This is a kind of . . . stalking time for us. We're on a hunt. We need to be clearheaded, we need to keep one thing and one thing only on our minds. This is no time to be going soft around the edges."

He wondered if it sounded as much like a rationalization to her as it did to him. But something changed in her eyes a few moments later, a subtle change in the shading, a dimming of light. She answered with a nod and a long, steady gaze. Eventually she smiled.

"I'm famished," she said.

He handed her a menu. "Then you've come to the right place."

▪ ▪ ▪

He sent Diana into the Brazelton library ahead of him, just in case Miranda might be manning the desk. If she remembered him— and he knew she would—she would go immediately on guard. It was two minutes after the ten A.M. opening time; Diana was to approach Miranda innocently, ask for help finding a book, form her own impressions of the young woman. Then Diana and Parris would discuss how next to proceed.

As it happened, less than one full minute after Diana stepped into the spacious lobby she reappeared outside, where Parris was lingering near one of the bronze lions. "She recognized me," Diana said.

"How could that be?"

"I hadn't gotten within ten feet of the desk when she looked up and saw me coming. I swear I saw the moment when she recognized me. Her face just drained of color."

"You're looking a bit pale yourself."

"I know that's her. She's Tony's girlfriend, I know it!"

"Slow down now. Let's think this out. You and she have never met, have you?"

"I've never met her," Diana said. "But that doesn't mean she hasn't met me."

"I don't follow."

"I think Tony used to . . . not spy on me actually, just . . . check me out from time to time? He even alluded to doing so. He knew where I lived, where I worked. And sometimes, more than once, I had the definite feeling that he was out there somewhere, watching me. I think it was his way of . . . staying connected."

"And she might have been with him."

"It's the only explanation of why she would recognize me. I never sent him a photograph because I never knew his address. He might have had some older ones, but—"

"They wouldn't have provoked instant recognition. You're sure she recognized you?"

Diana stared at the lobby door, her anger building. "Her eyes got wide, and her face went white, and then she turned away and headed upstairs before I could even say hello."

"She's spooked all right," Parris said.

"Should we call the police?"

"And tell them what?"

"Well, obviously she knows something, or she *did* something, or—"

"Or she thinks you do."

Diana turned abruptly to look at him.

Parris spoke softly, soothingly; as he did so, he glanced from window to window, certain that from behind one of them a shadow moved away from the glass. "Her reaction to you could be evidence of guilt, yes. But it could also be caused by fear. If she knows what happened to Tony, but doesn't know who did it or why. She's probably a little paranoid right now. She certainly has that look about her, don't you think?"

"But why in the world would she be afraid of me?"

"Just yesterday I was in there poking around and asking questions that made her very nervous. First thing today, you appear. Who knows what things Tony might have told her about his family?"

"He wouldn't have said anything bad about me."

"I'm sure he wouldn't have. But she is obviously a very nervous girl."

"Then let's go talk to her and find out what's making her so nervous."

She turned toward the door; Parris caught her by the elbow. "Whoa, hold on." He tried to calm her with a smile, but her eyes kept flashing, her mouth remained grim. She blew out a quick puff of air, a venting of exasperation.

Parris said, "I think the best course of action right now is probably *not* direct confrontation."

"And I think we're wasting time."

Still holding her by the elbow, he moved a step closer, bringing her arm to rest against his chest. He slipped his hand in hers, interlaced their fingers, leaned close and spoke very softly, as if they were lovers sharing a secret. One reason for this posture was to alter the way they must have looked to passersby on the street: People tended to avert their eyes from public intimacy sooner than from a public argument, and he did not care to draw attention to themselves. His other reason was simply to soothe her, to calm with touch that unreasoning creature inside her. He liked that she was a fighter, that she could be as protective as he where family was concerned; as vengeful, finally, when one's best efforts at protection had failed. And he was conscious too of how much he enjoyed holding her close, how he would never attempt such a thing except where their conspicuousness prevented him from doing more.

"One thing I've learned about frightened animals," he told her, his breath on her cheek, "is that once they spot you, you can forget about ever getting close by approaching them directly."

"So what are we supposed to do?"

Parris's hand slipped off her arm then and around her back. He turned her so that they were face-to-face and slipped his other hand around her too, his fingers meeting at the base of her spine. He felt his hips against her, a wondrous sensation even though he suspected that she, at the moment, was totally oblivious of it.

"Look," he told her. "You hired me for a reason other than that I'm such a wonderful dinner companion. But so far you haven't let me do much. In fact, I haven't done anything you couldn't have done yourself. If I'm going to be of use to you, it's because I can be a bit more objective than you. I understand your eagerness, and your anger, and your desire for"—he almost said revenge, but then stopped himself—"justice. So how about letting me take the wheel for a while, okay? You can still be the navigator, but let me decide when to apply the brakes."

That unflinching brown-eyed gaze of hers was as disconcerting as it was appealing. He did not know if she was going to spit at him or smile. Then he felt her hands touch lightly upon his ribs, he felt each fingertip, each scalding point of contact. "You're just hoping to milk this job for all it's worth," she told him, and had he not been so acutely aware of the warmth and pressure of her hands, he would have thought her tight-lipped smile a sneer. He felt something stumble inside of him then, a small jarring of control, as if whatever mechanism he employed to keep a check on his emotions had slipped a gear.

"I do need the work," he told her, and he drew away quickly, breaking contact, squinting into the glare of the morning sun.

■ ■ ■

Soon after Diana left Parris alone outside the library, the morning took on the air of expectant tedium he was so familiar with from his long days in the field. But Parris missed his camera and sound equipment, his binoculars and notepads, and all the paraphernalia with which he distracted himself when waiting in the woods or mountains for an animal to appear.

Diana had brought him a takeout coffee and a newspaper before heading off on her own—he had suggested a movie at the local mall, and she said that sounded like a good idea, though both knew she was too preoccupied to be seduced by Hollywood's skewed adaptation of reality—but the paper cup was soon empty and the news stories seemed just as ephemeral, so that he often forgot what he was reading before reaching the end of the paragraph.

In the end he dropped the paper in a trash can and walked the street across from the library. He was reasonably certain that even if Miranda were watching out a window, he could not be identified from that distance. Even so, he stayed as inconspicuous as possible.

There was no parking lot attached to the library, which told him that Miranda had either parked on the street somewhere or arrived by foot. The town was too small to have either bus or taxi service. So he strolled the street or perused the shopwindows or loitered around the corner of a building, all the time keeping an eye on the library's front door in the hope that Diana's presence earlier would flush Miranda out, would send her scurrying somewhere, anywhere that might be more revealing of Tony's fate.

Adjacent to the library was a small stone church with a wide, newly mowed yard. He could smell the grass clippings and the coolness beneath the two red maples in the side yard. It was the First Episcopal Church of Brazelton and it would have been the perfect place to sit and keep an eye on the library door. But he had not set foot on hallowed ground for over thirty years and he was not ready to do so today. Maybe he would never be ready. Probably it would not matter one way or the other. It was a lovely little building and there was something beguiling about the architecture of rough-cut fieldstone and stained glass and how the external solidity and squared corners and sure angles were no doubt home to soaring arches and vaulted ceilings and the almost sensual curves and shadowed colors inside. But that was mere craftsmanship, he told himself. It was a trick of construction, the art of artifice. Let the Christopher Wrens and Sir Thomas Mores ascribe something more to it if they wished, but as a filmmaker he knew the difference between hard work and divine inspiration.

So there was no reason not to take advantage of the grass and shade of the churchyard. There was no reason not to make himself more comfortable. Except that he could not shake the feeling that to sit quietly in the coolness of the church's shadow would be like staging a boxing match at a funeral.

And so he strolled the sidewalk, lingering here and there. Halfway up Perry Avenue, then back to Third, past the library, then halfway up Coolidge, then cross the street to the opposite side of Coolidge, and back down to Third. One round trip every fifteen minutes or so. It promised to be a tedious day. Made all the worse by the annoying sensation of having forgotten something. The sensation of wandering around naked and emptyhanded. In the field he was always well armed, especially when his subject was as large and unpredictable as a human, but out here on the concrete he had nothing, not so much as a can of pepper Mace. What if Miranda *did* recognize him, and telephoned some gorilla of a boyfriend, or even a small greasy-haired baboon—somebody capable of slicing and dicing a rival and scattering his pieces far and wide? Parris did not approve of hunting for sport, but he did approve of self-preservation. But what would he protect himself with out here?

In the field, when there was any danger of coming face-to-face with a dangerous animal, he would be sufficiently prepared so as to be able to put any concern for his own safety out of his head. In the Brooks Range in Alaska, for example, on the tundra above the Arctic Circle, he had carried a marine flare gun in a hip holster as his first line of defense against irate grizzlies and brown bears and moose. Twice he had had to send a flare sizzling across the ground when grizzly bears caught his scent and came to investigate his potential as a blue plate special. The first bear, startled by the light and the sulphurous stink of the blazing flare, had turned away while still fifty yards out. The second bear, which had charged his camp one morning just as he was pouring canned milk into his granola, ignored the first flare, sneered at the second one shot directly over its head, and finally stopped to reconsider the advisability of munching on a human only after Parris pulled his short-barreled Browning ten-gauge shotgun from the scabbard and fired a load of birdshot in the huge grizzly's direction. Somehow the grizz seemed to understand that the next two shells Parris pumped into the chambers were solid lead slugs that could tear off a good portion of ursine skull. The bear stood on its rear legs a few moments longer, stood to its full nine feet, roared, and pawed the air. It was an intimidating posture but not indicative of imminent attack. Parris kept his shotgun trained on the animal's forehead and told himself that if the grizzly dropped to all fours and came just five yards closer, he would have to pull the triggers. He prayed that he would not have to do so. He was in the grizzly's territory and the bear had every right to be upset. In fact, Parris even told the animal as much. He spoke in a strong, clear voice, his voice echoing off the mountains, and apologized for any concern his presence might have caused, and offered assurances that he was just passing through, and spoke with some regret about the curious and meddlesome nature of a man. After a very long thirty seconds or so the bear dropped down onto all fours. Parris felt the ground tremble beneath his feet. The bear gave its head a vigorous shake. Parris blinked the sweat from his eyes. Then, finally, the grizzly turned heavily and ambled away, over a half-ton of hairy muscle. Parris thought he had never seen anything so beautiful or graceful as that waddling ursine rump. He sat down in front of his tent, too weak to move. The air was so clean that it seemed almost to shimmer, the sky so china blue. He could smell the red dwarf rhododendron blooms on the valley floor a hundred yards away. Mosquitoes were everywhere—small throbbing clouds of whirring life. A golden eagle was cutting gyres in the sky. Mount Thunder loomed off to the west, wind-smoothed and ice-sculpted, and beyond it the silvery Utukok River, and beyond it the Chukchi Sea and Russia and the sweet slow curve of the globe. There was only nature and it was everywhere. And for a long time that morning Parris sat motionless at the mouth of his tent, smiling, with no desire to do anything but remain there quietly, living and breathing in the center of it all.

Not so here on the pavement of Brazelton. The traffic was not heavy but even so the stink of exhaust fumes stung his eyes. The glare of sunlight glinting off the mica chips. The bright colors and neon signs in the shopwindows. Too much glass and metal and concrete. The church and the library were the only truly attractive buildings and both were off limits to him. And now the coffee had worked its way through his system and he needed to urinate.

What next? he wondered.

Finally he had no choice but to take his eyes off the library for a few minutes. He hurried into the Sportsman's Bar & Grill half a block away, laid two dollars on the bar and, on his way to the rest room, ordered a Coke from the barman watching *The Guiding Light* on the barroom TV. A minute later Parris returned light-footed and smiling. He pocketed his change, took a sip of the soft drink, and hurried back outside. Diana was standing at the mouth of the sidewalk that led to the library, a grocery bag in hand as she scanned the street in one direction and then the other.

Parris caught the look of relief in her eyes when she saw him approaching, a look she quickly tried to veil behind a half-hearted scowl. "And Henry told me you would be reliable," she joked.

"Consider the source," Parris said.

Diana hoisted the grocery bag a bit higher. "I brought us some lunch."

He reached out to take it from her arms. "Why don't you have a peek in the library, make sure our lady didn't slip off while I was having my four boilermakers. I'll find us a comfortable place to sit."

She returned from the library two minutes later to find him seated on a bench near the street. "You call this comfortable?" she asked.

"Was she still inside?"

"Working at the computer at the front desk. And still looking like a rabbit in a dog kennel."

"Did she see you?"

"I made sure that she did. I even smiled."

"You have a sinister streak, don't you?"

She smiled again, this time with a slight widening of her eyes. Then she picked up the grocery bag and walked away from him, toward the churchyard. He watched until she had seated herself in the shade beneath one of the red maple trees and began to lay out the lunch she had bought.

What have you gotten yourself into here? he wondered.

He sat there on the bench with his hands clasped between his legs. It's just a bit of grass and shade and a building made out of stone, he told himself. It doesn't have to mean anything unless you let it.

He did not wish to let it mean anything and certainly not let it have any power over him, and so he finally stood and went to her and sat beside her. "You're very strange sometimes," she told him with a smile.

"Thank you very much."

She handed him a cardboard cup of iced tea. "It's unsweetened."

"Just the way I like it."

"I have sugar in here somewhere."

"None for me, thanks."

"We have bagel sandwiches too. Turkey or ham?"

"Your choice."

"I'll take the turkey, if you don't mind."

"Then I'll take the ham."

"We're being very polite, aren't we?"

"It's a character flaw I have. What's your excuse?"

"I think we're a little bit afraid of something in each other. Or maybe it's something in ourselves. Something the other person makes us feel."

He peeled the plastic wrap from around his sandwich and did not look at her. "Maybe we had better just have our lunch and not talk like that," he said.

Several minutes passed before they spoke again. "This is a good place," he told her. "We can see both the back and the front door from here."

"You like that, don't you? Being able to see both the entrance and the exit to everything."

"Would you stop?"

"Make me."

He looked at her, the way she faced him with her chin thrust forward in mock-challenge, and he could not suppress a small laugh. "You're amazing," he told her. "Here we sit, trying to find out whatever we can about your brother . . . and at the same time you can be like this."

"I'm a dual personality. Two for the price of one."

He laughed again.

"Why don't you want to like me?" she asked.

"Is this some kind of technique you learned somewhere? First you pet me, then you jerk my chain."

"Have you noticed that you never answer a question except with another question? You're a very guarded man, aren't you?"

"Could we keep our attention on the matter at hand, please? You watch the front door, I'll watch the back."

There was no denying what he felt when he looked at her smiling face and saw the sparkle of her dark eyes. He tried to squeeze himself shut against it, but it was so much like a picnic once in another place and time that he could not swallow for a moment.

"Episcopalians," Diana said after a while. "What is it they believe?"

He shrugged and swallowed hard. "Some variation on the original, I suppose."

"So," she said, "you never go to church?"

"I go to the woods."

"What about weddings and funerals?"

"I go to the woods."

"Sounds nice," she said. "Misanthropic, but nice. Anyway, I agree—churches are best when they're empty." She offered him a candy bar. He shook his head no.

"I used to go," she told him. "Every Sunday morning. I've missed the last few Sundays though. And now I don't know if I'll ever go back or not."

"You should try if you can. It might still work for you."

"Maybe I'll try the woods instead."

He nodded. "It's a wonderful place if you can get deep enough not to hear somebody's lawn mower or radio. Beyond where you might stumble over somebody's litter. Of course you can't be afraid of bugs and spiders and things that might crawl into your sleeping bag at night."

"I've been around those things for a long time now. I've gotten rather used to them."

He nodded again and drank the last of his tea. Then suddenly he sat up a little straighter. "There goes another one," he said.

She looked toward the library just in time to see a man in a pale blue summer suit entering through the front door. He carried a black leather attaché case. "Another patron? What's so strange about that?"

"He's the fifth or sixth businessman I've seen go in there this morning. How many businessmen do you know who visit the library during office hours?"

"Maybe they go there to read the papers."

"He'll be back in less than five minutes," Parris said.

And he was. He exited as he had entered, carrying nothing but his attaché case. "It just strikes me as odd," said Parris.

"Maybe they're using the fax or photocopy machine or something."

"Maybe," Parris said, but he did not sound convinced.

Twenty minutes later another man in a business suit entered the library. "Maybe one of us should follow him inside," Diana suggested.

"I'll go," Parris said. He waited another minute or so, then crossed to the library. The front desk was empty now. Parris went from one area to another but the man was not in the reference section or the periodicals. Parris checked the adult fiction and even the children's room in the basement, but there was no sign of the man. He gazed up the long spiral staircase and scanned the second-floor hallway. Finally he returned to Diana.

"Did he come back out?" he asked.

"No," she said.

"I can't find him. There are four or five offices and conference rooms on the second floor—he must be in one of those."

"Doing what?"

"Your guess is as good as mine."

■ ■ ■

It was September 1964 and they were young and everything good was about to end. Later he would blame himself for being so naive and unsuspecting. Or for not acting on his vague premonition of doom. Or for leading his family to their slaughter. It all depended on how cruel he wanted to be to himself.

It was a pleasant cool night with the smell of leaf smoke in the air, the scent of change. Something whispered from the corner of his consciousness, telling him to slow down, take it all in while you can, this will not last. . . .

They walked together for nearly half a mile, holding hands most of the way, Mackey riding on his shoulders, the little boy's hands tangled in his father's hair, pulling at it playfully, mussing it.

They walked from the soft safe twilight of their neighborhood into the harshly lit darkness of the east side. The sour odor of the brewery was detectable from eight blocks away. "I suppose you get used to it," Jennifer said. Parris nodded, his hands on Mackey's ankles. He was still too young to know that there are some things you can never get used to.

"Is that it?" Jennifer asked as they stood before a white frame house in need of painting. The house looked dark from the outside except for a yellow light in the front room. The covered porch was bare and empty.

"That's the address," Parris said.

"Maybe we should have called first."

"Too late now," Parris told her. The night seemed to have changed in the last few minutes, become stale and foul-smelling. He squeezed Jennifer's hand as they walked toward the porch. The steps were dry and cracked and the boards squeaked as he mounted them. He knocked on the metal frame of the screen door and then stepped away from the door and rubbed his hands up and down Mackey's thin legs. Even now he could remember the feel of Mackey's legs and the boy's weight on his shoulders and the warmth of the boy's hands lying flat on both sides of his head. He would remember everything, every sweet and ugly detail. The second knock . . . then the look he and Jennifer shared, as if to ask each other if they should leave. The door coming open then and the sleepy, surprised expression on Spangler's face, the momentary lack of recognition until Parris told him We're here for the meeting. Then, Spangler's face brightening, the spark of life coming back into those faded eyes as he pulled open the door and ushered them inside. The worn braided rug and the hardwood floor of the hallway. The heavy odor of fried food. Spangler barefoot in jeans and a T-shirt, his skinny feet and too-long toenails. Then the living room where Spangler had been watching *Have Gun, Will Travel* on a black-and-white television screen and Spangler kicking it off with his foot and suddenly nervous and animated to have guests in his house. He picked up a small pile of clothing from the corner of the sofa and tossed it into an adjacent room. My old man's such a slob, he explained. He's working the second shift at the brewery. He comes home polluted almost every night, gets drunk just from inhaling the fumes, I guess.

So where is everybody? Parris asked, and Spangler said Sit down, sit down. Huh? Oh, yeah, everybody fucking cancelled on me, everybody had some kind of fucking lame excuse, too busy to care about anybody but themselves, you know?

Parris felt Jennifer flinch with each careless obscenity. So you got yourselves a rug rat, huh? Spangler said. That must make it tough.

Parris and Jennifer looked at each other, and he saw something in her eyes he had never seen before, a kind of warning or fear or maybe it was just a question. It was the last look they would share.

Spangler took him roughly by the arm and said Hey, put the kid down and let's get us something to drink from the kitchen. Go ahead, he can't hurt anything in this dump, and then Parris was in the cramped kitchen holding the carnival glasses Spangler pushed into his hands and Spangler was banging a metal ice cube tray against the side of the rust-stained sink and the cubes were skittering about in the sink and Spangler was scooping them up and stuffing them into the glasses and Jennifer from the living room said Oh, you have a piano, do you play?

That thing? Spangler answered. That was my old lady's.

Do you mind if I try it? Jennifer asked, and Parris knew then how uncomfortable she must have felt, how out of place, so that even an ancient black upright piano with its varnish beaded and yellow would be a welcoming thing.

Hey, be my guest, Spangler said. He went to the refrigerator then and started pulling out bottles of soft drinks and beer and without turning to Parris he said Does the kid need juice or something? and then there was the sound of music from the other room and "Old Buttermilk Sky" played on an out-of-tune piano and two glasses filled with Coca-Cola which Parris carried into the living room where he stood beside the piano smiling and Spangler drinking a beer from the bottle grinning and standing too close to Parris and then Jennifer singing softly and Spangler leaning close to Parris his warm sour breath on Parris's face whispering Wait'll you see what we've got fucking planned and Parris's smile more of a grimace and then he looked around and said Where's Mackey?

He spoke too softly to interrupt his wife. *Do you darlin' do you do?* she was singing as he went back to the front hallway to look for his son, Spangler following after him talking quickly about getting into a generator at the dam site and something about the transformer coils and Parris not paying any attention but calling softly *Mackey?* down the narrow unlit corridor to what was probably the bathroom and then hearing Spangler's breathless *Jesus* at his back. Parris turning then to see Mackey emerging from a small room adjacent to the living room, walking toward his mother's back with some contraption awkwardly balanced in his hands. And Spangler shouted *Stand still, kid, don't fucking move!* And Mackey freezing for just an instant and then his face twisting up in fear from having been shouted at for probably the first time in his life. He began to cry and Jennifer stopped playing and turned at the waist on the piano bench and Spangler stepping backward bumping into Parris who now shoved Spangler aside and started forward. And Mackey wanting his mother's arms around him dropped the soft peculiar sculpture that he must have thought looked like the modeling clay he and his mother played with at home but was a softball-size clump of C-4 explosive with the shell and primer of a .38 pistol cartridge rammed into it and a spring plunger rigged to strike the primer when cocked and released. Parris never saw it hit the floor because his eyes were on his family and then the noise and the orange blast of roaring light that flung him backward down the hallway and then darkness for a very long time. And then the slow half-awakening into disbelief and the wish with every moment, every breath, every bruising heartbeat ever since that the darkness would come again and take him too and never end.

▪ ▪ ▪

It was well after one when the businessman emerged from the library. He walked jauntily, briskly, toward the sidewalk. Then turned right and headed for Main Street.

"Should we follow him?" Diana asked.

"He's headed back to work, wherever that might be. I doubt it will tell us anything."

"So what now?"

Parris studied the library for a moment. The door and windows and stones were all silent. "Time to change tactics," he said.

"Oh?"

"Sometimes the passive approach fails. Sometimes discretion *isn't* the better part of valor."

"Could you be a little more specific, please?"

He stood. "We go on the attack."

"Finally," she said.

"You're a bloodthirsty little thing, aren't you?"

She stuffed the remnants of their lunch back into the grocery bag and climbed to her feet. "Just tell me what to do."

"We need to beat the bushes a little bit, that's all. We'll both go inside and wander around, make ourselves painfully conspicuous. If there's anybody or anything hiding in those bushes, we'll know it."

"Let's go," she said, and headed quickly for the library. Even with a short detour to shove the grocery bag into a trash can she reached the library door two steps ahead of him.

"Don't you have a slow gear?" he asked as she yanked open the heavy door.

"Slow is for snails," she told him, and she let the door fall shut in his face.

He came inside to find Diana standing at the front desk, filling out an application for a library card. Miranda, at the other end of the desk, was typing furiously on her computer keyboard, eyes riveted to the monitor, trying her best to ignore Diana. The air around her all but shimmered with tension; she looked as if she might fly apart at the seams any second now.

Parris offered her a smile in passing. Miranda closed her eyes and became very still for a moment, a two-second faint. Then her eyes flew open again and she resumed her hysterical typing. Parris wandered toward the periodicals room.

A matronly woman dressed as if for high tea sat near the newspaper rack, a copy of *McCall's* balanced on her primly crossed knees. She was wearing a red dress and medium black heels and too much silver jewelry and way too much makeup. Probably a lonely widow on her single outing of the day, Parris thought. If he did not have a job to do he might have struck up a conversation with her. Of all the people he disliked, he disliked sad people the least. The more wounded they were, the less he disliked them. The really tragic ones could even arouse something like affection in him. What was it Enid Starkie had said? *Unhurt people are not much good in the world.* Nobody, to his way of thinking, was much good in the world, but the walking wounded were less likely to inflict further injury.

The only other patron in the room was a long-haired young man dressed in dirty fatigue trousers and combat boots and a black Mickey Mouse T-shirt. He sat facing the window, his boots resting on the radiator, knees raised, his face close to his knees as he squinted at a copy of *Scientific American*.

Parris lifted *The New York Review of Books* off the rack, then dragged a brown vinyl chair over to the window. He positioned himself less than a foot from the young man, and within seconds smelled a tangible funk of body odor and stale cigarette smoke and other indistinguishable scents as they settled around him like a cloud.

The young man was little more than a boy beneath all that dirty hair and grime. Skinny and hollow-eyed, with mostly peach fuzz on his cheeks, a few straggly whiskers hanging from his chin.

Parris snapped opened his paper and pretended to read. He could feel the young man watching him peripherally—quick, darting glances. "Fucking assholes," Parris said under his breath. He shook his paper once as if angry with it. "Shit for brains," he muttered. He snapped a finger against the paper. "What a bunch of snotnosed anal-retentive morons."

The young man swallowed a snort that might have been a laugh. "So why do you read it, then?" he asked.

Parris looked at him and smiled. "Gives me something to complain about."

The young man nodded and grinned. His teeth, in those few places not golden brown, were gray. When he lifted his chin, Parris could see the dirt in the creases of his neck.

"I know you, don't I?" Parris said.

The man squinted at him and pursed his lips. Then he shook his head. "Not that I can remember."

"Yeah, sure, you were at—hey, where's Tony these days anyway?"

"Tony?" the young man said.

"Yeah, that tall, skinny kid who used to work here. I haven't seen him around for a while."

"Yeah . . . now that you mention it . . ."

"I wonder where he's hanging out."

"I don't know, I . . . yeah, yeah, he used to slip me a couple of smokes every now and then, is that the guy?"

"Yeah, a real nice kid. Kind of quiet though."

"The best type."

Parris smiled. He leaned back in his chair. "So where are *you* staying these days?"

The young man blinked, then looked away. He stared out the window. "Fuck," he said softly.

Parris waited. The boy continued to gaze out the window—looking for something that isn't there, Parris thought; his past, his dreams, the road to second chances.

Half a minute later the boy faced Parris again; his eyes were different now, clouded. "So," he said, and paused long enough to smile, "you remember me from somewhere?"

"I'm sure I do, I just can't remember where."

"We ever party together?"

Parris pursed his lips and squinted, as if trying to remember. "Give me some clues. I'm better with places than people. . . ."

"In this town it would have to have been the Eagle's Nest."

The name sounded familiar; Parris closed his eyes for a second and allowed the image to form: a cement-block building of faded green, gravel parking lot, windows painted black. "Three miles back on the road to Jamestown," he said.

The boy nodded. "You're not a regular, though."

"Who is?"

The kid liked that; he grinned. "So," he said a moment later. "You interested in anything today?"

Parris reached into his hip pocket and took out his wallet. He separated two twenties, folded them in half, then held them between his finger and thumb, hand resting on a knee, concealed from everybody except this boy, whose eyes widened at the sight of them. "Just some conversation," Parris said.

"Such as?"

Parris leaned toward him. "Where's Tony?"

The boy blinked once; his eyes looked sleepy. "Don't know, man. Ran home to his mama, I guess."

Parris nodded. "How about you—don't you think your mama would like to know how you're doing?"

The boy blinked again, but this time it was quick, a flinch, a scratch in the eye. For a moment he looked as if he wanted to say more, engage in an argument, get into a fight. Finally he snorted softly and twisted around in his chair to face the window again. He picked the magazine off his lap and flipped it open and stared at it, eyes glassy.

Parris reached across the armrest and pushed the two twenties into the young man's hand. "You get yourself to Jamestown and get checked into a shelter there and get yourself cleaned up. All right?"

The boy did not look up or move; he stared at his hand.

"You get one life, my friend," Parris told him softly. "So do something with it. Don't piss it away."

Parris pushed back his chair and stood. He put a hand on the young man's shoulder; he could feel bone through the thin fabric. The young man sat motionless but for his blinking and the tremble of the small square of paper in his dirty hand.

"Thanks for your help," Parris told him. And then he walked away.

It was a small gesture and probably a useless one, but it did not cost him anything he needed for himself, and anyway what was the harm in taking a chance now and then? Life itself is a gamble, he told himself. It ain't all beer and skittles.

Must be the ambiance, he thought. It's got me waxing literary. Better I should wax investigatory and tend to my petunias.

He found Diana standing with her back to the front desk, smiling a melancholy smile. "So where's our Miranda?" he asked.

"I'm afraid I frightened her off."

"By doing what?"

"Nothing, really."

"Diana?"

"I just filled out my application form, that's all."

"In your own inimitable way, I suppose."

"Well . . . since I'm applying for a nonresident, temporary library card, I'm supposed to list the name and address of somebody local. As a reference, I guess. So . . . I did."

Parris turned to the desk and saw her application lying on the counter where Miranda had dropped it. He reached across the counter and picked it up. Diana had signed her name as Lizzie Borden. As a local reference, she had listed her brother Tony. For his address she wrote: "Leg bone, Dempsey Dumpster. Arm, landfill near Tyler. Other body parts, whereabouts unknown."

Parris pocketed the application form and bit back on his smile. "God, you're scary," he said.

■ ■ ■

Up the long, slow curve of the spiral staircase. The wide marble steps, the faded brocade of the wallpaper, the hand-worn hickory balustrade. It was a grand old building, built in the days when libraries still mattered to people, when money spent on the arts, whether private or public money, was considered well spent. When poetry and fiction and biography and drama were believed to nourish the spirit as well as the mind.

These days libraries served as little more than video outlets and social centers. Fat people met for aerobic classes in libraries, depressed people met for group counseling. Parents dumped their kids off for free baby-sitting. The homeless came in to get warm. Teenagers came in to rent videogames and movies and to get free access to the sex rooms on the Internet. In the meantime the books moldered on their shelves, devoured by no one but the weevils.

Parris wondered how the Brazelton library had thus far escaped that fate. Still, the place was not exactly bustling with voracious readers. No books were housed on the second floor and the terrazzo hallway was empty. Parris walked softly so that his footsteps would not echo.

There were five closed doors in all, five blank wooden faces distinguished only by a two-inch-high brass number mounted at eye level in the center of each door. Parris moved from one to the other in an unconvincing pantomime of innocent curiosity. Doors number four and three, on the left side of the hallway, each opened onto an unlit room furnished with a long conference table and several chairs. Door number five on the right side of the corridor was locked. Door number two, again on the left, opened onto another conference room. Door number one, on the right, was locked.

Parris jiggled the final knob, then turned and faced down the hallway once more. From there he could peer into the lobby, the still-unmanned front desk. He wondered if Miranda was cowering behind one of those locked doors, and if so, of what or whom she was so frightened. He supposed there were lots of good reasons why two of the doors would be locked, lots of reasons a trusting man would find perfectly acceptable. Fortunately, he was no longer a trusting man.

He stood at the railing and gazed down at the front desk, a fall of some twenty feet. Then he heard the click of a lock and turned to see door number one opening. He stepped into the center of the hallway and faced the door and had just a momentary glimpse into the room before its occupant stepped out and pulled the door shut again. It seemed a typical administrative office, well lit and perhaps a bit luxuriously furnished for a library—the sprawling oaken desk seemed ostentatious to Parris, but then, his tastes ran to the austere.

More interesting than the room, however, was the man who emerged from it. He came out smiling, a small bald man with a hawkish nose and a mouth as thin as a knife cut. He wore a tailored suit, navy blue with the thinnest of gray pinstripes, shiny black loafers, a white silk shirt, and a blue silk tie with white dolphins frozen in mid-leap.

"Can I help you with something?" he asked pleasantly. His voice was deep for a man his size and it held the trace of a New York City accent.

Parris did his best to look lost. "Well . . . I guess there aren't any books up here, are there?"

"Were you looking for something in particular?"

"T. E. Lawrence's *Seven Pillars of Wisdom*."

The man smiled more broadly. " 'I loved you, so I drew these tides of men into my hands/and wrote my will across the sky in stars. . . .' "

"That's the one," Parris said.

"Try the four hundreds, nonfiction."

"I must have walked right past it."

"Just ask Miranda if you need any help."

"Thanks a lot," Parris said. He turned as if to head down the stairs, but put his hands on the banister instead and gazed down into the silent lobby.

"It's such a beautiful building," he said. "Must be wonderful to work here."

The man smiled but did not answer. He was ready for Parris to leave.

"Are you the head librarian?" Parris asked.

"I'm the director," the man said.

"Ah! Then you would have known Tony."

If there was a minute flinch or muscle twitch around the man's eyes, any small evidence of fear or recognition, Parris did not see it. "Morrison or Curtis?" the director asked, still smiling.

Parris smiled in return. "Mr. and Mrs. Jakowski's son," he said.

"I'm afraid I don't know that name."

"Of course he might have been using an alias, he was known to do that from time to time. A tall boy, about fourteen years old? Very thin? He used to work here, up until a few weeks ago, I guess."

"Here? I don't think so."

"Really?"

"I would know, believe me. Miranda and I are the only full-time employees."

"Big library for just two people."

"We manage."

"I suppose you do. Well . . ." Parris pursed his lips, looked away, then turned to the director again. "You know, it's odd, but I was talking with a young man down in periodicals just a couple of minutes ago and *he* remembers Tony. He remembers him very well, in fact."

"What man would that be?"

"I didn't ask his name. He was wearing army fatigues and boots—"

"That would be Leon," the director said. "Who couldn't remember his own name if it weren't tattooed on his chest."

"He didn't seem to have any problem remembering Tony."

"I'm sure he didn't. Not if you mentioned Tony first."

"Ah," Parris said. "Well, gee, I feel like such an idiot."

"No problem," the director told him. He turned back toward his office. "Have a good day."

"You too." Parris waited until the director had pulled open his office door. "I guess I could talk with the IRS, or something like that. Check the W4s for anybody else who worked at this address."

The director turned, still smiling, holding open his door. He did not try to block Parris's view inside the office as Parris crossed toward him. "You can do whatever you like. But there are no other employees here. Nor have there been for the past several years."

"It's just that Tony has turned up missing, and there are some people very eager to locate him again."

"What people would that be?"

"People who care about him, and about what might have happened to him. People who were told by him that this is where he worked."

The director inhaled slowly through his nose, then released a long, weary sigh. "I'm sorry, but I can't be of any help to those people." He waited, his hand poised on the doorknob.

Parris smiled. "What other interesting tattoos does Leon have?"

Three seconds of silence . . . four seconds . . . five. The director turned and went inside his office and very softly closed the door. Parris waited until he heard the lock click into place, and then he too moved away, back down the long marble staircase, his hand gliding along the banister, his thoughts slipping easily down a wide, smooth avenue of heartening disbelief.

▪ ▪ ▪

At four o'clock Miranda finally emerged from wherever she was hiding in the library. Diana, watching from the churchyard, allowed her a twenty-yard headstart before following. Parris made a quick trip to his Jeep to pick up a pair of field glasses—he kept one pair in each of his vehicles at all times—then returned to keep an eye on the library. From his churchyard vantage point behind the maple tree, where he hoped he would be mistaken for a birdwatcher, he could move a few steps to either side and peer into the row of four tall windows that lined a wall of the nonfiction section, as well as into the lobby doors and the periodicals room.

Unfortunately he saw nothing of significance. Occasionally a patron straggled in, but no one to raise further suspicions. At one point Parris went up to the door and peeked inside and saw the director seated behind the front desk, reading a paperback novel, neatly eating an orange he had peeled and broken into sections and laid out on a paper towel.

Nearly an hour passed before Diana returned. "I saw where she lives," she told him.

"And?"

"It's a huge old Georgian about five blocks from here. Immaculate. With a little white fence and a manicured yard with not even a hint of crabgrass."

"Any signs of anybody else around?"

"No one. She unlocked and went inside and even then it was as if nobody lived there. I gave her maybe fifteen minutes and then I sneaked up close and started peeking in the windows."

"You take too many chances," he told her.

She shrugged. "I couldn't see much. Nearly all of the windows are covered with sheer white curtains, so it was like trying to see through cheesecloth. Except for the back door, that is."

"*And*?"

"I could see into a pantry—very neat, just like the rest of the house—and then into the kitchen. And there she sat."

"Doing what?"

"Absolutely nothing. She was sitting there at the kitchen table with her elbows propped up on the table and her head in her hands."

"That's it?"

"No cup of coffee, no soft drink, no snack, no anything. She just sat there, immobile, for at least ten minutes. It was as if she were paralyzed or something."

"And you find this somehow elucidating?" he asked.

They agreed that they were on to something. They agreed too that they had no idea what that something might be. But Parris believed that Leon had come closer to revealing the truth than the library's director had, and Diana felt certain that Miranda's quivering hand as she dropped the application form, and then Miranda's sudden flight and disappearance, and finally her cata-tonic posture at the kitchen table were all evidence of a guilty conscience, a fear, an escalating panic, a debilitating uncertainty.

Precisely an hour after she left the library, Miranda returned to it. Five minutes after that, the director came striding outside. He walked briskly, purposefully, an olive-green canvas book bag swinging from his hand.

"My turn," Parris said.

"Should I stay here?"

"Your choice," he told her. He allowed the director a forty-yard headstart, then turned to follow him. At the last moment Parris turned to look back at Diana.

"Please," he told her, "whatever you're thinking of doing in my absence, restrain yourself."

She answered with a devilish smile.

▪ ▪ ▪

The director maintained his vigorous pace back toward the center of town. He broke stride only long enough to glance both ways before crossing Main Street, then headed straight for the bandstand in the middle of the park. But as he came onto the grass he gazed in the direction of the bandstand and saw three children chasing one another up and down the short steps, climbing over the railing, hopping off the side.

He stopped, still twenty yards from the small wooden structure. He glanced at his wristwatch. Now he turned to the northern end of the park and, slowly rotating his head to the south, scanned the entire area. Kids kicking balls and chasing Frisbees, parents watching from the benches, an elderly man in a patio chair, reading an oversize book. And alone on the most isolated park bench near the rear of the park, seated in the shade, a man peeling plastic wrap off a sandwich, an open grocery bag resting against his leg.

Mac Parris saw all this from behind a van parked half a block away. He stood against the side of the van, binoculars to his eyes. He knew that to passersby he would look at worst suspicious and at best merely odd, but he could not afford to be concerned with his image just now. He watched the library's director cross to the rear of the park and take a seat beside the man, the director's book bag placed between them on the bench.

The director did most of the talking; the other man ate his sandwich and occasionally nodded and never once looked at the librarian. Parris wished he could read lips. But none of his previous subjects had been as garrulous as this librarian was now; his thin mouth seldom stopped moving.

The other man was nearly twice as large as the librarian. Dressed in a flannel shirt open over a white T-shirt, green work trousers, and heavy work boots, the man seemed an unlikely companion for the librarian. A study in opposites. One talkative, the other taciturn. One with manicured fingernails, the other with splotches of black on his fingertips and palms.

For five minutes the two men sat side by side. Finally the larger man shoved the last of the sandwich into his mouth. He crumpled up the plastic wrap, tossed it into the grocery bag, and then, a quick and anomalous gesture, he kicked the side of the bag with his boot, nudged it, in fact, until it was directly in line with the librarian's book bag on the bench.

Now the librarian reached into his bag, just as Parris instinctively knew he would. With one smooth movement he lifted something out of the bag and dropped it into the grocery sack. Parris saw the item for only an instant, hard and rectangular and black, but he was familiar enough with plastic videotape boxes that he did not doubt for a moment what he had seen.

And so, he thought, a librarian who makes deliveries.

Half a minute later the librarian stood and picked up his book bag and came back across the wide green lawn. Parris ducked down a side street. The binoculars hung from a strap around his neck and bounced against his chest as he walked, heavy and reassuring, as repetitious as a heartbeat, a satisfying thud.

■ ■ ■

To Parris's relief, Diana had done nothing more than keep an eye on the library until his return. Together they watched the building a half hour longer. Convinced finally that this tactic had yielded all the information it was likely to, they returned to their hotel. Over dinner in the hotel restaurant they discussed what they had learned.

"I bet it wasn't a copy of *Schindler's List,*" Diana said.

"And this morning, all those businessmen coming and going." Parris cut a triangular chunk from his porterhouse steak and stabbed it with a fork. The steak was rare and a pool of pink juice shimmered around it. "I need to get into that room on the second floor. There's something going on in that room."

"Such as?" Diana asked. She had chosen the seafood fettuccine but she merely picked at the flakes of crab meat and now and then ate a scallop. Parris was ravenous to a degree he could not justify; he had devoured his salad and the baked potato and had eaten four of the five rolls in the basket, each one heavily buttered and then used to sop up the bloody juices from his steak.

"Such as something very unlibraryish," he told her. He sawed another chunk of meat off the steak.

If she needed further explanation, she did not ask for it. She picked at her food and sipped from a glass of white grenache and watched him trimming the last of the meat off his steak.

"Go ahead and chew on the bone if you want," she told him. "I don't mind."

He grinned sheepishly. "I don't know why I'm so hungry tonight. I'll probably regret this in the morning."

"That's what mornings are for, isn't it?"

He let that one pass and made a conscious effort not to chew so quickly. When the waiter asked if they would care for dessert, Parris wanted to say "One of everything" but he declined and asked for the check instead. He felt bottomless, as if some hunger had been tapped in him by the day's events and no amount of food could satisfy it.

They stood in the hallway outside the dining room and talked quietly about what they should do in the morning, how best to proceed with what little they now knew. They had come out of the dining room and simultaneously slowed and then stopped walking as if by previous agreement, as if neither wanted to take this conversation upstairs and into their room with them, and now they stood side by side with their backs to the wall, their voices low. When anyone came down the hallway they stopped talking until that person had passed.

"I think we should go back to Miranda's place in the morning," Parris told her. "What time does the library open?"

"Ten o'clock."

"Okay. Let's say we're at Miranda's by nine, maybe eight-thirty. She'll have had all night to get even more jittery. Ready to either head for the hills or to somebody else who's involved or . . . somewhere. In any case, we should be able to step up and say boo and have her—"

"Fall completely to pieces."

"We can only hope," Parris said.

"And what if she doesn't?"

"There's always that possibility."

"So what then?"

"I need to get into that locked room somehow," he said. "I need to see what's so important in a public library that the door is kept locked."

"What kind of lock is on the door?"

He stared across the hallway at the opposite wall, trying to remember, to see the lock again in his mind.

"Was it a dead bolt?" she asked. "Or was it one of those through the knob things?"

"I don't remember a dead bolt," he said.

She nodded. "An old building like that, it wouldn't originally have had those conference rooms. The second floor might have had an elevated stage for traveling shows, or an artist's apartment, a place for, say, Mark Twain to stay when he came into town for a reading. So those conference rooms were probably partitioned off twenty, thirty years ago. And since a lock on a conference room in a public library is hardly a requirement, my guess is they're fairly inexpensive, almost decorative locks. Nothing more than a hole in the knob, with a spring-loaded mechanism inside that can be depressed by any solid object skinny enough to fit through the hole."

Parris could only look at her and blink.

She grinned, enjoying his surprise. A moment later she said, "I'll be right back." She headed down the hallway toward the dining room, but then disappeared into the cloak room on the left. Before long she returned carrying a black wire coat hanger. As she approached she straightened the hook and then twisted the hanger back and forth in her hands until a six-inch length of wire broke free. She handed it to Parris.

"If the doorknob has a little round hole in the middle of it," she told him, "just stick this wire in and push and jiggle it around while turning the knob back and forth. They're the easiest locks in the world to open."

Parris looked at the wire for a moment, then slipped it into his pocket. "You're just one surprise after another," he said.

"Where I used to work, we lost the key to the supply room door. So I kept a piece of coat hanger in my desk. I used it every day."

"Remind me to check the bathroom door when I take a shower tonight," he said.

She turned and stood very close, facing him, and playfully shoved her fist into his belly. "You'd better," she told him.

She smiled up at him a moment longer, then turned and headed for the elevator. She left him braced against the hard glazed wall, watching the heart-stopping sway of her hips, the sweet curve of her legs, and wondering whether or not, just to be safe, he should spend the night in the bar.

■ ■ ■

The elevator seemed to take forever getting to their floor. Neither spoke during the ride up or during the walk down the hallway. Only when Parris was digging in his pocket for the room key did she say anything more.

"Things are going to start clicking tomorrow, aren't they?" she asked.

"We'll do our best."

"I'm a little bit afraid of what we might find out."

He inserted the key, then turned to smile at her. "You? Afraid? I don't believe it."

He turned the key in the lock and pushed open the door, then he reached inside and flipped on the light and stood aside to let her enter. She came in slowly, in no hurry. "A week from now," she said, "or two weeks, we'll both be back at our regular lives again."

"I suppose so." He turned to relock the door, the key lock and the dead bolt and the safety chain.

"As if none of this ever happened."

"Not exactly," he told her. "Every moment leaves its mark."

He turned away from the door and she was still there, still close to him. "So tell me, Mac. What's your ambition in life? Another film? Five more films? Ten?"

"My ambition," he said, and he eased past her to toss the key onto the dresser, "is one good night's sleep before I die."

"Maybe that could be tonight," she said.

"Which part?" he asked.

She chuckled softly and he did not look back at her but went straight to the window and slowly drew the cord to open the curtains. Below and beyond their room lay the last two blocks of Jamestown on its gradual slope to the river, the gray bridges and the traffic and the ugly geometry of functional architecture. Out there to the north and west of the river lay Lake Erie, and beyond it Canada, and beyond it the sunset at the end of the world, purple and scarlet, a long, gaping wound in the sky.

He did not like this city or any other and he wished his business here were finished. He felt closed in, as much by this girl and the feelings she aroused in him as by her dead brother and the asphalt and concrete outside. He always seemed to get into trouble in cities. There were too many people in the cities. A city might be a nice place to visit if it were unpopulated. He could enjoy the museums and parks and the stores, he could enjoy strolling up and down the sidewalk, window shopping, he would take in a concert of birds and chipmunks at the gazebo in the park, he would attend a play of clouds.

Cities were a place to stay out of unless he had business there. A producer or distributor to meet, a contract to sign. A city was no place to visit for any other reason either with company or alone. Anyplace, in fact, could be ruined with the wrong kind of company. Woods and mountains and even deserts were ideal for being alone, however. Solitude could be enjoyed there, reveled in. Only in cities was one's solitude oppressing.

A small town was a compromise made for the daily tasks of living. Until such time as one's job was done and he could go into the woods for the final time, post-Spangler. With no camera this time and no recording equipment. No extensive plans or preparations. Nothing to do in the morning. No animals to stalk. With nothing to do but to sit by the fire, unencumbered, finished, and wait for the memories to come, slowly at first, like wary animals approaching the strange warmth and light of his campfire, but hungry too, too hungry to turn away, and finally circling around him, closing the circle, enveloping him, the golden eyes of memory swarming over him finally, the last light he ever sees.

Well, all that's for another time, he told himself. All that is for later. He let his hand fall from the curtain cord and started to turn from the window, and that was when he saw her in the glass, the reflection of the girl standing not three feet behind him, waiting, watching, arms at her sides, her small, lovely body naked and motionless, as if it had risen from the careless pile of clothing at her feet, Aphrodite rising from an oyster shell.

His heart caught on something sharp and he felt the pain all the way into his throat. He closed his eyes for just a moment and then, knowing there was no escape from this, no way to disappear from this moment, to walk out through the glass without ever looking back, he turned and faced her and smiled and did not say anything or move a single step closer.

"Are you getting the hint yet?" she asked softly. Her voice was warm and deep and raised just above a whisper. Her eyes were damp. The room seemed very small somehow. He could feel his heart thrashing against the wall of his chest.

Only with humans does our nakedness make us smaller, he thought. She seemed small enough to enfold in his arms and cover with his body and protect forever. Her hair fell over one delicate shoulder and over the top of a breast as lovely and perfect as a smile from a beautiful stranger. She was breathing shallowly, rapidly, her stomach rising and falling with every breath, her uncertainty as bright as fear in the eyes of a startled fawn.

She stood with her right hand laid against her cheek, head slightly cocked, her left arm hanging down and across her lower abdomen so that her hand rested on the pelvic bone of her right hip, her wrist not quite covering the small triangle of short brown hair. Just above her forearm there were three short parallel scars, three faded pink stretch marks etched straight across her abdomen.

He had no idea what to say to her or the right thing to do. Maybe there was no right way to handle such a moment. He knew what he wanted to do and what every cell of his body seemed to be urging him to do, but on the other hand there was a lifetime of discipline to consider and the reasons behind that discipline. And there was always the question of why a girl like her would want to be with him. To fulfill some need of her own, he told himself. And then he tried not to think about it. He tried not to think about anything because it was all too painful in the end, and when had thinking ever provided any answers?

He moved close to her and she lifted her face to his. He leaned down to press his mouth against her cheek. She did not yet reach for him nor he for her. He felt the warmth of her cheek on his lips. He imagined that if he let himself he could lie beside her in this same position, his mouth pressed lightly to her cheek, and fall into the deepest of dreamless sleeps.

A moment later he drew back and turned away. On his way to

the door he scooped the room key off the dresser. The brief jangle of keys shattered the silence and every hope. "I'm going down to the bar for a while," he told her, his voice hoarse and low. "I'll try not to wake you when I come in."

He fumbled with the locks and was afraid she would say something, but she made not a sound and then he was out in the hallway and headed for the stairwell and walking quickly, and it was then that the strangest mixture of relief and anger he had ever felt washed over him.

In the bar he drank a double Jack Daniel's and then, blinking with the jagged heat in his throat told the barman "Just singles from now on" and while sipping on the next one felt himself separate finally from the other customers and the music and the interplay of neon light with the smoky deliberate darkness. The smell of the sour mash whiskey reminded him of Henry Carlyle, and like a man sinking down into a dark warm pool he forgot about the girl for a while and he wondered how Henry was coming along with the music. Henry is coming along fine, he told himself. Henry in his own mysterious way always comes along fine.

Parris was only mildly surprised then to realize that he had not thought about his wolverine film for quite a while now. When he returned home Henry would be finished with the music and then there would be more work for Parris to do and then the film would be complete. He no longer felt any great excitement or exhilaration upon the completion of a film, and that, he told himself as he watched his third whiskey pouring from the squarish bottle into his stout little glass, that is very sad. He had not felt the excitement of completion ever since his second film.

The first creation is the only magical one, he told the man who was looking back at him from the mirror behind the bar. Then the second is a relief because it shows that the first was not a fluke. And with the third there is no great emotion at all in the end, just the sigh that comes after a great deal of hard work. You are glad to be finished but you wish you had done better. You wish you knew what to fix to make the weak parts stronger and the dull parts brighter.

But there are also those moments that shine clear and bright and sure, aren't there? And so you hold fast to these and hope they will carry the whole.

But there are always more moments slightly out of focus for you, shots made at too great a distance, risks not taken or bad choices made that can never be unmade. This is what plagues you. You remember them late at night when you cannot sleep. In the four A.M. of your soul, when the need to create gets turned inside out into the need to destroy. To create by destroying. The serenity of violent action.

The barman came down behind the bar and nodded at Parris's glass and Parris nodded in return. "One more," he said. One more to keep the blood warm tonight. One more to douse the fire.

But the fire was not so easily extinguished and when he looked up at the stranger in the mirror the stranger was smiling at him. She had to go that extra step, didn't she? the stranger asked. She had to take it out of the realm of possibility and fantasy and shove it right up there into take-it-or-leave-it land.

Well, I left it, he told the stranger. I sure as hell left it.

Did you really? the stranger asked. Is that how it looks to you?

No, it did not look that way to him, not even after all that whiskey. The desire was still there and he resented it. After all these years he had never been able to completely extinguish the physical desire, but over time he had managed to make the very notion of sex repugnant. He had certainly filmed enough animals doing it to know how little magic and mystery and sharing of spirit was involved in the act. It was a simple mechanical maneuver to which society unreasonably attached an importance and mystique. It was nothing more than a biological imperative left over from the earliest of times. Too common to be so valued. A simple acrobatic accomplished with ease even by the tiniest-brained.

Take the dragonfly, for example, he told his smiling reflection. The dragonfly has been around for 150 million years now—a lot longer than we bipedal know-it-alls. And after all this time what is the dragonfly's grand scheme? His purpose is to live underwater in the muck for three-fourths of his short life, eating whatever morsels happen by while he molts again and again, changing from larvae to dragonfly. Finally he climbs onto dry land, shimmies out of his skin a final time, and takes to the air, awkwardly at first because his body is still soft.

Like softshell crabs, most of the soft-bodied dragonflies get eaten—not by tourists visiting the Outer Banks but by voracious birds. Those few who survive long enough to harden become expert aviators and then embark on fulfilling their one and only purpose in life—procreation.

Males and females lock together in flight. The male uses his penis like a miniature snow shovel to scrape out any sperm that a predecessor might have deposited, and then he deposits his own seed.

Successful mater or not, the dragonfly lives about a month. Its only concern is to survive long enough to get laid. After 150 million years of evolution, that's all it wants.

Reminds me of some people I know, Parris thought.

But not you, the man in the mirror said, and now his smile seemed more of a smirk. You couldn't care less, could you? You don't feel a thing. That girl who risked her pride and self-respect and bared her soul and lots of other parts to you is probably lying in bed now, and crying herself to sleep, and you don't feel a thing, do you, Parris?

"Don't tell me what I feel," Parris muttered aloud.

The barman crossed to in front of him. "Sir?"

"Nothing. Sorry," Parris said.

"Can I get you a refill?"

"Better not. Thanks all the same."

Parris looked at the sip of whiskey remaining in his glass. The glass was warm in his hand, the liquid lovely and dark and speckled with artificial light.

So maybe it is love, Parris told his sour mash and his glass. All right, call it that. But of a different color and depth and amplitude than the love I feel for Jenny. Which is different too than my love for Mackey.

So if you indulge in the first, does it necessarily diminish the other two? somebody asked.

Probably not, he admitted. Arguably not.

And so?

But it *will* destroy the commitment to experience none but the latter two. As masochistic and neurotic and impractical as that vow might be. And so how can romantic love be anything but a betrayal of something more enduring and complex?

On the other hand, the maggots of guilt and rage have been chewing on your brain for a good long time now, Parris, my boy.

Tennessee sour mash can't kill them and work will silence them only for a while. They're always in there, man, gnawing away at you. So maybe you should consider the possibility that you are more or less insane already and you shouldn't believe anything you tell yourself.

Well, there's the paradox, he said. He looked up at himself in the mirror. That's the everlasting paradox, isn't it?

He reached into his pocket then and pulled out a handful of bills and dropped a twenty onto the counter. He walked unsteadily out of the bar and into the hallway and tried to remember his room number and hoped that he would get lost somewhere along the way.

▪ ▪ ▪

The room was dark when he let himself in and the curtains were drawn. He closed and locked the door and then stood just inside the door, listening. Her breath was as light as a whisper across the room. He waited until his eyes adjusted to the dark and he could make out the low bulge of her body on her bed, the colorless shadow of a well-worn blanket.

He went into the bathroom and closed the door and undressed without turning on the light. Then he stepped back out in his underwear and retrieved the pajama trousers he had hung on the clothes rack that morning. He pulled them on as quietly as he could.

Aware of every grating breath and every creak of the floorboards and squeak of the mattress springs, he eased himself into bed. He pulled the cover to his chest and then lay there, looking up at the bright red unblinking eye of the smoke alarm.

He thought she was asleep, but even so her voice did not startle him. It was as soft as the darkness itself and there was no coldness in it. "You keep rejecting me like this," she said, "and I'm going to start thinking that there's something terribly wrong with me."

His own voice in comparison sounded harsh to his ears. "The only thing wrong with you is that you allow yourself to have thoughts like that."

"I know you're not gay," she said.

"How do you know that?"

"I have eyes."

"And very nice ones too."

"So is there somebody else?"

He wished that small red light would go out. He wished the batteries would die. "In a manner of speaking."

"She's not alive, is she?"

Nothing if not perceptive, he thought. "Only in my heart."

He heard her body shift slightly beneath the light blanket. He tried to keep the image from his mind. "Do you think that's healthy?" she asked.

"Not in the least."

"But you want me to honor it anyway."

"I'd be grateful if you would."

Another ten seconds passed. Every breath was an effort, as if there were something sitting on his chest. He could smell the barroom smoke on his skin, the whiskey on his breath.

"Could I ask you one last thing?" she said.

The red light glowed above him, the only star in his bottomless sky. "The answer is yes," he told her. "Yes so much that it hurts."

"Me too," she answered, her voice so small and broken that he squeezed shut his eyes.

He pushed his head down into the pillow, trying to stretch a soreness from his neck. When she did not say anything more, he opened his eyes again and began a series of exercises that sometimes helped him to relax. He tightened the muscles in his feet and then slowly released them. And then he flexed his feet to extend the calf muscles, and then the muscles in his thighs, gradually working his way up the body, one set of muscles after the other. He was pushing both shoulders down hard against the mattress when she spoke again.

"Good night, Mac."

He let out a slow breath then and felt something lift up from his body, some heaviness, some fear. "Good night, beauty."

"Just so you know," she told him, "I'm still naked under this blanket."

"Good God," he groaned, and rolled onto his side to stare at the empty wall.

■ ■ ■

He dreamed that he was flying and it was unlike any flying he had ever done before. There was no engine noise and the ride was as smooth as a sigh and the Cessna 172 responded to the controls with an alacrity it had never before possessed. All around him was a cloudless sky like a great high dome whose peak he could never reach, and below was the gently curving earth with its smoothed-out mountains and rivers and the geometric fields of corn and wheat. From five thousand feet even the highways looked benign below.

On the ground the sun had just now set and he watched the long great shadow pouring over the land from the west to the east, but for him the sun was still visible over his left shoulder, still a curving top edge of fiery light. He wanted to go higher then, so he eased back on the yoke and throttled up and still there was no engine noise and the small plane climbed effortlessly as if there were no such thing as gravity and the earth had no desire to restrain him.

At eight thousand feet he applied a gentle left rudder and the plane tilted unerringly with the right wing lifting twenty degrees higher, and still climbing, he corrected for the turn and applied the right rudder and felt the sureness of the craft responding a moment before his foot actually pressed down. He realized then that he was controlling the plane by thought alone and so he leaned back and crossed his arms over his chest and with his thoughts he began a series of maneuvers he would never have attempted before, a series of loops and turns and free-wheeling rotations he would never have trusted his hands and feet to control so expertly.

When he closed his eyes he felt the pull of the turns in his body and that was when he knew how an eagle must feel and what it must be like to be free of every earthly constraint and so like an angel, and with that thought he leaned back and thought *higher* and he felt the pitch change abruptly and the sudden sharp climb and he could sense the speed increasing against all laws of physics and he smiled at that too. It was only when he realized that the wind was also rising in pitch and almost squealing and now there was engine noise as well, a mechanical drone building quickly to a roar, it was then that he opened his eyes and saw the red quarter-ball of sun filling the lower half of his windshield. He saw too the position of his body, not weightless on his back as he floated skyward, but pushed back hard against his seat as the plane in a hard impossibly oblique dive was being pulled into the sun. The engine noise roared in his ears and his nostrils burned with the acrid reek of smoke and his stinging eyes blurred with tears. At the moment when his rattling cockpit filled with the searing light of the sun he squeezed shut his eyes and thought nothing and then there was the explosion of the crash.

Then only silence and darkness. Then out of the darkness the low, muted crackle of flames, the sound rapidly increasing as of a fire approaching, of flames racing toward him.

As the sound of the fire increased, so did the blackness decrease until the fire was brilliant and scorching all around him and he found himself standing in a blinding blue and orange atmosphere of flames. He stood in an ocean of flames and the wind was howling and blowing the flames into his face and off in the distance a child was screaming. Parris struggled toward the small, shrill voice and literally waded through the flames even as the skin peeled curling from his face and hands and he could smell his own hair burning and could feel the blood in his veins beginning to bubble. He called out *I'm coming sweetheart!* and with every breath seared his lungs and swallowed fire and the fire was everywhere and he had no idea where to go. He pushed on through the fire and struggled for that distant dying fading and finally silent voice and all the time a part of his mind separate from the panic kept whispering calmly even as he turned this way and that blinded in a confusion of helplessness and fear *He never called out, he never uttered a sound. . . .*

■ ■ ■

And after the dream it was all as before. He had fallen asleep quickly, dreamed the familiar dream, and awoke trembling to find that fewer than two hours had transpired. He stared at the darkness until midnight. One minute Diana's soft breathing would be annoying, the next minute arousing. As always, the dream left him feeling unbearably alone. At home he might get up and turn on the television, or if he was feeling clearheaded enough he would go to his editing table and distract himself until dawn. Here he had other options—and that was the problem.

She's just a child, he kept telling himself.

And kept answering, She's a woman, you fool. Ready and willing.

He had to get out of that hotel room. Get out before your weakness catches up with you, he told himself. Get out while you still can.

He climbed out of bed and gathered up his clothes and dressed in the bathroom. By the time he slipped into the hallway and heard the lock click behind him he knew where he could go for a while, where he could put his insomnia to practical use.

It felt good to be behind the wheel of his Jeep again, alone and driving through the darkness. But the drive was too short and soon he had to pull over into the gravel parking lot. There were only a few cars in front of the Eagle's Nest, and at first he assumed that he had made the trip for nothing. But he could hear music thumping inside the cement-block building, and then a pickup truck came speeding out from behind the building, with another vehicle, a station wagon, close behind it.

Parris drove to the rear of the building and there saw another three dozen vehicles parked. In the time it took him to drive from one end of the rear lot to the other, he counted eight men standing together in pairs, drinking beer, smoking, leaning against one another.

He drove around front again and parked close to the wall. He pocketed some cash, slipped his wallet and car keys under the seat, then climbed out and crossed to the door. The moment he stepped inside he was blinded by a glare of white light. The music was so loud that it seemed to thump against his skin, and he stood there momentarily helpless, blinded, until he raised a hand to shield his eyes and moved forward two steps, out from beneath the row of track lights shining down from the ceiling, pointed at the door.

Now he was blinded by darkness. He waited a moment for his pupils to adjust, and when he could make out the shadowy outline of the bar with red and green neon signs mounted behind it he walked in that direction.

He was aware that he was being watched and scrutinized every step of the way, aware that the undercurrent of shouted conversation had diminished upon his entrance, and began to swell again only after he had settled onto a stool at the bar. To his right a four-piece rock band was hammering away at their instruments, each man bathed in a different-color spotlight. On the small dance floor in front of the band a dozen sweaty couples gyrated against each other.

"What can I get you?" the barman said.

Parris squinted in the direction of the voice. "Jack Daniel's, straight up."

A moment later the drink was set before him. Finally something he could see. He sipped it slowly, the slow burn down his throat, the ember in his belly, the subtle wash of confidence. He took another sip and then turned on his stool to face the open room.

Every table was occupied, men of every size and shape, every economic persuasion. Studded leather mingling with Brooks Brothers, yuppie with slacker, farm boy with schoolteacher. There were a few individuals who might have been women but probably were not. Parris smiled at all of them as if sizing up his own private smorgasbord. A few returned his smile.

He finished his drink and signaled for another one. This one he nursed, barely sipping enough to wet his lips, always smiling, pretending to enjoy the music which to his ears was ninety percent bass thump, nine percent guitar squeal, one percent discernible melody. Then from somewhere behind the clamor came a tinkling of piano keys, five high notes, and he glanced quickly toward the bandstand but saw no piano player, no keyboard, just four guitarists and a drummer.

Glasses clinking, he told himself.

And all the while he could not shake the feeling—like the time in Costa Rica he had had to outrun a fer-de-lance, a snake so aggressive that it will actually pursue an intended victim—that he had better keep moving, better not look back.

He took it as a personal favor when the band announced that it would return after a fifteen-minute break. Parris downed the rest of his whiskey and signaled to the barman.

"Ever get any jazz groups in here?" Parris asked as the barman poured another drink.

"Second Sunday of every month," the barman said. He was a

stocky man of average height, with a full white beard and thin white hair. He wore a crisp white shirt with the sleeves rolled to the elbows.

"No kidding?" said Parris. "That's great; I'll look forward to that."

The barman nodded. "I don't care much for this loud stuff either."

"I can't even hear myself think," Parris said.

"Try having to work with it."

Parris raised his glass to the barman. "To jazz."

The barman smiled. "The Delta blues."

"Chicago blues," Parris said.

"I'd even take Dixieland over this noise."

"How about swing and bebop?"

"All of it. All except that fusion shit."

"Fingernails on a blackboard," Parris said.

The barman nodded and grinned. "You come back next month. Second Sunday, nine P.M. You'll enjoy yourself."

"I'll be here," Parris told him.

The barman moved down the bar then, mixing drinks and serving beer and glasses of wine. A few minutes later he returned to Parris, but when he saw the whiskey remaining in Parris's glass he began to turn away.

"You know," Parris said, and the barman turned to look at him. Parris smiled and nodded his head toward the crowd. "This is all very nice here, very collegial. But the thing is . . ."

He smiled and waited. The barman stepped closer and leaned toward him slightly.

"The thing is," Parris told him, "my interests are somewhat more specialized than this room appears to offer."

The barman glanced up at the ceiling as if checking it for cobwebs. "In what way?"

"Well . . . have you ever been to the public library in Brazelton? A good friend of mine works there."

The barman looked down at him for a moment. Something had changed in the barman's eyes. "Is that right?"

"As a matter of fact, he runs things there. And . . . you know . . . we share a certain interest."

"Why don't you just say it," the barman told him. "I'm not your wife."

Parris's smile felt pinched. "A younger man," he said.

"How much younger?"

"Well . . . I try to be flexible in that area, but . . . there was a boy by the name of Tony who used to work at that library. About fourteen years old? He and I hit it off very nicely."

The barman pointed to a small sign mounted on the wall behind him. WE DO NOT SERVE MINORS, it said.

"Actually I didn't expect to be served one here," Parris told him. "I was just hoping that you might . . . have a suggestion or two."

He smiled and held the barman's gaze for what seemed to Parris too long a time. And now when the piano notes played he flinched at the sound of them, five shrill screeches inside his head, a quick stab of pain in his ear.

"I'll ask around," the barman finally said, and walked away, down along the bar and then off to the side somewhere. Parris did not turn to watch him go. He held the small glass steady on the counter and stared into it.

A while later the band began to play again. The barman returned. He washed a couple of glasses and then came down the bar, wiping the counter with a damp blue cloth. He lifted Parris's glass and wiped the counter and then set the glass back down.

"Ten-fifty for the drinks," the barman said.

Parris handed him a ten and a five. "Keep it," he told him.

The barman nodded and wiped the counter. "Why don't you finish your drink and have a walk out back?"

"I'll do that. Thanks."

Parris waited another two minutes, then he downed his drink and slid down off the stool and walked out the front entrance.

Outside the air was cool and clean. He blew out a long breath and then inhaled slowly, hoping to chase out the smoke and the noise and the fear. Even so, he felt slightly off balance, as if there were water in his right ear. He shook his head once, but the feeling did not go away, and as he walked around the side of the building a humming began in his ear, a barely audible vibration that without increasing in volume rose in pitch to an electrical whine.

There were no couples in the rear parking lot now, no glow of cigarettes, nothing but cars and trucks and the single yellow light over the closed rear door of the bar. Parris went to the door and tested it, but the door was locked. He turned and looked out over the rows of vehicles, the music still thumping at his back, his head still feeling lopsided.

Out in the third row of cars an interior light came on, a soft white glow in the darkness. My signal, Parris thought. Let's hope that he knows Tony.

Parris was still twenty yards from the vehicle when its interior light blinked out. Parris froze. Suddenly he realized that his ear was no longer screeching, his head felt clear again. An instant later something struck him at the base of his skull and everything disappeared in a flare of red. He staggered and blinked and went down on his knees, both ears crackling now, a string of firecrackers exploding inside his head.

Somebody pushed him over and he felt his cheek scraping gravel. He smelled the dirt and the limestone chips and he felt at least two pairs of hands rifling his pockets. Somebody was wearing too much cologne, a nauseating scent.

"Nothing," somebody said, and then Parris wondered if he had only imagined it, so distant a word, as amorphous as fog.

He tried to push himself onto his hands and knees, but somebody kicked him hard in the stomach, the blow lifting him up momentarily before he went down flat once more. Somebody moaned and Parris thought That was me and he knew he was going to be sick now, the crackling red inside his skull draining like poison into his stomach and groin, and he pushed himself up again, struggling to get his face off the ground before he vomited, fingernails digging into the dirt, fists grasping stones.

He felt the whiskey burn in his throat and then his stomach bucking. He thought the sound of his vomiting extraordinarily loud but a few steps behind it somebody said "*Now,* gentlemen," and then the sound of footsteps and car doors and an engine rumbling to life and then Parris felt the tremble in the ground as the vehicle sped away.

He vomited two more times and then his stomach was empty. He breathed hard and fast and felt his heart pounding against his chest, but the nausea was over now. He felt his breathing begin to slow and he forced himself to move sideways until he could sit up against one of the cars. Except for the throb of music inside the cement-block building, the night seemed as empty now as his stomach. He looked up at the stars and they seemed particularly bright tonight.

Now, gentlemen, he heard again in his head. He climbed to his feet eventually and made his way around to his own vehicle and climbed in behind the wheel. He sat there for a while before he finally reached for the keys.

Now, gentlemen, he heard again and again. He opened the windows and did not go over fifty miles an hour on the drive back to the hotel. At least once every mile he replayed the two-word phrase in his memory, waiting to see if the wind or the road noise might whisk away the familiarity of the voice that had spoken those words, might somehow alter the image that voice brought to mind, the picture of a small bald man in an expensive tailored suit. But when he returned to the hotel the image was still there, the familiarity as clear as ever.

His head had stopped pounding finally. He lay on his bed fully dressed. Diana did not stir. After a while he sat up and slipped off his shoes and then lay back again. No bed had ever felt so soft and welcoming. Even the red eye of the smoke alarm looked friendly.

His ribs hurt when he rolled to the side but he did not mind the pain and only hoped that the ribs weren't cracked. He thought it was probably just a bruise. He would be sore and stiff in the morning but the injuries wouldn't show.

Overall it had been a very productive day. He had made several new acquaintances and had gotten to know the area better. He had found a place where he could listen to live jazz one night a month. He had learned a lot today, especially in the past two hours, and all it had cost him were fifteen dollars and a quick beating. He had wasted some good whiskey, yes, but he had still made a good trade. Yes, it had been a good day. And isn't good a good word? he thought. A very functional word for a change.

And isn't it amazing, he asked the smoke alarm, how good a kick in the ribs can make a man feel?

FOUR

═══════════════

I have run less than a mile but for the last five minutes the voice of doubt has been taunting me to give up the chase. It is ridiculous to think I can keep up with these wolves. My knees ache and my eyes are blurred with sweat and the hot tears of exertion. This camera under my arm gets a few ounces heavier with every gasping breath. And my legs get heavier, and my boots. I am more stumbling now than running, and there is a pain in my side like a yard of barbed wire sawing back and forth. The wolves are nowhere in sight. I'll never catch them, I'll never catch up. I blew it.

And so finally I stop. I stand there panting, wheezing, disgusted with my pathetic mobility. I'm wiped out, exhausted. I can't run another step.

But God the air is sweet and ripe with rain. There is a pucking sound of fat rain drops striking the soft earth. It isn't a heavy rain, not even a bona fide rain at all, just a few early drops, forward scouts, come to test their welcome, no doubt.

Well, you're welcome here, I tell them, and turn a smile at the charcoal sky. Just don't get my camera wet. I bend over then and kneel on the ground so as to unbutton my shirt and cover the camera for the plodding trip back to camp. And it is then I see that the trail I have been following, the single path through the scattered dry needles, separates into a Y just a yard or two ahead.

The wolf pack has split. And I know what that means.

Boogie time.

It's like an injection of adrenaline, a blast of pure oxygen into my lungs. I'm on my feet and moving again, not exactly running but in a shaky-legged trot. It doesn't matter which path I follow so I stay more or less with the one on the right, but somewhat inside it as it veers wider and wider beyond its companion path. The wolves know better than I do what lies up ahead, apparently; they're flanking their prey now, moving in.

A hundred yards more and I break onto a meadow, a wide, grassy clearing that runs another fifty yards on a gradual slope to a lake. The lake is maybe a quarter-mile across, and beyond it heavy forest. I make a mental note to locate this lake on my topo map; it's plenty long enough for my float plane, and judging by the blue-black waters, plenty deep.

But that's for later. For now I'm inching forward in a crouching duckwalk on screaming knees, headed for a gray boulder behind which to hide. I have the camera on again and zoom in at 15X so as to hold the entire pack in my field of view, eight bristling animals in a wide half-circle converging on the lake, converging, more accurately, on the single animal that has paused there on the bank, and has turned to face its pursuers, the stolen carcass still hanging from its traplike jaws.

The wolverine is a fearsome fighter and the wolves are appropriately cautious. Wolverines can be very clever at avoiding steel traps and stripping bait from them without being caught, and a wolverine though half as big as a wolf might drive a single wolf from its kill, but there are seven wolves now and they are smarter than any steel trap ever invented.

They move in slowly, each animal weaving slightly back and forth in its path, side to side edging ever closer, yellow eyes always on that low-slung enemy against a backdrop of water. The wolverine looks from left to right and left again, backing to the very edge of the bank. She drops the carcass finally and bares her teeth; she looks more weasellike than ever now, her snarl more frightening than a rottweiler's. If she can find a wolf's throat with those teeth, the wolf will go down howling, never to rise again.

But there are too many wolves and only one wolverine, and the end is inevitable. If there were a tree nearby, the wolverine could easily climb it, maybe even with the heavy carcass still in her mouth, and remain there in safety, eating her fill, grinding up bones and hide and skull and hooves while the wolves watch helplessly from below, leaping and yelping. But the trees are all behind her now.

She moves away from the carcass, she sidles away, head low, ugly teeth bared. It is easy to see why this animal is called the hyena of North America. An opportunistic and indefatigable scavenger, a homely collection of mismatched parts. Not fast of foot nor particularly keen of hearing or sight but with a brute strength that keeps even seven healthy wolves from moving in too quickly.

I have the camera on the boulder now, I am on my knees in the grass, my breath slowing but my heart still racing. The camera motor hums. I hope the battery holds out.

And then from the left of the half-moon circle a strike—a wolf rushes in and grabs for the wolverine's rear leg. The wolverine spins as if on a pivot, heavy-jawed head swinging the rest of the body around, mouth wide. But she snaps at only air, and in the next instant is hit from behind from the opposite side, another wolf moving in. She spins again, almost whirling on her stubby legs, and a wolf from the center flies in to clamp its teeth on her flank, heave her around, let her fly. The wolverine goes sliding and scrambles for her feet, but she is attacked by two at once now and the larger of the wolves has seized her by the nape of the neck, he's all but astride her, riding her with his teeth plunging in. A shrill yelp echoes across the lake but it is impossible to tell which animal it comes from, the air is alive with yelping and strange barking noises, high-pitched yips of savage glee or fear or pain.

And two minutes later, maybe three at the most, it is over. The wolves take turns sniffing at the wolverine, dragging it back and forth like a dirty cloth, tossing their heads and whipping the limp but heavy trophy through the bloodied grass.

And then they leave it there, they leave it to rot. They will not eat the wolverine, its scent is foul. They sniff at the deer carcass, pick it up, flip it over. The wolverine scent is there too, but not so strong, not so offensive. And there are pups to be fed.

A few of the animals clamber down to the lake and drink. One stands guard, panting over the wolverine. Then it too wanders toward the lake's edge. They clean themselves, lick their fur, lick one another, nip and roll in what must surely be a kind of victory celebration. But a tired one at that, marked more by relief than exultation.

I sit back on my haunches and let the camera hum. Only now do I again become aware of the blackening sky and the flares of lightning. The lightning seems to be coming straight at me from across the lake, carried by the wind. I had better hotfoot it back to camp soon. I won't beat the rain, but that doesn't matter now, I feel as satisfied as those wolves must feel, as vindicated, as empty of remorse.

There was nothing malicious or evil in their calculated attack, I need to make that clear. That is why there will be no narration on this or any other film, none of that anthropomorphizing language that no matter how hard it tries to avoid doing so paints the natural action of animals with the brush of human morality. I will not even use any of Henry's music here; there will be the crashes of thunder and the hiss of wind through grass. The distant yips and whines. But no commentary.

That little society of wolves acted purely and simply, as necessity dictated. It acted out of the oldest urge of all, the urge to protect itself. Not every threat is head-on and face-to-face. Some of the worst threats of all will come when the house is empty, when the larder is left unattended. And when that happens, the sneak thief must be dealt with. Even if this cache is lost, the next must be protected. One threat at a time, that is how you deal with them. This wolverine will never steal again.

I can't help but wonder how anyone could view this wolf attack with horror. In light of their situation, their always precarious and tenuous existence, this attack, this death, this execution, whether conscious or instinctual, it was the wisest and surest thing they could have done.

▬▬▬▬▬ A cold morning for the first of May, even for Jamestown. The sky was low and thick and gray. Parris awoke before six, eased out of bed, and showered as quietly as he could, though he fumbled the soap a half dozen times and nearly tripped into the mirror when climbing out of the tub. He toweled off and peeked into the still-dark room and saw Diana asleep, or pretending to be, so while he shaved he brewed two cups of weak coffee in the little coffeemaker bolted to the bathroom wall and drank both cups himself and thought What a stupid place to put a coffeemaker. Why not just bolt it to the toilet?

There was a dark blue bruise on his right side, but he was sure now that his ribs were okay. He could stand straight and move naturally, and as long as he kept his shirt on Diana would never know the bruise was there. He saw no reason to tell her about his little adventure last night.

When he emerged from the bathroom fully dressed and caffeinated, Diana had not yet stirred. He went downstairs to the coffee shop and bought a large black coffee to go and then walked outside and down to the river. He wore no jacket and hoped that the combination of shivering and more caffeine would chase the cobwebs from his brain, the thickheadedness and cynicism that always came from too much alcohol or too little sleep. With the sun burning behind the clouds the sky was as pale and hard as an eggshell, the river a slow and dirty stream.

At times like these he longed to be in the wilderness again. He usually boiled or filtered his water in the wilderness because the wilderness was not pristine either, but at least in the wilderness *he* could be cleaner somehow, cleaner of spirit, purer of thought.

139

And God how he wanted to be clean again. If only for an hour, just like any normal man. If only in the scorched austerity of Diana's brown eyes. The cleanliness of her scarred embrace.

But it would never work, no matter how long or hard she held him. There could be no release for him, no purifying moment other than the one predestined some thirty years ago. His desire for it might build and build in her embrace, escalating toward that point of absolute surrender and self-negation, but never reaching it, always nearer the impossible, but never there. There could be no transcendence for him, no *heureux petit mort*. And when she realized finally that she was not enough to keep him from the inevitable, not enough to erase the imperative of Spangler from his brain, everything would fall apart in frustration and pity and regret and where would either of them be then?

He only knew where *he* would be, where he always was, where he hated and yet never wanted to leave, in this wallow of self-absorption, this muck of mnemonics, wanting only violence, expungment of the basest kind, destruction in lieu of creation, the vile for the infinite. In fact just knowing how it must end roused the same tremulous feelings in him, that lust to destroy.

The big zero, he called it. The day he lived for. The moment of completion. The *nada grande*. God in the Buddhist sense, the nothing containing all.

For a long time now he had done nothing to move any closer to that moment, he had lived his life and done his work and had watched the days crawl past dragging their nights like the aging exhausted mourners in Camus' *The Stranger*. When what he should have been doing was taking a risk now and then, flipping over some rocks and rotted logs, looking for the serpent. After all this time could he chance a phone call to his parents, or would just the sound of his voice send them hurtling toward their graves? Surely the FBI had forgotten about him by now. Or did the FBI ever forget? And what of Jenny's brother?

For a couple of years after first leaving town Parris had checked in with Tom from time to time, a call from a public phone every three or four months, asking for any word of Spangler's whereabouts, any rumors overheard. But Tom's seething anger and vague suspicions sent Parris on one wild-goose chase after another, from Virginia to New York to Ohio to Idaho. Until finally, in New Braunfels, Texas, after three years of chasing a phantom and coming up against one dead end after another, Parris collapsed in a motel room with his traveling companion Jack Daniel's, and emerged from the darkness three days later to walk headlong into the motel's litter-filled but otherwise empty pool, where he lay baking for four hours in the afternoon sun before somebody called an ambulance and he was carted off to the local hospital. Of course the police insisted on discussing this incident with him, but his identification cards were all in order thanks to a small, gentle criminal in Nuevo Laredo who for eighty dollars could perform miracles with a bottle of Liquid Paper and a razor blade, so after Mac Parris paid off his motel and hospital bills he was released with little more than a stern warning to do his drinking in some other state from now on. He took the New Braunfels Police Department at their word and even beyond by driving due north through five other states, not stopping until he reached a whole other country. In Winnipeg he bought a tent and sleeping bag, a rifle and some fishing gear and a few other supplies, and he swung east for that place on the map of the Ontario province that had no printing and no black dots of cities or towns and no evidence whatsoever of human habitation. He stayed there through the summer, drying out, learning to live with the mosquitoes that plagued him through the day and the ghosts that swarmed around him every night.

One morning in late September he awoke to find that his breath had condensed and frozen in his mustache and beard, and he knew it was time to head back to civilization for a while. He made it as far south as Kalamazoo, where he worked several jobs before landing a position as a security guard at the university. Every evening on his rounds he strolled the corridors of the communications department, and now and then lingered for a cup of coffee with a young assistant professor who spent nearly every night in the editing room with a couple of graduate students. The next summer Parris accompanied the professor and three of his students up to Petoskey for a three-week shoot of a thirty-minute film about Hemingway's early days, and by the time the new semester started, Parris knew what he would do to survive for the rest of his life until somehow his path and Spangler's crossed again.

He had no doubt that their paths must cross. In the world of humanynamics, chaos can not exist without its opposite, and in every chaotic system, whether individual or universal, there must be as verification of the chaos random moments of order—moments when yin comes into contact with yang, points of contiguity. It is only at these moments or along these points that, if one is sufficiently prepared for the contact, yin can overpower yang or vice versa. Light can swallow dark, cold can extinguish heat.

In the end it will not matter which force survives because the survival will be brief. No force can exist without its opposite. When yang dies, so dies yin. The final result of this dual annihilation would be what Parris most desired anyway—the big zero. Death without end, amen.

■ ■ ■

"Well, aren't you in a lovely mood this morning?" Diana asked.

He had come back to the hotel to find her waiting in the lobby, and because he was still distracted and in his mind elsewhere until he walked through the door and saw her, and seeing her sitting there not angry or scornful of his rebuff of the night before but as lovely as that first time he had seen her standing on his front porch with the snowlights of an April sunset glinting in her hair, he felt suddenly resentful of his situation, this perennial condition of self-denial, and maybe even a little embarrassed by the foolishness of it all, so that when she asked him how he was feeling this morning he answered in a voice too loud for the stillness of the tiled lobby, not meant to sound as sarcastic or accusative as it did, "I feel fine, how are you?"

"Well, aren't you in a lovely mood this morning?" she replied.

She sat there with her legs crossed at the knee, her eyes calm, steady on his, waiting.

"Have you had any breakfast yet?" he asked a moment later, careful now to soften and modulate his voice.

"No," she said. "Have you?"

"I've had about a gallon of coffee. Which leaves me still a pint low. Care to join me?"

He held out his hand and she took it and stood. They walked together, no longer touching, to the coffee shop. "Sorry about that," he told her.

"About what in particular?"

"About everything, I guess."

"Oh, so you're the one responsible for everything, are you?"

"Didn't you know?" he asked.

She gave him a playful shove with her elbow. "I've had my suspicions."

"Smoking or no smoking?" the hostess asked as they came into the coffeeshop.

"Smoldering," Diana told her with a smile.

▪ ▪ ▪

By eight forty-five the clouds had broken and drifted east and the sky was once again as blue as a slice of lapis lazuli. They took up a position across the street from Miranda's home. Parris had parked the Jeep in the shade of a large tulip poplar, with the rising sun at their back, so that when Miranda stepped out of her front door she would be looking into the glare of the sun and would not be able to distinguish the occupants of the vehicle some thirty yards away.

"How do you think she can afford that place?" Parris asked. It was a stately and impressive Georgian that would not have been out of place in Georgia, a grand old box of a white-pillared house which by virtue of its size and iceberg-white paint and its stoical air of detachment on a double-wide lot dominated all the other grand old boxes on the street, the red and yellow brick Georgians modeled after a slightly more modest ideal than in-your-face affluence.

All of the houses were post–Civil War palaces, constructed probably during those frenzied years of greed following Colonel Drake's serendipitous discovery. But the oil was gone from Brazelton now, and so were the southern aristocrats who had rushed north with their remaining fortunes to suck the earth dry. John D. Rockefeller had come here and so had Horace Greeley. John Wilkes Booth once owned a share in a local well and had spent a summer here reading poetry and charming the ladies before heading off to Washington in his fawn-colored waistcoat, his tapered trousers and gauntlets, to put a bullet in the president's head.

Most of the houses along this street had long since fallen on hard times, only to be rescued in the 1980s by bankers and artists and double-income childless couples who were able to purchase a crumbling mansion for about $3000 per room, closets included at no extra charge. Renovations more than doubled that expense, but the market value had quadrupled and now even closet space cost extra.

"Maybe she inherited it," Diana said. "Or maybe she's only renting."

"Are sixteen-year-olds allowed to live alone?" Parris asked.

Diana shrugged. Parris knew what she was thinking, that until a few weeks ago Miranda had not been living alone, Tony had lived in that house, walked through those rooms, slept in one of the beds. And that was what the house had become to Diana, what it represented: Tony's place.

Another five minutes passed. Parris saw somebody move past a window on the second floor.

"Do you think she's attractive?" Diana asked.

"Who—Miranda? I guess maybe she could be, in a certain light. She has that gaunt, dissipated look that some men find appealing."

"What men?"

"Frenchmen during the occupation of the Third Reich," he said.

"And boys like Tony," she told him. "Somebody who might see her as a reflection of his own spirit."

"*Felix qui potuit rerum cognoscere causas.*"

"Does that come in an English version?"

"Lucky is he who has been able to understand the causes of things. Or so said Virgil."

She studied him critically. "You're just a little too literate for a man who avoids all human language in his films."

"What do you know about my films?"

"Henry showed them all to me. We watched them together."

"Henry doesn't watch my films. He told me so himself."

"And Henry told me that you're a charming, even-tempered man."

They looked at each other and spoke simultaneously. "Henry lies."

Then they smiled self-consciously, and Parris was the first to look away. His eyes fell to her right hand resting on the dashboard, the long, lovely fingers with a sliver of golden sunlight falling across them. But he did not care to look at that either, so he turned to his left and looked back through the row of houses at the yards and the swing sets and the small-town facade of cultured normalcy. The sunlight coming over the distant hills fell across the neighborhood in long shafts of yellow, long shards of light illuminating backyard swimming pools and a Frisbee on a roof and a bicycle in the grass. Up the street a woman in a bathrobe was watching her Pomeranian urinate against a bloomless rhododendron. A man kneeling in his driveway tinkered with a lawn mower. An older gentleman was sitting on his front porch steps, barefoot, watching his yard take on the light.

"Son of a gun," Diana said softly.

Parris turned to look at her. She in turn was staring at Miranda's house. He followed her gaze and saw the director of the library coming off the porch. He was dressed just as impeccably today as yesterday, a gray pinstripe this time, and carrying his olive-green canvas book bag, the same bag he had carried yesterday to the park. He walked briskly in the direction of the library.

"Son of a son of a gun," Parris muttered.

"What do we do now?"

"Damned if I know." He popped open his door and jumped out. "You wait here. No use both of us going off half-cocked."

She raised her eyebrows.

"It's just a figure of speech," he told her.

He had to jog to catch up with the director, whom he caught half a block from the house. "Hey, good morning!" Parris called.

The man turned, smiling, until he saw who had hailed him. His smile faltered and he took one small, involuntary step backward. Then he recovered sufficiently to stand his ground. "The answer is still no," he said.

"Fine with me," Parris told him. "But what's the question?"

"Miranda told me all about you and that woman harassing her yesterday. And if it happens again today, I'm calling the police."

Parris nodded and smiled. "Tell them I said hi." He moved a step to the right, hoping to get a look into the canvas bag. The director shifted the bag to his left hand. He eyed Parris steadily for a beat, then turned and continued on his way.

Parris trotted up beside him. "That's a great house Miranda's got," he said. "You shacking up with her, or is it vice versa?"

The director shifted the bag to his right hand again and lengthened his stride. "Miranda is my daughter," he answered.

"No kidding? How coincidental. Whatd'ya got in the bag?" Parris reached toward him as if to grab the bag. The director leapt backward, jerking the bag away. Parris heard something click and caught a glimpse of black.

"What's in the bag?" Parris asked. "Books on tape? Don't tell me that a librarian is contributing to our national illiteracy."

Angrily the director told him, "You could be a bore if you were just a little more interesting."

Parris stepped in front of the man, blocking his progress, dwarfing him by half a foot. "Why is it that the only time I hear a brilliant saying like that is when I don't have a pen to write it down?"

"You want a pen?" the man asked, and he reached for one in his inside pocket. "I'll give you a pen. I'll even shove it into place for you too."

"Thanks for the offer, but I'm not into that. I could maybe give you a couple of references though. Point you toward a pickup joint a couple miles out of town. Interested?"

At this a wash of apoplectic pink came into the director's cheeks. He shook the fountain pen in Parris's face. "You stay away from me and you stay away from Miranda," he said.

"She's a very nervous girl, have you noticed?"

"I'm telling you right now—"

Parris seized the fountain pen in his fist, at the same time gripping the director's hand. He then pried the pen loose and still squeezing the man's hand delicately returned the pen to the pocket of the director's jacket. He then squeezed the man's fingers even harder and moved very close to him, speaking softly. "Two things. First, you shouldn't carry a fountain pen in a nice coat like that; you're bound to have an accident. Secondly, I've been in the mood for a long time now to hurt somebody. Just so you know, I think it's going to be you."

He released the man's hand, smoothed down his pinstriped lapel, and stepped back. "Other than that . . . have a good morning."

Parris turned and strode back to his Jeep, smiling broadly, filling his lungs with arcadian sunshine and the scent of freshly watered rhododendrons. Diana met him on the sidewalk, looking aghast.

"That felt frighteningly good," he told her.

∎ ∎ ∎

They watched the house for another fifteen minutes, but there was no sign of Miranda. Not so much as a shadowy figure slinking past a window.

"My guess is she's a bit under the weather today," Parris said from behind the wheel of his Jeep. "The poor girl's a bundle of nerves. And that ghoulish little note of yours yesterday couldn't have done much to improve her health."

"It's only ghoulish if it's fiction."

Parris nodded. "She's probably still in bed, neck deep in blankets, afraid to come out."

"She's got a lot to be afraid of." There was an edge to her voice now which, though it did not surprise or worry him, set the tone for the day. He knew there would be no more playfulness now. They were at two thousand feet and the engine was sputtering and they needed to focus all their attention on the ground; they needed to find a clearing where they could set down without too loud a crash.

"We're into some serious stuff now," he told her. "At this point nobody really knows who we are. We can turn around and get out of this just as cleanly as we got in."

"Miranda knows me," Diana said, "so there's nothing clean about it. There never has been."

He nodded. They sat very still for a while, watching the house. Then he reached out and laid his hand atop hers. He spoke very softly. "In my line of work," he told her, "there comes a time when you have to decide whether to go wading into the bush or not. You don't know exactly what's in there but you know it's something dangerous. And you know that once you step inside, there won't be any maps or plans to tell you what to do, and there won't be anybody there to help you if you get into trouble."

She turned her hand beneath his, palm to palm. "The point of no return," she said.

"One more step and that's where we are."

She turned to look at him. "You always go into the bush, don't you?"

"I always have, yes. But only because I felt I never had anything, or anybody else, to lose."

"You're sure that Miranda's father is involved in this?"

"Do I feel it in my gut? Absolutely. Do I have any proof? Not a shred." The incidents of the previous night, which he had not yet shared with her and maybe never would, accounted in large measure for the strength of his hunch. It was enough for him, but it would never be enough for a court of law.

She squeezed his fingers and stared hard into his eyes. "Then maybe we should go get that shred."

"Maybe?" he asked.

"Definitely," she told him.

▪ ▪ ▪

At exactly ten A.M. Arthur Best unlocked the library's front doors. He stepped inside to turn on the lights, then came back outside for just a moment, looked up and down the street, and peered across the sidewalk at the empty churchyard. Then he turned and reentered the library.

Parked in his Jeep halfway up Coolidge Avenue, Parris lowered the field glasses he kept in the netting behind the passenger seat. "Open for business," he said.

"So how do we do this?"

He slipped the field glasses back into the netting, then patted his shirt pocket. The short piece of coat hanger was still there. "Very carefully," he told her.

The problem was how to get into the library and upstairs without being seen. There was only one public entrance to the library. And with Miranda still at home nursing a massive case of nerves, her father, Parris guessed, would be manning the front desk.

"He's never seen me yet," Diana suggested. "Maybe I could divert him somehow."

"He hasn't actually seen you, but he knows about you through Miranda. And you can bet that she gave him a good description of you."

"So . . . maybe we can use that to our advantage. What if I simply walk in and—"

"And what?"

"And . . . head downstairs maybe? Down to the children's section? If he recognizes me from Miranda's description, he'll think I'm up to something, won't he?"

"And he'll follow you downstairs."

"Giving you an opportunity to go upstairs."

"And if he doesn't?"

"If he doesn't . . . I come back outside and we try to come up with a better plan."

"And what if he accosts you somehow?"

Diana reached to the floor of the Jeep, picked up her purse and opened it. She took out a can of pepper Mace. "Then I spice up his life."

"Well," Parris said, and held his smile in check, "we've bumbled along this far, let's bumble some more."

Two minutes later Diana shoved open the heavy library door and strode inside. By the time Arthur Best looked up she was already halfway across the lobby, taking long almost haughty strides, purse hanging from her shoulder, left arm swinging military fashion. She looked straight at him as she approached, smiling a cold and steady smile.

Not a trace of smile graced Arthur Best's thin lips. "Something I can do for you?" he asked.

"I doubt it very much," she said. Just in front of his desk she turned on her heel and without breaking stride headed for the stairwell.

Best watched her disappear down the staircase. He listened to the echo of her footsteps. He glanced toward the front door and then toward the stairwell again. A moment later he stepped out from behind the desk. He started for the stairwell but turned at the last minute and stopped midway between the front door and the basement stairs, looking in one direction and then the other.

Parris watched all this from a side window, peeking down along the stacks of the nonfiction section. He knew that if the librarian turned fully to his left he would be coming to lock the entrance, and Parris could not let this happen. He did not know how he could stop it except by direct confrontation, but he knew he could not allow himself to be locked out with Diana still inside.

Parris made it to the front door just as the librarian was reaching for the lock switch near the top of the frame. Parris jerked the door open and stepped inside, Arthur Best's arm still raised in the air, his mouth hanging ajar.

"Now you can lock up," Parris said. The door hissed shut behind him.

Best stepped backward into the lobby. "I don't know what you think you're doing here. . . ."

"It's called playing the hand you've been dealt," Parris told him. He flipped the lock switch above the door, then came forward to lay a hand on Best's shoulder, fingertips digging in, squeezing a tendon. He drew the librarian toward the basement stairwell.

"You're one of those small-boned guys, aren't you?" Parris said. He squeezed the librarian's clavicle. "I bet you break very easily." Each time the librarian squirmed, Parris squeezed harder.

At the stairwell Parris pushed the librarian forward, down the first two steps, low enough to be out of view from the lobby doors. "Come on up," he called into the basement. "We have a bit of a complication here."

A few seconds later Diana appeared below them. "What's going on?"

"He tried to lock me out."

She came up the steps until she was one step below the librarian. "That wasn't nice," she told him.

"You people are going to be in very big trouble," Arthur Best said.

Diana looked up at Parris. "Can I hit him?" she asked.

"Maybe later."

"Then what can we do for fun right now?"

"I'm thinking," he said.

"Try not to make a day of it, okay?"

"We've sort of painted ourselves into a corner here," he told her.

"How's that?"

"The usual method is to find the evidence first, and then catch the bad guy." He gave the librarian a shake. "You are a bad guy, aren't you?"

Arthur Best glowered in silence.

"He doesn't want to talk to us," Diana said.

"He's not a people person," Parris answered. "In any case, we either have to let him go, or we find the evidence to prove that he is the bad guy."

"I vote for the second one," Diana told him.

"Somehow I knew you would."

He gripped the back of the librarian's neck. "How about a tour of this lovely old building?"

Diana said, "What if somebody comes?"

"I locked the door, but you'd better make a sign and stick it up on the glass. Closed Due to Illness, something like that. Then stay out of sight but keep an eye on the sidewalk. If Miranda shows up, get rid of the sign and let her come in. I have a feeling she'll be more talkative than her daddy."

With that Parris escorted the librarian back into the lobby and up the marble staircase to the second floor. "It must be nice to work in a place like this," Parris told him. "So peaceful and quiet. When did you first discover your love of books?"

"I should have reported you to the authorities the first time I saw you," Arthur Best said.

Parris chuckled softly and rubbed the librarian's shoulder. "Yep, you certainly should have."

The door to Arthur Best's office stood wide open, the room brightly lit by the morning sun. Parris paused for just a glance inside, but deemed it worth little more than a glance; otherwise the door would have been closed. In any case, he saw nothing unusual, a desk and chairs and the standard furnishings. They continued down the hallway to its end, past the three open conference rooms, to room number five.

This door, as he expected, was locked. But the lock was not of the type Diana had described, not simple and decorative but an actual keyhole, a narrow notched opening in a heavy-duty lock.

"I'm guessing that you have the key," Parris said.

Arthur Best turned his face to him and smiled.

The telephone rang in Best's office then, the jangle echoing down the hallway like a shattering of glass. After four rings the answering machine beeped, but whoever had called chose not to leave a message and hung up instead.

Now the silence felt deeper somehow. Parris realized that his grip had tightened on Best's neck. He released the librarian and flexed his hand, which had grown stiff with tension. Best's slender neck was flushed pink except for the white imprints of Parris's fingers.

Mac Parris watched the pale circles fading on the man's neck, the skin reddening, and he felt a wash of nausea in his belly, a constriction in his throat. What sickened him was not the violence but that he had been enjoying it, the surge of adrenaline, the heat of revenge. But now he only felt ashamed.

The evil which I would not, he thought, a line unbidden from the Bible, a Sunday school admonishment, and he realized with a shiver how serious the situation had become, how grave.

Even so, there was no going back, no place to turn around. The only option now was to push on.

"Let's make this simple," he told the librarian. "You either produce that key immediately, or I pick you up and shake you by the heels until you flip inside out."

Arthur Best stared at him, blinked once, and sniffed imperiously. Then he reached into the breast pocket of his suit coat and produced a single key.

"It's just another room," he said. "You won't find anything."

Parris pulled the key from his hand. "Let's have a look."

He unlocked the door and pushed it open. With his first glance inside, his heart sank. What he saw was a nicely furnished living room: a comfortable sofa, four chairs, small coffee tables and lamps, a thick blue carpet. Floor-to-ceiling windows ran the length of the far wall, the heavy draperies opened wide, the room bright with sunlight.

"It's just another meeting room," Arthur Best told him. "The women's reading club holds its monthly meeting here, as do the chamber of commerce and the library's board of directors. The only reason I keep it locked is to protect the furnishings."

Parris shoved him through the doorway, then stepped in behind and closed the door. Something about the arrangement of the furniture struck Parris as odd. The sofa faced a thirty-one-inch television set and a VCR in a wood-grained cabinet. The chairs were set in the four corners of the room, as if they had been pushed out of the way. Certainly not an arrangement conducive to group discussion, he thought.

But there was little else to arouse his suspicions. On various wooden stands about the room were a forty-pound Random House dictionary, a copy of *The New York Public Library Desk Reference,* and a two-volume copy of the *Oxford English Dictionary.* One entire wall was covered with glass-enclosed bookshelves, and behind that glass were hundreds of dun-colored leatherbound volumes. By all appearances save the arrangement of furniture it was just as Arthur Best claimed.

"What are the TV and VCR for?" Parris asked.

"The various organizations that use this room sometimes bring tapes to watch. And this is where I preview educational films; I'm very selective about what I make available to our patrons."

Parris nodded to himself. "The kind of videotape you delivered to the park yesterday?"

He felt the small man stiffen, saw a flush of pink go up the back of his neck. "I demand to know who you are and why you are harassing me like this."

"Take a seat," Parris told him.

"Excuse me?"

"Sit down and shut up."

Arthur Best stood motionless for a beat, then turned sharply and strode across the room. Parris wasn't certain, but he thought he noticed a tiny hitch in the man's stride as he passed the sofa and then continued on to sit instead in a chair on the other side of the room, adjacent to the cabinet that held the TV and VCR. The librarian crossed his legs at the knee and laid one hand atop the other in his lap.

"What's wrong with the sofa?" Parris asked.

"Not a thing. I simply prefer not to sit with my back to you."

Parris crossed to stand beside the librarian. He studied the sofa. Half a minute later he crossed to the sofa and lifted off the middle seat cushion. A cloth strap lay flattened atop the folded mattress.

"A sleeper?" Parris said. "Interesting choice for a library."

Arthur Best said nothing. Parris turned to face him. "Where do you keep the satin sheets—in your office?"

The librarian sat motionless, perfectly calm. Only his eyes betrayed him; they were sleepy with disdain, black with fear.

Parris replaced the seat cushion and sat facing the TV set. He stared at the blank screen for a while, then let his gaze trail slowly around the room once more. Nothing. No evidence of anything criminal. No proof, no hint, no clue.

"I suppose I could beat a confession out of you," Parris said. "Or let Diana do it."

The librarian merely smiled.

For the next five minutes Parris watched him. Parris knew how to be still, as quiet as a stand of reeds, as inconspicuous as a bush, and now he would see if Arthur Best possessed the same skill. Or if he would somehow betray himself, give his position away. Every animal did sooner or later, a twitch of the ears, a flutter of tail. It was simply a matter of time.

The librarian was not without talent, Parris had to concede as much. Arthur Best understood what was happening and he acted accordingly. He looked out the window for a while, then turned his head and gazed at the ceiling. Then at the door across the room. Then at Parris. Then at his own shoes.

He's feinting with his head, Parris thought. Using his head and eyes like a mama killdeer dragging a wing, trying to draw me away from the nest.

But the librarian's hands, they were another story. Motionless, as good as dead, the left one curled over the slope of the man's right hip, the right hand atop it. At one point Best moved his right hand to scratch his cheek, but the left hand never moved. Not so much as a finger twitch. Only deliberate stillness could account for such immobility.

"What's in your pocket?" Parris asked.

And there it was again, that shadow across Best's eyes.

"Now, see here," Best said.

"Stand up, you weasel, and empty your pockets. *Now*, gentlemen."

With those two words, delivered with exactly the same inflection Best had delivered less than twelve hours earlier, Parris felt the atmosphere change. It was almost as if the air began to glimmer, just as it always did for him the moment he found the perfect shot for one of his films, the culminating image. Sometimes it was the moment of birth and sometimes the moment of death, but in every case it was what all the previous footage had been moving toward, the defining moment, the justification.

Best stared at him flatly for another ten seconds, then pushed himself to his feet. He reached into both trouser pockets simultaneously and pulled them inside out, spilling their contents onto the carpet.

From the left pocket came three quarters and a dime, a breath mint wrapped in green cellophane. From the pocket on his right, a small rectangular object made of black plastic, not much bigger than a Wheat Thin. It lay with its face to the floor, the back side blank.

Parris crossed to the object and knelt beside it. With a fingertip he flipped it over. Seven tiny gray buttons. One red power button. And the manufacturer's name across the top: Panasonic.

Parris covered the tiny remote control device with his hand, then he closed his fingers around it. An instant later he saw the peripheral blur of movement as Arthur Best bolted for the door. Parris grabbed him by the ankle and jerked hard. Best slammed to the floor, hands and then belly slapping the carpet.

Holding the remote in his left hand, Parris stood and grasped the librarian under one arm, lifted him up, and tossed him into the chair. "Sit," Parris told him.

He stood in front of the TV then, aimed the remote at the screen, and thumbed the power button. Nothing. He lowered the remote a few inches and aimed it at the VCR, but the effect was the same, the digital display remained blank.

He depressed the power button a third time, this time listening rather than watching, and yes, there it was, he hadn't imagined it after all, the vaguest of clicks. Again he pushed the button, and again heard the click. It was coming not from the remote but from somewhere behind the TV cabinet, from somewhere above.

The wall was blank but for the white enamel cover over the heating duct near the ceiling. Parris aimed the remote at the vent, then he pushed the button. A click, very small, muffled, and then a nearly inaudible hum. Only a person trained to hear the anomalous would ever notice it.

"Smile," Parris told the librarian. "You're on *Candid Camera*."

▪ ▪ ▪

After checking the tape, which was blank but for a two-minute show of Mac Parris thumbing the power button on and off, head cocked like a dog listening for a distant whistle, he left the small camcorder in place and pounded the vent cover back into position.

"It's for surveillance," Arthur Best said.

"That would have been my guess." Parris sat in the middle of the sofa again and gazed at the librarian. So, he thought, we're both filmmakers. We're both voyeurs. What makes your version any dirtier than mine?

"Let's see some of the tapes," he said.

"I don't know what you're talking about."

"In other words, you're going to make me look."

"You won't find anything."

"Somehow I don't think I should take your word on that." Parris stood and unbuckled his cloth military belt and pulled it through the loops. "Let's have yours too," he said.

"This is absolute nonsense."

"Isn't it though?"

Parris crossed to him and seized him by the belt and roughly unbuckled it and pulled it free. "Alligator, right?"

Arthur Best said nothing. Parris grabbed him by the shoulder and pushed him toward the door.

In the smallest of the three conference rooms, and the only one without windows, Parris shoved the librarian into a straight-back chair. "Hands behind the chair," he said. He lashed his cloth belt around the librarian's wrists, cinched it tight, and secured his arms to the back of the chair. With the librarian's belt he secured the man's right leg to the chair leg. He then yanked off Arthur Best's silk tie and secured the left leg.

At the conference room door, Parris paused to look back. "One sound and I shove a dictionary down your throat, understood?"

The librarian sniffed twice, lips curled in a snarl.

Parris searched all of the second-floor rooms and came up with nothing—nothing but the certainty that he was looking in the wrong place. Downstairs he found Diana crouched in a chair pushed into a dim corner, positioned so that she could keep an eye on the street without being seen.

"So?" she said when he came toward her.

"See anything interesting?"

"A couple of patrons came by—one businessman and that over-dressed old lady from yesterday—but they saw the sign and then left. No Miranda though."

"That means she's probably still at home."

"What about you? You've been upstairs with him for an hour. Did you learn anything or not?"

"Not what we need," he told her. He looked toward the back of the building. "There's got to be a fire exit around here some-where," he said.

"There's one in the basement."

He reached into his pocket then and brought out his key ring. "I need you to get the Jeep and bring it around to the fire exit. Pull up as close as you can, and then just wait for me. Try to be incon-spicuous. I have something to load into the backseat and I'd prefer that nobody sees us do it."

"What's going on?" she asked.

He handed her the keys. "Mr. Best has invited us home for tea."

▪ ▪ ▪

Parris pounded on the back door of the Best house a second time. Again there was no answer, no sound of any kind from within the house. And yet he sensed that Miranda was inside there some-where, maybe hiding just around the corner, cowering in the shad-ows. It was in her nature to cower, he knew that much about her already. She lacked her father's arrogance and self-righteousness, his ability to look you dead in the eye and lie through his teeth.

He pounded on the door a third time. "Just kick it in," Diana told him.

"And come face-to-face with a double-barreled shotgun? I'd rather not."

"Then get out of the way and let me, damn it."

He took her by the arm and turned her to face him. "Slow down," he said evenly. But her arm was as tense as a sapling, her entire body rigid. Her nostrils flared when she breathed. He wished he hadn't told her about the camcorder in the library, the pull-out sofa.

They had left Arthur Best hog-tied and gagged in the back of Parris's Jeep, the Jeep now parked out of view inside Best's spacious garage, whose side door had yielded nicely to a short length of wire clothes hanger.

Now Parris eased his grip on Diana's arm. "Once we get inside," he warned, "you keep your hands off her."

"Just get us inside," she said.

He stepped to a small window just beyond the edge of the back porch and peered through the glass. He had to lean out over the railing to look into the window, but he could see through the screen and into the pantry, the washer and dryer, a freezer chest, a cupboard probably filled with canned and boxed food. A perfectly normal household. Except that it wasn't.

The window was raised two inches for ventilation, two inches of wire mesh screen between him and the pantry. Enough to keep his body out, but not his voice.

He leaned awkwardly over the railing, the wood pressing into his pelvis, his mouth to the screen.

"We know about Tony, Miranda," he said through the wire. His voice was loud enough to carry through the empty house, but there was a calmness to it as well, a resignation, a tone of, almost, apology. "We know that he worked with you at the library. We know that you and he were lovers. He cared about you a lot . . . more, I think, than he had cared about anybody in a very long time. He said that you were going to be his salvation, did you know that? He thought that being with you was going to make everything right again, make his life . . . worth living for a change."

He paused then, waiting. He turned his head slightly, his ear to the screen. He thought he heard a sound somewhere back beyond the kitchen, a small, animallike whimper. And it struck him as odd, as it had many times in the past, how alike all voices sound when reduced to a mere cry, the vocalization of pain. A wolf caught in a leg trap, a rabbit pinioned on dirty talons. A dog struck by a car, a moose calf brought down on the spongy tundra, an abandoned baby.

He tried to think of what to say next, what word or phrase could bring the wounded crawling closer to its predator. In this way at least we humans are different, he told himself; we always think we can explain our defeats away, talk our way out of them. But he could think of nothing to coax Miranda closer. And he could feel Diana's body leaning into his, straining for a look through the window, her breath on the back of his neck. Her nearness both irritated and aroused him.

In the end it was the silence that drew Miranda out, a silence she felt compelled to fill. "I don't know what happened to him," she said in a tight whimper, shrill, her voice rasping with phlegm. "I don't know where he is."

He turned to look at Diana. Her eyes were bright with surprise.

And then he put his mouth close to the screen again, tasted and smelled the cold metal, the ancient shadows inside the house. "He's dead, Miranda."

Another tiny yelp of pain. And then one long, impossibly shrill moan of anguish.

"Somebody killed him, Miranda. Somebody killed your Tony. And then the murderer cut his body into several pieces and scattered them all over New York and Pennsylvania. And it was somebody you know."

He felt more and more of the weight of Diana's body collapsing against his own. The warmth of her tears on the back of his shirt, her hands warm and still, holding to his sides. And in her agony and Miranda's he felt the pulsing soreness of his own chest and all the pain his own disappearance had surely caused, was still causing, and he wondered if his mother still cried each night as he had too for the first couple of years, he wondered if his father walked the darkened streets at night in futile search, vainly hoping that a figure might emerge from the shadows and call to him softly, a figure so like his own, and he wondered about Jennifer's brother and her own parents and if they after all these years still believed in and missed him or if in his absence they had learned to blame him too, and if such blame brought them the same unrelenting agony it brought to him.

She appeared through the blur of his tears and the thin gray gridwork of the window screen, appeared in the half-lit kitchen like a specter of a woman, disheveled, barefoot and still in her robe, hair uncombed, face streaked with grief. The lock turned in the door and then the door squeaked open. He stepped back from the window, stepped back from the door. Diana's hand gripped his arm, her fingers tight.

The screen door did not open though. Miranda stood on just the other side of it; she looked too frail to do more. Parris put his hand out and turned the latch and pulled open the door, and what felt like the coolness of the pantry rushed outside and washed over him.

■ ■ ■

It was a very ordinary house inside, if ordinary for the director of a small-town public library is a place lifted right out of the pages of *House Beautiful,* with an antique sideboard or armoire or desk in every room, handwoven area rugs you would no sooner tread across than blow your nose on. To Parris it seemed more like a museum exhibit of an oil baron's turn-of-the-century house than like a home where two people—and, until recently, three—lived secret, shameful lives.

By the time Parris and Diana sat on the living room sofa— though to call it a sofa seemed a gross insult to the forest green brocaded fabric and its eiderdown stuffing, and to call it a living room seemed a gross exaggeration—he had glimpsed only four rooms but each one looked as if a troop of anal-retentive chambermaids had just passed through. He could tell with just a glance that Miranda was not the mistress of this house. There was still sleep in the corners of her swollen eyes. A cleanliness fanatic would not forget to put on her face before falling apart at the seams. She would be better dressed for the occasion. No, Miranda was definitely a girl who would sweep a bit of dirt under the carpet if nobody was watching. She would forget to dust.

She sat now on the edge of a Queen Victoria chair and wept into her hands while Parris and Diana watched. Diana laid a hand on Parris's knee, and when he turned to her she looked at him with questioning eyes, as if to ask *Is this for real?* He nodded once and patted her hand.

"How long has Tony been gone?" Parris asked.

It took her a while to lift her face from her hands. Even when she looked in his direction eventually, Parris doubted that she was actually seeing him. Her eyes were focused somewhere on the far distance, watching shadows and auroras and other tricks of the light.

"Two weeks ago tomorrow," she said.

"Was it in the morning . . . the afternoon? When was the last time you saw him?"

Again the long delay in answering, the vacant, beyond-all-hope stare. There was something broken inside her.

But this time when she came back to them it was Diana's eyes she met, and for a moment Miranda's eyes were dark and bright and clear.

"Are you sure he's dead?" she asked.

Parris could not tell in the intervening moments if Diana was about to scream at her or spit on her or leap up and strangle her to death. He knew Diana well enough to suspect that all these responses were in her repertoire.

But in the end Diana offered only a nod, a slight tilt of her head, eyes closed briefly as if in prayer.

Miranda's eyes squeezed shut momentarily too, the fingertips of both hands pressing hard against her mouth, so hard that when she lowered her hands a minute later there were white impressions on her thin, pale lips.

"We didn't always see each other that much during the day," Miranda explained. There was a peculiar flatness to her voice now, a soft gray flatness as thin as yesterday's plans.

"We made a point of getting together for lunch, usually upstairs in one of the conference rooms. Arthur kept Tony upstairs most of the time. In fact the only time he came downstairs was when Arthur was out of the building."

"You call your father by his first name?" Parris asked.

"I always have. As long as I can remember."

Everything she said brought another question to Parris's mind. When had she lost her mother, and how? Was it her father's wish that he be called by his first name, or Miranda's?

He knew, however, that her answers would be other stories for other times, if ever he had the time and the opportunity to inquire of them. As for now, time was at a premium.

"Was that the last time you saw Tony, then? That day at lunch?"

She nodded.

He put his hand to the left as casually as he could, picked the telephone off its cradle, and laid the receiver on the glass-topped end table. For a while he could hear the small and distant beeping of the phone. Then even that stopped. He could only hope that none of Arthur Best's customers, upon finding the library closed, would appear at the house.

Miranda had watched Parris take the phone off the hook but nothing registered in her eyes, no fear or question. She said, "Arthur kept him busy with cataloguing and mailing and things like that. So at five o'clock I locked up out front and came home to get dinner started. That's more or less the way it always went."

"But Tony didn't come home that night."

She shook her head no.

"Was your father on time?"

"He sometimes stayed late for . . . private business," she told him. "So there wasn't anything unusual about that."

"I think I know about his private business, Miranda."

She looked up at him then, not startled or fearful, past caring. He felt Diana's eyes on him too. Without looking in her direction he put a hand out and let her take it.

"And when your father finally did come home, how did he explain Tony's absence?"

"He said he had caught Tony trying to open the safe in the office. And that Tony . . . threatened him."

"Physically?"

She shook her head. "He would never have done that. He was very gentle."

Parris felt something warm fall onto his hand and he realized that Diana was weeping—noiselessly, helplessly, unabashedly weeping. To Miranda he said, "Tony threatened to report your father's other activities, is that it?"

She nodded. "And so Arthur gave him the money from the safe and told him to get out and never come back."

"And did you believe that explanation?" Parris asked.

She did not answer immediately. She had tried to believe it, her eyes said. She had wanted to believe it, painful as it was to believe, because to believe anything else would be even more painful. To believe the warnings of her heart, for example, when she lay in bed each night and remembered what he had whispered to her, the promises they forged together, the soft-voiced plans they had made . . .

And so yes, she had believed her father. Because he came home that night and Tony did not. Because he was still there and Tony was not. And when there is no one else to trust, no one to share and alleviate your misery, and when you can no longer trust the one you love, you trust by default the only person left, you trust the jailer who has locked you in your misery, you trust the one you hate.

Parris asked, "Would Tony really have stolen from your father?"

She shrugged. "We always said that when we had ten thousand dollars between us we would leave."

"Together. But he wouldn't have left without you, would he?"

No, her eyes said. No.

"How long has your father been marketing pornography?" Parris asked.

He heard a small gasp from Diana and felt her hand tighten around his, her fingernails biting into his flesh. If Miranda noticed Diana's surprise, she gave no sign of it. She gave no sign of anything.

"It's what he's always done. In one place or another."

"And that's how he got this job at the library?" Parris said. "A client on the board of directors?"

She nodded dully.

"So all the materials—which are what? Books and tapes, photographs, things like that?"

Miranda raised her eyes to the ceiling; she breathed through her mouth; her lower lip trembled.

"So all the materials get sent out in library mailers," Parris continued. "And the postal service has no cause for suspicion."

Her hands in her lap moved against each other, back and forth, nail-bitten fingers sifting the elusive air of dreams and finding nothing to hold.

"And we're not talking now about run-of-the-mill pornography, are we?" Parris asked. "It's not the kind of thing I could rent at the local video store."

Her silence was his answer.

"And then," Parris said, his voice dropping a register, softening, losing all hint of challenge or accusation but assuming a tone of commiseration, "and then there are the local customers. That's what the room at the library is for."

Miranda blinked once, twice, sleepily, wanting to sleep, wanting to close her eyes to all of this forever. Parris felt exhausted too. He wished he knew some way to turn this thing around and go back to where he came from, back home to last week, last year, back to the womb, back to nonbeing.

"There aren't that many," she told him. "A dozen or so. They come by once a week or so to pick up a tape or drop one off."

"What about the clients you take upstairs?" he asked quietly. "The ones who come to see you or Tony."

She looked at him now as if he had suggested she was a freak of some kind, had publicly revealed a truth she thought that only she knew, had always known, a knowledge so deeply imprinted on her sense of self that to have it stated by another was not insult but a strange kind of relief, the sharing of a shameful secret.

"As soon as we had ten thousand dollars between us," she said, "we were going to quit."

"Except that your father would never have let you."

"He couldn't have stopped us."

"He stopped Tony."

They sat in silence for so long that he became aware of a clock ticking in the hallway. It seemed so loud, he wondered how he had missed hearing it until now.

Miranda lifted her eyes to Diana again. "We went to Pittsburgh every now and then," she said, almost smiling, just the trace of a crooked and heartbroken smile. "We used to sit in my car outside your apartment late at night, and Tony would talk about how you always took care of him when he was little. How you were the one to always bandage his cuts and make sure his hands were washed and—" Something caught in her throat and she swallowed hard; it went down like broken glass.

"If you had ever come out and seen us there," Miranda said. "I know he would have loved that. I think it's what he really wanted to happen. I know it is."

Diana swallowed her own jagged sobs. "Why couldn't he just come up and ring the doorbell?"

"He was just so . . . He hated the things he did. He knew you would too."

"But I wouldn't have hated *him*," Diana said.

It was a startling revelation for Miranda, this separation of act from actor, of deed from doer. Parris could see the surprise in her glistening eyes. The flare of—what should he call it? hope? expectation?

Whatever it was it was short-lived, too frail to survive. Her eyes soon clouded again.

"Did you know you were being videotaped?" Parris asked.

Both women stared at him.

"In the conference room upstairs," he said. "Your father had a video camera hidden in the heating duct. He probably taped everything you and Tony did there. For his own . . . reasons. Whatever they might have been."

Slowly Miranda's head moved back and forth, no, no, no. . . . But it was not the no of disbelief, not denial or incredulity that what Parris suggested might have actually taken place, it was a no of self-recrimination, the guilty recognition of one's own horrendous gullibility.

"Where would he keep those tapes?" Parris asked calmly.

A full minute passed before she answered. Her voice was different now, even more lifeless than before, and yet as deep and foreboding and hypnotic as death. "With the rest of his inventory, I suppose."

"And where is that?"

"There's a walk-in closet in his bedroom upstairs. There's a false door behind the clothes. He had it installed when we first moved here."

Parris nodded. A few moments later he stood. He held out his hand to her. "Will you show me?"

She looked at his hand but did not move. "I've never been in his room. Nobody is allowed to go in there."

"You don't have to be afraid of him now," Parris said.

She moved only enough to lift her eyes to his. She blinked dully and smiled dully and it was the most frightening expression he had ever seen.

Finally Parris turned and started toward the hallway. Diana stood to follow. He turned and stopped her at the bottom of the stairway.

"I need you to watch the door," he told her.

"I want to see what's up there."

"No, you don't," he said.

"I have a right to see what's up there."

"Maybe you do, but I'm still not going to let you."

"You think you can stop me?" she said, suddenly angry, needing to get angry. He understood everything she was feeling and had understood it long before she was even in kindergarten learning her ABC's. But his seniority in no way diminished the damage done to her in a shorter time, it made her rage no less valid than his.

He put a hand to her cheek, touched her with the tips of his fingers. Her skin was flushed and warm and soft. He felt something for her he had felt for no one ever before, not even for Jennifer or Mackey. A kinship that only the desperate and the damned could fully comprehend.

"I need you to watch the door for me," he told her, his voice little more than a whisper. "I need you to remember Tony the way you do now, and not the way you will if you come up those stairs with me."

She stood looking up at him and he heard the grandfather clock ticking behind him and finally he felt something go out of her. Her posture sagged and her eyes softened and he leaned forward to kiss her very delicately on the bridge of the nose. For just a moment a dizziness washed through him and he wondered if maybe he really could lose himself in her.

"If you see anybody coming, give a whistle," he said. And then he turned and he strode heavily up the stairs.

▪ ▪ ▪

It was not difficult to determine which of the four bedrooms belonged to Arthur Best. The door was closed, of course, but there was no lock—no expectation from Best that his word would ever be disobeyed or even questioned in his own house—and the old door swung open easily, swung wide open onto the eccentricities of its inhabitant.

The bed was small and high off the floor, a four-poster with no canopy. Parris knew just by looking at the queen-size mattress that it would be firm to the point of hardness. Like the rest of the furnishings, the bed revealed a curious mixture of indulgence and austerity: the pillowcase and sheets navy blue, crisp, and freshly laundered, all corners tucked in military-style, a single brocaded coverlet of matching hue spread evenly atop the sheets, not a wrinkle to be seen, not a hint of disarray.

Across the room from the bed was a solid oak cabinet containing another thirty-one-inch television, this one accompanied by two VCRs, piggybacked for the duplication of tapes. All but a two-foot perimeter of the polished hardwood floor was covered by a thick Persian carpet, red vines and leaves on a background of eggshell white. A pair of open-backed leather slippers protruded from beneath the bed. And all around the room, on small marble pedestals or wooden shelves, on the floor and one small table and on the oak dresser and even on top of the television cabinet sat the statuary. Plaster reproductions of Michelangelo's *David,* Verrocchio's *Boy with Dolphin,* a black-faced lawn jockey. There were a few original pieces as well, a little girl stroking a sleeping kitten, a boy and a girl on a teeter-totter, the half-scale bronze of a pre-school boy standing naked with his face and hands to the sky, mouth open as if to catch rain or snow or golden gleams of sunlight on his tongue—a piece which, like the others, would have been redolent of innocence and joy were it not for the sheen of a thousand handprints on the small, molded bodies.

To the left of the door was the walk-in closet. Parris pulled open the slatted door, folding it back on itself like a Japanese screen, and saw the rack of expensive suits in various shades of gray and blue and solid or pinstriped black. A dozen white shirts, heavily starched. The rack of conservative silk ties, the shoe tree holding ten pairs of brown and black leather shoes. Not bad for a librarian's salary, Parris thought. Not bad for fifteen or twenty thousand a year.

Parris shoved the expensive clothes into one corner and stepped into the closet. He found the light switch, flicked on the fluorescent tube, and waited a moment while it crackled to life. Then he leaned closer to the rear wall of the closet, running his fingertips over the textured floral wallpaper, pressing on each of the seams. Finally, near the shoe tree, one seam separated from another and depressed by a quarter of an inch, just enough that Parris was able to slide it easily behind the adjoining panel, and the second behind the third, and the third into a slender cavity in the wall.

Ingenious, he thought. And so damn nonchalant. No locks, no secret combinations, no booby traps. It's almost as if Best believed that he was doing nothing wrong and therefore had nothing to hide. Or maybe it's just the arrogance of thinking he's too smart to ever get caught. That his bedroom is inviolate. A sanctum sanctorum.

But, Parris told himself, sanctum sanctorums can exist only for those who believe in holiness or sanctuary, only for those who have something left to fear.

As for Parris, any residue of fear had departed, ever since he first looked on the bronze child with his laughing eyes turned skyward. He quickly scanned the shelves before him, an area perhaps two feet deep, ten feet long, and eight feet high. It was divided into four compartments of more or less equal size, each crammed full from the floor to the ceiling. On the far left were the commercially produced videotapes, some still in their original cellophane wrappings, others still in their boxes, many with titles in German or French or Japanese. But even in a foreign language there was no mistaking the contents of the videos; the amateurish illustrations and grainy photos of the artwork left little to question. It was pornography of the vilest kind, not just tits and asses and the mutual gratification of consenting adults, but the kind of prurience for which the United States Postal Service and the FBI tended *not* to look the other way, pedophilia and sadomasochism, simulated and maybe not so simulated heterosexual and homosexual rape, pederasty, brutality, self-mutilation, every variation of violent sexual act the human mind could conceive.

In the next compartment were the books, a few volumes of erotic literature but mostly oversize photography books, none of which Parris felt inclined to open. Next were the paraphernalia, the metal and leather, the spikes and rubber and plastic and prods required by some practitioners to augment their own basic equipment.

And finally there were the privately produced videotapes, the smaller 8mm cartridges from Best's heating duct camcorder. The tapes were labeled only with dates, each one neatly typed, dating back nearly two full years. Parris ran his finger from one row of tapes to the next until he found the label marked April 16. The date Miranda had last seen Tony.

Beside the VCR was the empty conversion tape into which the 8mm cartridge fit. Parris then turned on the TV, slipped the tape into the VCR, and pressed play. He turned the volume off; there was no need for an audio accompaniment.

Ten minutes later he whacked the stop button with the heel of his palm. He stood there for a long time then, leaning against the cabinet.

Eventually he removed the 8mm cartridge from the larger one. He went back to the closet and stood there, looking at the shelves. And now what do you do? he asked himself. What do you do with all of this and with everything you know?

You do what you have to, he answered.

He slipped the 8mm tape into his jacket pocket. And there were a couple of items among the paraphernalia that interested him too, so he pocketed these as well.

He slid the panels back into place, and then the dozens of wooden hangers full of expensive clothes, taking care to space each hanger evenly, just as Arthur Best would have done. No wrinkles for Artie, Parris thought. Not for our man, no sir.

He closed the slatted door and turned away.

Parris took a last look at the bronze child. And that was when he remembered something Saint John Chrysostom had said: *Sin is a suppurating wound; punishment is the surgeon's knife.*

The room seemed small and dark and foul to him now. An immaculate bedroom that was filthier than any burrow or cave or den he had ever crawled into. He turned away finally and closed the door behind him and went back downstairs with his pockets heavy and his spine stiff and his eyes as cold and as hard as a blade.

▪ ▪ ▪

In the living room he found the two women sitting side by side on the sofa. Diana had an arm around Miranda's shoulder; Miranda held Diana's hand in both of hers. Parris wondered where that capacity to forgive and comfort originated and why he had been passed over during its distribution. He could have used some of it now. Or maybe, like voodoo and psychic energy, it didn't work on one's self; it couldn't be used for selfish means.

Diana looked up as he entered the room; she questioned him with her eyes.

He went to the chair opposite them and sat down. He studied his hands. "We've got some choices to make," he said.

Diana answered, "Just tell us what they are."

Another minute passed. His hands were trembling. Finally he looked up at them and smiled at Miranda. "I think you had better go."

Judging by her reaction, which was no reaction at all, Miranda had apparently reached the same conclusion. All she needed was a nudge.

Diana asked, "Where would she go?"

"We always talked about moving to Maine," Miranda said to no one in particular.

"You and Tony?" Diana asked.

Miranda nodded. "I don't know why, but that was where we had decided we'd go. Maine . . . it just sounds as if it's so peaceful and slow and, I don't know . . . so clean there. It's probably not, but—"

"If that's what you want it to be," Parris told her, "you can find it there."

Diana held her awhile longer. "Do you have any money?" she asked.

"Everything Tony and I saved together. Eight thousand seven hundred dollars."

Diana choked back a sob. "You were so close," she said.

And then she did the strangest thing, strange, in any case, to a man watching from a few yards away—she leaned toward Miranda and slipped both arms around her and pressed her mouth to the other woman's cheek. A moment later Miranda returned the kiss. It was such a feminine thing to do, this exchange of warmth and touch, this inarticulate something, this healing gesture beyond anything Parris felt remotely capable of.

"I'm glad you had each other," Diana whispered.

"I'm glad he had you," Miranda said.

Parris studied his hands again. They were large hands and strong. He wondered what man they really belonged to.

"How did your father explain my and Diana's presence here?" he asked.

"He said that Tony had sent you to try to get more money out of him. That Tony was trying to blackmail us."

Parris smiled. "Whose idea was it for you to stay home today?"

"I was sick all night," she told him. "My stomach feels like—"

Like pounded veal, Parris thought. I know the feeling.

Miranda continued, "Anyway, I couldn't go in to work today, I just couldn't. He wasn't very happy with me but—I don't think he wanted me at the desk looking like this either."

A moment later her dark eyes narrowed. "What are you going to do to him?"

So, Parris thought, Diana told her. "What would you like me to do?"

She lowered her eyes, then she squeezed them shut. Her head rocked slowly from side to side. "Never mind," he finally told her. "It's not your decision anymore. Just rest assured that it's over. It's in my hands now."

When she looked at him again it was with sleepy, exhausted eyes. He knew that she would have that look for a very long time, would trudge through at least the next couple of years on an emotional flatline, wondering if she would ever experience happiness again, and not really wanting to, craving nothing but an end to all feeling.

"I need you to identify somebody for me," Parris told her. "One of your father's clients."

"All right," she said.

"He's at least as tall as me, maybe a bit taller. He looks like he might have been a weightlifter once—broad shoulders and thick arms and chest, but he's also got a pretty good paunch now. I'd guess that he goes at least two hundred fifty pounds. He looks to be maybe in his mid-fifties, with very thick, wiry hair, black and silver, and black-framed glasses—"

"My God," Miranda said. "Is he the one?"

"The one who what?" asked Diana.

"He was there that day," Miranda said, her voice rising slightly in pitch. "He had an appointment that afternoon. Is he the one?"

"An appointment with Tony?" Diana asked. "Goddamm it, Mac—did he kill Tony?"

Parris tried to counter the excitement in their voices with the calmness of his own, a calmness that was nothing if not illusion. "What's his name?"

"That's Mr. Diffenbaugh," Miranda told him. "Kenneth Diffenbaugh."

"I saw him talking with your father in the park yesterday. Is he local?"

She nodded. "He has a print shop on Seventh Avenue. Seventh and Wrangell."

Parris nodded to himself and chewed on the inside of his cheek.

"Is he the one?" Miranda asked again.

"You'd better go pack your things," Parris told her. "You don't want to stay here any longer."

But she sat there, leaning forward, staring at him, breathing hard. Her hands were clenched into white-knuckled fists, and after a few moments Diana covered both fists with her own open hands. She stroked and kneaded them softly, pulling at the fingers, coaxing them open.

"You'd better go now," Diana told her. "Go as soon as you can. Mac will take care of everything else that needs done. Won't you, Mac?"

"That's why I'm here," he answered. And for the first time since coming to this town, for the first time since meeting Diana and hearing of her brother, for the first time ever perhaps, he understood that what he had said was the only truth he really knew.

▪ ▪ ▪

Miranda went upstairs to pack a suitcase and get dressed and Mac stood in the hallway looking out the front door at the well-swept porch and sidewalk and the neat yard and the lovely, well-mannered neighborhood. Diana came up behind him and touched him on the elbow.

"What now?" she asked.

"I wish like hell I knew."

"Who's that man you were asking about? That printer."

He stood awhile longer with his face close to the glass. He wished he could throw open the door and stride out of there and drive back home with the wind in his face and get into his airplane and climb to eight thousand feet and look down on the world to see nothing but an endless field of soft white clouds, a thick, cottony bubble of clouds enveloping the entire planet, no sign of life at all below, no evidence of anything at all except the impenetrable sky above and the high white death below.

"It's getting ugly," he told her, and saw his breath fog the glass.

"It's always been ugly," Diana said. A moment later she slipped a hand around his arm and leaned against him. "Sometimes we just can't stand to look at it anymore so we make jokes or talk about silly things or find something to distract us for a while, but it's always been ugly, Mac. And it's always been there."

" 'Excess of sorrow laughs,' " he said.

"That's one I used to know. Alexander Pope, right?"

"Could be. I forget the source. I forget the source of a lot of things."

Her hand moved up and down on the inside of his arm. In thirty years he had not had as much physical contact with a woman as he had had with Diana in the past twenty-four hours. He thought it amazing how such contiguity could alter one's perspective so drastically, could precipitate hope where none had existed before, could rouse tenderness from its slumber, affection from its drugged and restless sleep. But he also wondered which awareness was the proper one for him, which was straight and which was skewed. There was a comfort in the hard white glare of the noonday sun, but there was a different kind of comfort in the soft glow of a moon-bathed night. Both fire and ice held an appeal. Yet both, in the end, could burn. At the heart of Dante's inferno was a lake of eternal ice. So maybe the two opposites were not mutually exclusive. Maybe they were variations on the same theme.

"Tony was such a handful when he was little," Diana said, more to herself than to him, as if the evocation of memory could resurrect the corporeal. He looked down at the top of her head, he leaned down and kissed her hair but she did not feel it, she did not know.

Her voice was Rashomonlike—haunted. "Even when he was only five or six years old he hated being told what to do. It wasn't that he was mean, he was just so . . . independent. Whenever I'd make him eat his vegetables or help with the dishes or do anything he didn't want to, sooner or later that day he'd trick me into going outside. He'd tell me there was a woodpecker out in the mailbox, or a fire in the neighbor's house. And I always fell for it. Those big sweet eyes of his . . . he was so angelic. And then, of course, when I'd get outside, he'd lock all the doors. After a half hour or so of me screaming and threatening to kill him, he would unlock the bathroom window or the basement door or some entryway that I practically had to risk my life getting into.

"But once I got inside, there would be a piece of candy or a cookie or maybe even a picture he had drawn for me. It was my reward for finding a way back in. And then I'd go looking for Tony, and there he'd be, off in a corner somewhere playing by himself, or taking a nap on my bed, and it was like—

"No matter what he did, no matter how angry he made me, he knew and so did I that we loved each other more than anything else in the world. Maybe more than anybody else ever would."

And as she trembled against him and he felt her tears soaking through his shirt, he knew what she was thinking, what the survivor always thinks. He also knew that nothing he might say could change her thoughts. That of all human emotions and their impact on the heart, guilt leaves the most ineradicable stain of them all.

He held her and listened to the clock ticking relentlessly and to the soft scraping sounds of Miranda in a room upstairs, dismantling her life. After a minute or so Diana drew away from him. With both hands she wiped the tears from her face. "All right," she said. "Let's get on with it."

He tapped the videotape in his jacket pocket. "As soon as we get Miranda out of here safely, I'll take this video to the police and tell them where to find Diffenbaugh."

"You're absolutely sure it was him?" she asked.

"Absolutely."

"How did he do it?"

Parris paused while he considered his answer. "Asphyxiation," he finally said.

"*How?*"

"He strangled him."

Her sob was a familiar sound to him, an animal reflex, a guttural cry. "*Why?* Why, why, why would somebody do that?"

"Diffenbaugh got . . . carried away."

"Were they having sex?" she asked.

He looked at her again. This almost clinical curiosity of hers—this compulsion to know the details while being able to dampen all emotional response to them, this inability to be shocked—she amazed him again and again. Her eyes were cold and hard, unflinching. And yet he knew how warm they could be too, how inviting and accepting.

Why don't you have that duality? he asked himself. You've got the yang but where's your yin?

"Were they?" she asked again.

"Diffenbaugh was, I suppose. If you want to call it that. Tony was on his stomach, Diffenbaugh on top. And Diffenbaugh's a masochist. For him sex and violence go hand in hand. And this time he went too far."

"Is he the one who cut Tony up?"

"I don't think so. The tape shows him getting up afterward, getting dressed, and getting out of the room as quickly as he could."

"Did he know what he'd done?"

"He knew all right."

"And where does the tape end?"

"With Arthur Best coming into the room. He used his little pocket remote to shut the camera off."

"So it was him, then."

"We don't know that yet."

"You know damn well it was him. He had to get rid of the body, he didn't want Miranda or anybody else to know. So he got it out of the library somehow, he cut it up, and he scattered the pieces. Trying to make it more difficult to identify Tony."

Parris blew out a long slow breath. He fogged the glass, then watched the circle of fog shrink and disappear. "Well," he said, "we'll leave that up to the police to prove."

"Like hell we will."

"Diana—"

"No. You just think about it, Mac. Just think about how this will turn out. Even with the videotape, what's the worst that's going to happen to Diffenbaugh?"

And she was right, of course. He knew that she was right. But he could not bring himself to admit it just yet.

"His lawyers will plea-bargain him down to voluntary manslaughter, an act of passion. He'll serve maybe ten years . . . in a place where he's free to do the very thing that got him sent there!"

Parris felt himself trembling again, felt the chill and perspiration in a vague and distant way, as if a part of his consciousness had separated from the rest and was watching him from across the room, waiting to see how he would proceed. "It's not our decision," he told her.

"It's *only* our decision. Who has more of a right than I do to make this decision? And what about Best, what's going to happen to him? He'll be in and out of jail in no time at all, living the same kind of life and hurting people all over again."

Even as he answered her he knew how hollow his argument was, how specious and phony. He didn't believe a word of it. He had already had this argument with himself a hundred times. And every time, he lost.

"We'd be no better than the criminals," he told her. "We've got to let the system work the way it's—"

"The system doesn't work! Jesus, Mac, I know you're not this stupid."

What he didn't like was the collusion involved. The open acknowledgment of what he considered his most vile and savage desire. Maybe he would not be so reluctant if Diana were not a part of it. His was a secret which, no matter how he had rationalized it through the years, he considered as dirty as Best's, as repugnant as Diffenbaugh's. And he did not want to share it. There had been a sweet and dirty pleasure in keeping it to himself, of thinking it applied only to Spangler and nobody else in the entire world. Spangler was his evil, his Armageddon. Yet here was a lovely and loving young woman with an evil of her own. And she was right, the justice system was clogged with evil and inefficiency and filth as well. So was what Parris had planned for Spangler, what Diana wanted for her brother's murderer, any less fair?

"Diffenbaugh," he finally told her. "All right. Because we have the absolute proof. It's irrefutable. But we've got no proof against Arthur Best."

"We can't have everything on videotape, Mac."

"I'd settle for a confession."

"Then go get it."

He heard Miranda coming toward the top of the stairs, dragging a suitcase. Quickly he removed the videotape from his jacket. He reached for Diana's purse as it hung from her shoulder, popped it open, and shoved the tape inside. "You keep this somewhere safe. Just in case I don't come back."

"I'm going with you."

"No, you're not."

"You're not giving the orders, damn it. I'm going and—"

He held her by the shoulders. "No!" He saw the fury in her eyes, and he heard Miranda pulling the suitcase down the steps now, one slow thump at a time, but he did not look away from Diana, he held her firm.

"When it's time," he told her softly, his grip relenting, "all right. When it's safe for you to do so. If you really need to—"

"I need it more than anything," she said.

"All right. I understand. But you wait until I call you."

"Wait where?"

"Back at the hotel. You get Miranda on the road, then use her keys to go to the library and get rid of that sign you put on the door. If you've ever been fingerprinted, make sure you don't leave any prints behind in this house or at the library. Then you get back to the hotel and stay in the room until I call. Don't open the door to anybody but me."

"What about . . . out in the garage?"

"I'll go out now to bring Miranda's car around front. Once we get her on the road, you head for the library. In the meantime I'll move the Jeep out to the street so that you can pick it up later. I'll leave the keys under the seat."

"All right," she said.

"Promise me that you will go straight to the hotel afterward. That you'll leave the rest to me."

"What would I do?"

"Promise me."

"All right, I promise."

He leaned down and kissed her on the forehead. "And one last thing. Do *not* look at that videotape."

"Never," she said. "When you're back, and everything's over, we'll burn it together."

"I guess I'm ready," Miranda said. She was standing behind them now, looking frail and exhausted. She had changed into a flowered granny dress and sandals but had applied no makeup and had scarcely run a comb through her hair. To Parris she resembled a gentle flower-child from the sixties, a slightly stoned waif who, like Rip Van Winkle, now found herself in a time and land she could not possibly comprehend.

But she was on her way to Maine, and that was good. If time moved slower anywhere in this blood-soaked country, it was in New England. Maybe she would be okay there, out on the fringe of the nation. Out in the salt spray and the numbing Atlantic chill.

As for Parris, still with one foot caught in the leg-trap of the sixties—

"Take this," Diana whispered. He looked down to see what she had lifted from her purse. With her back to Miranda she held the 9mm automatic close to her stomach and pushed it toward his hand.

"What are you doing with that?" he asked her.

"I'm giving it to you. Take it."

"Put it back in your purse," he said. He looked at her briefly, eyes stern. Then he stepped aside and went to Miranda and picked up the suitcase. "Give me your keys and I'll take this out to your car. You wait here."

Keys in hand, he started for the door, then looked back at her. "Do you know how to get where you're going?" he asked, and immediately realized what a stupid question it was. Did *he* realize how to get where he was going? Did anybody ever?

"I thought I'd just head north," she answered. And then she remembered something and turned to Diana. "I almost forgot," she said. "I left some pictures for you upstairs. Some pictures of Tony."

"I'll get them," Parris began, but it was too late, Diana was already running.

▪ ▪ ▪

The scent of September on fire, a September mowed and raked and dried out and smoldering. A group called the Beatles is singing that she loves him, a strange visceral harmony, it mixes with the smoke, it wafts in and out of his head yeah yeah yeah while nurses in blinding white uniforms pad noiselessly in and out of the

smoke, there is something malicious about their smiles, the trays
of food, the stink, every touch is another shock, every clang the fall
of a soft blob of clay . . . .

After the explosion he was kept in the hospital for eleven days,
under watch not so much for the second and third degree burns as
for the concussion and vacant silent stare with which he greeted
everyone who visited. He did not attend the funerals and did not
want to and nobody guessed that as he lay there wide-eyed day
after day staring at the yellow ceiling that he was attempting to
reverse time through the power of his will, trying through unwa-
vering concentration to wrestle time to a stop and then drag it
backward to a cool September evening pre-Spangler. The police
came to question him and then the FBI and his only reponse to
their interrogatives was a slow half-smile, because that small part
of his brain that acknowledged those somber faces saw them at a
distance and heard their voices in the distance and from such a far
perspective they all seemed slightly absurd to him. Theirs was an
exercise in futility because one of these mornings he was going to
awaken to a breathless giggle and the feathery touch of Jennifer's
hair as she swung it lightly across his face, back and forth and back
as she knelt atop him, waiting for his eyes to flicker open, for him
to swat at that tickle troubling him out of sleep. And then he
would open his eyes and see her there and she would ease herself
down atop him and his hands would slip easily around her waist
and up her back and pulling her closer he would taste her sweet
sleepy mouth and inside her and a part of her and their very souls
would wrap around each other in that rising falling timeless time
until later they fell apart exhausted, breathless, glistening with
each other's perspiration, and he would hear Mackey's susurrous
breathing from the other room and he would look to the rectangle
of sunlight in the high basement window and ask her *What time is
it getting to be?* And she would pinch his buttock and tell him *Time
to get up and make breakfast for your wonderful wife.* And there
would be no police and no questions and no tears or stink of
antiseptic and no stiff seared skin and no moans and coughs and
wails from down the hall no clanging of orderlies' carts no music
playing no nurses padding in and out on soft-soled shoes no taste
of fire in his mouth and smoke in his nostrils and the maddening

distant song on an out-of-tune piano *Old buttermilk sky* over and over and over again like a doorbell ringing in his ears.

But his concentration failed in the end. His willpower was not sufficient. One day it was October and he felt the chill of the season coming off the window. He told the FBI what little he knew and they looked at him without expression and he was released from the hospital. He went to Spangler's house and walked around sifting through the cold gray rubble until Jennifer's brother Tom found him there and took him home again. Spangler's old man is going around saying it was all your idea, Jennifer's brother told him sometime later, how long he could not say because he scarcely knew when one day ended and another began. He's saying that you must have brought the bomb with you that night. He says you were at his house on other occasions and he remembers you making sketches and getting very excited and angry when Spangler said he didn't want to get involved in any of it. And how you and Spangler even got into a fight one time and how both Spangler and his old man were afraid of you.

It was ludicrous to everyone who knew him. Unfortunately the FBI could not find Spangler to confirm or deny anything. The neighborhood was in a state of panic that there might be terrorists living among them. The newspapers bemoaned the deterioration of society and the apparent inability of the authorities to do anything about it. The Kinzua Dam Commission demanded that appropriate action be taken. A representative from the Seneca Allegheny Nation came to Jennifer's house to extend condolences, but then on his way to the convalescent's home he was intercepted by the FBI and taken away for questioning. Then Jennifer's classmates were questioned and a list was obtained of all the students who attended Spangler's meeting to protest the building of the dam and somebody remembered that the man who would become Mac Parris had traveled in Spangler's car and somebody else remembered overhearing him say to his wife at the Seneca graveyard that he was going to do something about this. He was questioned again by the FBI and everywhere he looked they were watching him and the second time Jennifer's brother found him sitting in the rubble of Spangler's house he knew it was time to leave and Jennifer's brother urged him to do so. He could not withdraw the money he and Jennifer had been saving for a house of their own because the FBI was watching all bank transactions, so Jennifer's brother gave him four thousand dollars in cash and sent him into the darkness with an embrace and a hoarse whisper, When you find Spangler, call me.

At four A.M. he kicked in the door of the sixth-floor apartment where Spangler's old man was living, and the first bullet ripped into the dry wood of the door frame and sent splinters flying and the second one whizzed past his ear to thud into the hallway plaster. By then he realized that Spangler's old man was shooting at him and he dove inside, sliding headfirst the way he had been taught in the Pop Warner League. Then from behind a sofa that reeked of beer and dirty bodies and cigarette smoke he watched the darkness overhead light up with four more streaks of lightning blue. He was not afraid and strangely calm as he thought to himself, I must really be crazy to think I can see bullets flying past, but then the percussions stopped and he stood from behind the sofa and walked across the room while the drunken old man sat fumbling with a box of .22 longs, spilling the little blunt-nosed projectiles across the twisted sheet and blankets. Parris walked over to him very calmly and seized him with one hand around the neck and the other beneath a sweaty arm and lifted him off the bed and marveling at his strength he said aloud in a whisper as sibilant as a writhing snake, *Where is he?* The old man swung the Smith & Wesson revolver against the back of Parris's head, but Parris's upraised arm as he held the man aloft partially blocked the swing so that the blows lacked full force and Parris felt them as dull, distant thuds not unlike the knocking on a door penetrating sleep and again and again he heard the heavy jarring thuds as he asked repeatedly or only imagined he did, *Where is he?* Then finally the dull explosions against the back of his head ceased. No more pulsations of red that rocked his brain and knocked his vision out of focus. *Where is he?* he asked one last time, and heard his voice coming back to him clear and alone, the angry scream of a stranger in a hollow room. He stood there, listening for what seemed a long time. He heard the echo of his voice falling away, fading into silence. His vision gradually cleared like the lifting of fog and the air stopped buzzing and he was surprised to find himself surrounded by broken glass. A fine dusting of broken glass glittered in his clothing, illuminated by the moon which he now stood facing, looking out across the balcony through the shattered double doors, and he realized that his hands were empty and something warm on the back of his neck was trickling slowly down his back. The room smelled of old beer and night air. He turned to the door and there was somebody standing in the hallway looking in, but whoever it was moved away as he approached and he picked up his suitcase where he had left it in the hallway and he walked calmly toward the stairs not quite remembering what had happened and it was not until a woman started screaming that he realized he was running over pavement with the clap of his footsteps chasing him and his blood stiffening on his neck and the powdered glass on his clothing magically ashimmer in the moonglow with a strange, ethereal light.

■ ■ ■

Diffenbaugh Printing consisted of a single cement-block building painted white. There were spaces for eight cars in the macadam lot out front, but all the spaces were empty. In the back was a small loading dock and a gravel lot, and here a lone automobile was parked. It was a 1985 Lincoln Town Car in excellent condition, deep sea blue, one of the last of the land cruisers. A big car for a big man, Parris thought.

He had left his own vehicle for Diana and he assumed that she would be on her way back to Jamestown soon. Diana heading south and Miranda in the opposite direction. He hoped they would both be safe and could think of no reason why they shouldn't be except that there were a lot of people between them and sanctuary and therefore a lot of chances for unfortunate events. But they were out of his hands now and there was other business to attend to.

Trying to look nonchalant, he knelt in the corner of the parking lot to tie his shoe and peered through the front window of the print shop. A plump but pretty woman in a green dress was eating her lunch at the desk, a tossed salad in a clear plastic container to her right, a magazine to her left. Behind her was an open doorway into the print shop, but the area was unlighted and he could see no sign of anyone else.

Still kneeling, Parris slipped both hands in his jacket pockets.

Briefly he squeezed the objects there as if they were talismans of a sort, objects from Arthur Best's closet, something to bring him luck or at least a knowledge of what he should do next. Maybe you shouldn't have been so quick to decline the 9mm, he told himself.

Finally he told himself to get on with it, whatever it turned out to be. He walked to the rear of the building again and peeked into the smaller door beside the loading dock. Now he could see the heavy printing machines, all dark green in the muted sunlight that came through the dust-filmed windows. And to the left near the front of the building, only a few feet back from the secretary's room, was a lighted doorway, a rectangle of dirty fluorescent light.

Parris tested the rear door. It opened with a slow squeak. He stepped inside onto the stained concrete and eased the door shut behind him. Staying close to the machinery and keeping an eye on the secretary's back, he moved closer to the room behind her. She held a fork in her right hand and now and then stabbed it into the container of lettuce, then held a forkful of salad poised in the air until she flipped two pages in a magazine. A radio was playing softly in her room and he could hear Stevie Nick's melancholy voice as if it were beckoning to him from the bottom of a well, inviting him into a tranquil, shaded doom.

Parris crouched behind a linotype machine and peered into Diffenbaugh's office. The big man sat there in profile, scowling at a computer screen, one thick hand on each side of the keyboard as if he were about to heave the contraption into a wall. He was wearing a white T-shirt and green work pants and heavy, thick-soled boots, the same outfit he had worn yesterday to the park. He looked even more massive in person than he had in the videotape.

Parris inhaled slowly through his nose, filling his lungs. He smelled ink and concrete, a deep and cold uncertainty. Only after he closed his eyes and allowed the videotaped images to replay in his head did the weakness dissipate from his legs. He felt his blood warming again and the stiffness leaving his hands.

He stood and moved quickly past the door at the secretary's back. He caught the scent of her perfume as he then stood with his back to the wall, something inexpensive and wonderful, a dime-store fragrance of jasmine and oleander. He suddenly felt something for her which on a dark night in a warm bed a man might be inclined to call love, but which at the moment he preferred to leave unnamed.

He stood erect and put a smile on his face and took three steps to his left and sauntered into the doorway of Diffenbaugh's office. He took his hands from his pockets and rested them on both sides of the door frame and leaned slightly inside. Still Diffenbaugh did not look up at him.

Another fifteen seconds passed. "I wish I had your concentration," Parris said. He hoped to keep his voice at a natural level and yet too low for the secretary to hear over her music. He did not like to think of what he might have to do if she left her desk to investigate the voices.

"It's not concentration," Diffenbaugh said, "it's confusion. I hate these things."

"Computers? I would have thought that they simplify your work."

"They sure as hell have done that. Every office in town does its own printing now, and I can't even figure out how to shut the damn thing off."

Parris smiled. "Arthur Best suggested I get in touch with you."

Now Diffenbaugh leaned back in his chair. A moment later he swiveled his chair around so that he sat facing Parris directly. He clasped his hands over his belt. "About what?"

"I have a manuscript that I would like to get printed. Just a few hundred copies to start. More if it turns out to be a . . . marketable work."

"What kind of manuscript is it?"

Parris glanced briefly toward the secretary. To Diffenbaugh he said, "Would you mind if I stepped inside and closed your door?"

Diffenbaugh put one hand in the air, a finger leveled at Parris's chest. "I asked you what kind of manuscript it is."

Parris stepped inside and eased the door shut against his back. "The kind that Arthur Best thinks could be very profitable."

Diffenbaugh stared at him without blinking. There were tiny beads of perspiration on his upper lip and forehead, ink stains on his hands, smudges on his T-shirt. Obviously he was a hardworking man, but Parris could not let that distract him. What was significant about Diffenbaugh was not his work but his play. Being stand-up in one capacity did not exonerate him. Ted Bundy was one heck of a tennis partner. Jeffrey Dahmer was the king of home cooking.

"So that's the way it's going to be now," Diffenbaugh said. His voice had the kind of flatness that precedes either eruption or resignation.

"Excuse me?"

"This is how he's going to squeeze me."

Parris smiled as stupidly as he knew how. "I'm afraid I don't know what you're talking about, but . . . All I know is that I showed a manuscript of mine to Arthur, and he thought that a printed volume might be received with some interest."

Diffenbaugh continued to stare at him.

"Of course I want to go first-rate from beginning to end. Hand-stitched leather cover, Smythe-sewn binding, acid-free paper. The cost really isn't important to me, I'm much more interested in aesthetics than in profits."

Diffenbaugh stared at him awhile longer, his face as hard and cold and expressionless as a stone. Casually Parris slipped a hand into his right pocket and fingered its contents.

Finally Diffenbaugh released a long, fetid breath. "What the hell," he muttered. "I guess it's not like I'm in any position to be turning away business. So where's the manuscript?"

"I left it in my car."

"So go get it and I'll have a look at it."

"It's, uh . . . Maybe we could talk outside?"

"Why would I want to do that?"

Parris could think of no good reason. He smiled sheepishly. "I'll be right back," he said.

He turned and exited the room, leaving Diffenbaugh still facing the door but with his head inclined to the left, looking askance at the computer monitor as if it had somehow betrayed him.

Parris paused for a moment behind the doorway that opened into the front office. The secretary was sitting as before, her salad half eaten, jaws moving absently up and down, grazing, docile, bovine. She was still listening to Fleetwood Mac, and now he saw the cassette player on top of a filing cabinet. The *People* magazine under her left hand lay open to a two-page photo of Don Johnson and Melanie Griffith strolling arm in arm along some unnamed beach, both with their designer jeans rolled to the knees, and it was captioned *In happier times*.

He wondered what the secretary felt when she looked at such a photo, when she read all the gossip and half-truths of her celebrity heroes, when she browsed through their addictions and surgeries and their relentless clamorings for attention. How were her own dreams fueled by the public indiscretions and peccadilloes of the silicone set?

She was living on salad and trying to lose weight and everybody's life was more glamorous than her own. Her boss's business was failing and she probably earned little more than minimum wage and she didn't even know that her boss was a murderer and a masochist and a buggerer of dreams. She would not have believed such a depiction even if you showed her. If her parents were alive, she was very good to them, and she was generous to all the neighborhood children and so what if she drank too much at the Holiday Inn on Saturday nights and so what if she wandered across the street once a week or so during her lunch hour and always ended up in the stockroom giving a blow job to the owner of the sporting goods store, who was married and had no intention whatsoever of ever taking her on that cruise to the Caribbean.

She was pathetic and innocent and Parris's eyes stung from the perspiration that trickled off his forehead as he checked one last time to make sure the parking lot out front was still empty.

He blinked and wiped his eyes and then striding quietly but quickly toward her back, he slipped the stun gun from his pocket and thumbed the on switch and before she even felt his presence looming behind her, he touched the contacts to the nape of her neck and squeezed the trigger. There was a short hiss of electricity and her body jerked. He caught her as she slumped forward. Careful to remain fully behind her he held her head in both hands and gently turned it so that she was staring at the wall. He let her head come down softly on top of the *People* magazine, her cheek next to Don Johnson's.

Her eyes were open, wide and bright with an appropriately stunned look. With his fingertips he eased her eyelids shut. Quickly then he went to the front door and locked it. From the outside she would appear to be taking a nap. He came back to her desk and eased the plastic fork from between her fingers and placed it in the salad container.

What must she be thinking right now? he wondered. Her body has suddenly stopped working, all muscle control gone. But she can hear the sound of somebody moving about and she felt my hands positioning her. Her mind must be racing with explanations. She's probably thinking she had a stroke, he thought as he lifted a sheaf of papers off her desk. Thinking about being spoon-fed and sponge-bathed for the rest of her life. All the places she wishes she had visited, all the things she wishes she had done. All the things she shouldn't have done for which she is now being punished. It was too bad she had had to be here. Too bad an innocent has to suffer.

He had maybe three minutes now. Impossible. Still, it was all he had. Carrying the sheaf of papers in both hands with the stun gun underneath it, he returned to Diffenbaugh's office. He strode inside and said, "Here it is," and dumped the papers in Diffenbaugh's lap. The startled printer did not even try to catch the papers as they fell; he looked at them for a moment and then looked up at Parris just in time to see the crackling blue arc of the stun gun an inch from his arm. The spark touched him at the same moment he swung a massive arm into Parris's stomach. Diffenbaugh jerked rigid in his chair and Parris felt the stun gun go flying from his hand, the wind exploding from his lungs.

Diffenbaugh groaned and shook his head and Parris groaned and tried to breathe. The room swam in a watery crepuscular light for Parris and he could not suck in any air. Nor could he believe that Diffenbaugh was struggling to climb out of his chair, his arms not wanting to support his weight as he tried again and again to lift himself up. Parris had no air in his lungs but he had no choice either and so he swung a fist at the side of Diffenbaugh's head. Something crunched. The jolt that raced up his arm and into his shoulder suggested that it had been his knuckles.

He turned, still gasping, to look for the stun gun. It was lying on the floor not five feet away. Parris staggered toward it. He was still two feet from the weapon when Diffenbaugh seized his right arm and, twisting it back, spun Parris around to face him. Diffenbaugh was grinning and his face was very red. Only his right eye appeared to be focusing on Parris. With one hand gripping Parris's tricep and the other around his wrist, he exerted pressure on Parris's arm in opposite directions, trying to break it at the elbow. Parris knew that in a matter of seconds his elbow would indeed snap. He could feel the cold black pain and the nausea already pulsing in him. He leaned toward Diffenbaugh for leverage and lifted his left foot and kicked it hard against the inside of the big man's right knee. The ligament ripped away from the bone and all the tension went out of Diffenbaugh's grip and he crashed onto the floor, landing on his buttocks, writhing in pain.

Parris wanted very badly to swing his fist into Diffenbaugh's face. Unfortunately he doubted that he could make a fist. Instead, he retrieved the stun gun and quieted Diffenbaugh with a double jolt to the small of his back. The printer went rigid again and trembled briefly and then tumbled onto his side, frozen in position still clutching his ruined knee, a whale of a baby in a tight fetal curl.

Parris rubbed his arm and felt for a protrusion of splintered bone. He flexed his elbow and was relieved to find that it still hung in the standard position, its hinge not reversed.

He stood over Diffenbaugh and looked down at him. "And now what am I supposed to do with you?" Parris asked. His knuckles throbbed and his stomach felt as if he had stopped a cannonball with it. He allowed himself another thirty seconds to get his breath back and for his vision to clear. Then he went looking for something with which to restrain Diffenbaugh while he was still in a mood to be restrained.

By the time he found the rolls of duct tape in a tall metal locker, the secretary was making shrill whimpering sounds and slowly rocking her head back and forth. Parris went back to her. "You slobbered all over Melanie," he whispered. He laid his left hand on the back of her head and then lifted the hair off her neck and gave her another quick jolt of blue electric sleep. Later she would no doubt check in a mirror and try to see what had bitten her on the neck, and she would find two small burns side by side. There was something very lovely and vulnerable about her neck with the hair lifted up like that, and besides, he did not want her to worry inordinately, so he leaned down and kissed her lightly on the burns and whispered in his best Transylvanian accent, "I vas going to suck your blood, but you are much too beautiful for an animal like me."

As quickly as he could then, he bound Diffenbaugh's ankles and wrists with several yards of tape. Another yard was allocated for the mouth. It took Parris a full minute of grunting and sweating to drag Diffenbaugh up into his swivel chair. "Did it ever occur to you to go on a diet?" Parris asked. The printer stared at him with huge predatory eyes.

It took him another fifteen seconds to find Diffenbaugh's car keys in a desk drawer. Twenty seconds to get Diffenbaugh's over-burdened wheeled chair moving across the concrete floor to the loading dock.

Parris checked one last time on the secretary. She was breathing regularly and was drooling freely. She would be immobile for another minute or so, then afraid to do so much as wiggle a finger for a while longer. Long enough, he hoped, for him to finish up unnoticed.

He backed Diffenbaugh's Lincoln up to the loading dock and popped open the trunk. Inside was the spare, plus a wooden crate containing jumper cables, cans of oil, road flares, and other sensible items. Parris pushed all this to the rear of the trunk and made room for something that was not very sensible. He wheeled the chair to the edge of the loading dock and dumped Diffenbaugh in. "Time to contemplate the error of your ways," Parris said.

He slammed the trunk lid down and hurried back inside the building and put everything in order again, the chair in front of Diffenbaugh's computer, the computer turned off, the duct tape pocketed, the sheaf of papers returned to the secretary's desk. She was trying to lift her head off the desk even as Parris tiptoed away from her. It would take her a while to realize that she had not gone blind but that the magazine was sticking to her face. It would take her even longer to realize that her boss had taken the rest of the day off. She would sit there and wonder if her boss had been the one who put the bite on her, and if so, what did that auger in terms of job security.

Parris left her to these and other ruminations while Stevie Nicks warbled about being taken by the wind and Diffenbaugh the printer wriggled dazed and trussed and uncomfortable in his dark and speeding womb.

▪ ▪ ▪

One-nineteen P.M. Half past perdition.

Parris pulled the printer's land cruiser into the librarian's garage, climbed out, and lowered the door. There was no telling whether he had been seen or not. No telling how many neighbors were watching from behind their windows; voyeurs were everywhere. He would simply have to proceed under the assumption of anonymity, just as he had been doing for most of his life. Someday he would be caught—by the FBI or by God or by an animal in the woods—but there was no use worrying about that day until it came.

For now he knelt beside Arthur Best, who lay on his side on the concrete floor, elaborately trussed, gagged, and tied to a support beam.

"Where do you keep your whiskey?" Parris asked.

Best squinted and blinked. He groaned something that might or might not have been an answer.

"Never mind," Parris told him, "I'll find it myself. You stay here and work on your articulation. And by the way—pay no attention to any sounds you might hear coming from the trunk of that car."

He had left the back door of the librarian's house unlocked after sending Diana and Miranda on their respective ways, knowing he might have to return, if for no other reason than to give himself a quiet place to think. And that was what he needed now, that and something wet to burn the confusion from his brain. He let himself in and closed the door very quietly; every sound was grating now, every squeak too loud.

He went in through the pantry and the kitchen, then turned the corner into the living room. Suddenly he was seized by the strangest feeling—the certainty that somebody was there just behind him in the corner. It was a knowledge that did not depend on any of the physical senses, but an intuitive knowledge which, though intricate and subtle, he had learned over the years to heed, even when it contradicted logic.

This time there was nothing to do but to accept it. He smiled and accepted whatever might happen, his hand in his pocket, fingering the stun gun. Then he turned very slowly, still smiling, and saw Diana braced hard against the corner, the 9mm gripped in both hands but canted upward now, aimed at the ceiling. Parris knew that a moment earlier the little Beretta had been pointed at the side of his head.

"How close did you come to shooting me?" he asked.

She smiled crookedly.

Close enough, he thought.

He looked at her a moment longer, marveling more at his own indifference than at his near-death. Then he turned away and went to the window. He stood to the side, the curtain lifted just enough that he could see the sidewalk out front.

"I thought I told you to go back to the hotel," he said a few moments later.

Diana came forward and sat in a brown leather wing chair. Her voice quivering, hands still trembling from what she had almost done, she answered, "I test very high for insubordination."

It was a line once uttered by Philip Marlowe and it made Parris feel like laughing. He did not care now what happened to him. He did not want Diana hurt and he wanted to live long enough to come eye to eye with Spangler one last time, but in the final analysis it was all just chance and happenstance anyway. The luck of the draw out here in the animal kingdom.

"I thought you promised that you wouldn't look at that tape," he said.

"What makes you think I did?"

"The fact that you're sitting there waiting to shoot somebody."

"Maybe I just feel like shooting somebody today."

"Maybe you'd better put that thing away."

She laid it atop one knee, her fingers spread over it. "I heard a car pulling into the garage. I didn't know it was you."

"It's Diffenbaugh's car," he told her.

"And where is he?"

"Asleep in the trunk."

She did not even attempt to conceal her smile. "Permanently asleep?"

"Just practicing," he said.

"What are you going to do with him?"

"I haven't decided yet."

He turned slightly so that he could look at her directly and yet take an occasional glance out the window. "I want you out of here, Diana. Please go back to the hotel."

"Who cut up the body?" she asked.

"Don't do this to yourself."

"Don't do what?"

"Don't poison yourself with this."

"Do I look healthy to you?" she asked.

"You look wonderful to me. You look beautiful. You look so beautiful that it breaks my heart to see you sitting there wanting to kill somebody."

"*Now* I get a compliment. Not when I'm standing naked in front of you, or trying to get you into bed. But now."

"Must be the gun," he told her.

She smiled again, but this time it was not a happy smile. "Just let me scare him a little bit. Let me make him think he's going to be shot."

"I don't want you going anywhere near that garage."

"Why not?"

He glanced out the window. The sidewalk was empty. "Because you can still be saved," he told her.

She laughed once—quick, deep, derisive. "Which turnip truck did you just ride in on?" she asked.

He listened to the clock ticking in the hallway. For some peculiar reason it made him think of Edgar Allan Poe—*It is the beating of his hideous heart!*—and he smiled in spite of himself, in spite of the situation, in spite of the chill that trickled up his spine.

"Who cut up the body?" she asked again.

"You know who," he told her.

She nodded. "Then why?"

"You know that too. To blur the trail. Make identification difficult."

"What about the fractures—how did those happen?"

He blew out a breath. It was beginning to taste sour. "Do we have to do this now?"

"You have somewhere else you need to go?"

And so he tried to look at the situation objectively. She had hired him to do a job and he had done it. So now he could turn around and walk away if he wanted because nobody had paid him to stand here at a window and try to decide what to do with two grown men. Nobody had paid him to risk a hernia by wrestling two hundred and fifty pounds of perversion into the trunk of a stolen car.

Come to think of it, he told himself, nobody has paid you anything yet.

So he could turn around and walk away from this if he wanted. But on the other hand, he couldn't. All she asked for was the truth and the catharsis, if possible, of retribution. It was what he wanted from his life too and maybe somebody would help him someday. It was an Old Testament idea, but he had never claimed to be Jesus.

And maybe that was what was wrong with society too. Nobody got any retribution anymore. Nobody ever got clean of the wrongs done to him, nobody ever healed and moved on. Are the Muslims this fucked up? he asked himself. Somebody steals from them, and the thief loses a hand. One needs only to look at the wrongdoer's stump after that to feel good and clean and safe and to know that justice has been served. But here in the land of forgiveness and rehabilitation, if somebody does you wrong and if the wrong is flamboyant enough, you will see him on TV talking about his book and movie deals. Something is rotten and it isn't in Denmark.

"I had a little talk with Diffenbaugh before I brought him here," he told her. "It's amazing how cooperative a man can be when you're threatening to hold a stun gun to his testicles."

"Oh," she said softly. "I'm all aflush just thinking about it."

He flashed her a disapproving look, then both of them smiled. It had taken him a while, but he was getting used to this proclivity of hers for making light of the most serious of subjects. An irreverence that had evolved, he guessed, as an astringent to pain. A numbing agent. The alcohol swab that precedes the hypodermic. He could scarcely imagine what her life must have been like as a child. How many times had she grinned through her teeth or smirked through her tears? The scars across her abdomen were only a part of the story, the visible tip of the iceberg of pain.

"According to Diffenbaugh," Parris said, his eyes on the manicured yard across the street, the small-town order gleaming in a clear arcadian light, "Arthur Best stepped in and took control of the cleanup. Unfortunately, Tony's body was a little too much for him . . . ."

"He dropped him coming down the library stairs," she guessed.

Parris nodded. "Over the railing. Hence the fractures."

Diana squeezed shut her eyes. And now she had this image to add to her archives as well. Now every time she closed her eyes she could choose from the repulsive white obesity of a grunting printer with his ink-stained hands on Tony's neck, or a long fall onto unforgiving tile, or Best's fastidious saw work as he bent over the frozen corpse, or any number of imagined scenarios that would fill in the gaps of factual knowledge. In any case, there were no entertaining images in the entire rack, not from now on. Now there could be just one colorful image of hell after another, Bosch after Beardsley, horror after horror. No wonder she was sitting there with a gun in her hand.

"So now they're both out in the garage," he told her. "And you're going back to the hotel."

She sat there for a long time, staring at the floor. "So what happens if we do turn them over to the police?" she asked.

Dirt under the carpet, he thought. Only to work its way back out again, sooner or later. But what he told her was, "That's what I need to think about. And I can't think very well with you sitting there staring at me. So get back to the hotel and stay there until you hear from me."

"Will you let me know if you need any help?"

"There's nothing more to do. Nothing I can't handle alone, in any case."

"I don't want you getting hurt," she said.

"Then the safest thing to do is to get you and that gun back to Jamestown."

▪ ▪ ▪

"Sometimes I get tired of pretending to be polite," Parris said. His knuckles stung from backhanding the librarian across his thin, sneering mouth, but at least he had managed to wipe the sneer away.

"So let me ask you this one more time. Did you or did you not cut up that boy's body in an attempt to protect your perverted friend?"

He took another drink from the bottle of bourbon he had commandeered from an elegant cherrywood armoire in the librarian's dining room. He had sat alone in the house for a couple of hours, hoping for an insight, a miracle of wisdom. Convinced finally that none was coming, he cracked the seal on the bottle of bourbon and returned to the garage. And now Arthur Best regarded him with a glower of disgust.

"I know how this must look to a man of your refinement," Parris said. "Drinking from the bottle, it's just not good form. But you need to understand—I don't give a damn about style points."

He took a second drink and held it in his mouth for several seconds, then leaned his head back and let the bourbon trickle down his throat. He thought of Henry Carlyle at home in his dark rooms, probably doing the same. Henry with his music and the mystery of creation. Henry with his memories that made the outside world too glaring and harsh.

And then there was Caroline Paglia with her Glorious Morning muffins and her old movies and the spacious sunny rooms of the Whiffenpoof. Henry was one side of the equation and Caroline was the other. Some people retreated into darkness while others sought the light of companionship. You should give Caroline a call when this is over, Parris told himself. If you know what's good for you, you had better give her a call.

He sat back against the wall then with his feet nearly touching Arthur Best. Best's eyes were black with rage and wet with fear. His lip had begun to swell and there was a fleck of blood in the corner of his mouth. Parris smiled at him and sipped his bourbon.

"I'm going to ask you two questions," Parris told him. "If you answer my questions, and don't say anything irrelevant for now, we can still be friends. But if you say one syllable that you shouldn't, I think I'll cut off your dick and then throw it outside in the dirt. Okeydoke?"

It amused Parris that the librarian seemed to be trying to kill him with his eyes. Parris felt nothing but the bourbon going into him, just the warm, slow sting of bourbon and maybe some distant gathering heaviness, some vague but amorphous gloom like the gathering of a storm at sea.

After a moment the librarian nodded slightly.

"Wonderful," Parris said. "Cooperation is the key to human advancement, you know."

The bourbon was doing its magic, he could feel it now. Turning tragedy into comedy, reality into cartoon. But he would have to slow down soon and be careful; the bourbon could take him only so far. "Question number one: I know you keep a money safe somewhere. Where is it?"

The librarian ran his tongue over his lips. "My bedroom," he said. "Floor safe, under the bed."

"Very good. Now then—can you guess what question number two is?"

"Sixteen right, twelve left, four right."

"Excellent," Parris told him. He went to Diffenbaugh's car then and got the roll of duct tape he had left on the front seat. He peeled off a long strip and smoothed it over the librarian's mouth. "You saved your dick—for now."

Twenty minutes after leaving the garage, Parris returned carrying thirty thousand dollars in a black flight bag. "I hope you don't mind, but I had to borrow one of your bags," he told the librarian. "Would you like to know where your money is going?"

Arthur Best glared at him.

"It's going to New England," Parris said. "You're sending it on a vacation. New England in the spring, tra-la. Isn't that nice?"

Parris picked up the bottle and took another drink.

Then he crossed to Diffenbaugh's car and opened the driver's door and sat down sideways, his feet still outside the car. He stared at the garage wall, the bare, unpainted wood.

After a while he put the bottle between his legs and leaned back against the seat and closed his eyes and he watched the skies darkening at sea. He watched the thunderclouds gathering on the horizon, boiling toward him as in some time-lapse cinematography. He had never cared for such tricks himself and always preferred that the camera tell a truthful tale. There was no camera now, but the longer he sat there the more he felt like the subject of his own documentary, as if he and Best were two animals who had reached the final minutes of their story. He could almost hear Henry Carlyle's brooding score in the background.

"The question now is what to do with you," he said. He turned his head to the side, looked toward the floor, the man in the thousand-dollar suit. "Any ideas?"

The librarian's eyes turned softer. How many wounded animals had Parris seen with just that look in their eyes?

"Do you believe in paying retribution for sins past?" Parris asked. "Paying off the old karmic debt?"

The librarian tried to move his mouth. Parris slipped down off the car seat and knelt beside him and peeled back the tape. Then he returned to his position behind the wheel.

"This is . . ." the librarian began, "this isn't right."

"What isn't?"

"What you're doing to me. And what you're thinking of doing. I know what you're thinking of doing to me."

"Of course you do."

"And if you do it . . . it makes you as bad as I am. It makes you just like me."

"There's some truth to that argument," Parris said. He smiled and felt the bourbon warming his belly.

"Unfortunately, certain aspects of my personality have been asserting themselves lately," he said. "I'm not sure I understand why. And I'm not sure I care . . . I'm not sure it matters. Except that I'm finding this . . . what shall I call it—my black side? I'm finding my black side very useful when it comes up against other black sides. It's sort of like starting a fire so as to put another fire out."

The librarian licked his sticky lips and considered his words. "Could I have something to drink?" he asked.

"Maybe later," Parris told him. "Maybe not. What we have to do now is to come to a decision. And since it directly affects you, I guess I should let you make that decision."

"I'll tell the police everything, I promise."

"Sorry, but that's not an option anymore. That would just make matters too complicated, and more people would get hurt, and it would cost the taxpayers a lot of money, and . . . it's all just too fucked up these days. I'm afraid I can't permit it."

"What do you want me to do?"

"Here's what I'm thinking. I can put an end to all this suspense and kill you right now. Cut your body up in a half-dozen pieces and scatter it around at various landfills."

The librarian squeezed shut his eyes and slowly rolled his head back and forth.

"Or . . . I can give you a chance to get away. Give you a chance to think about things and maybe even change your life."

"Please," the librarian said.

"Are you sure? Because I'm not going to make it easy, you need to understand that. I don't want you to survive, and I don't really believe that men like you and your overgrown friend can ever be redeemed. Sow's ear and silk purse and all that. So I'm going to make sure that your chances of surviving will be . . . maybe a hundred to one. Maybe a thousand to one.

"Choose life, the Bible says. 'I have set before you life and death, blessing and cursing: therefore choose life . . .' "

Parris lifted the bottle of bourbon toward his lips, but then he set it down again. "Damn Bible," he said.

He sat motionless for a moment, fingers curled around the neck of the bottle. "The thing is, it's all up to you. I'm going to let you make the decision for both of you. You are, after all, the cleanup man. So if you would rather do the right thing and pay off your debt cleanly, I promise that you won't feel any more pain. I'll put a bullet through the back of your head, right about here, and it will all be over for you. Everything. The good with the bad."

The librarian had not yet opened his eyes. His face remained tight, mouth tight, forehead furrowed. Parris looked away, toward the naked wood. He knew that the sky would be graying now, that side of the house in shadow, the sun low in the back. Out back there would still be the lemon sunshine of a spring afternoon, the soft crystal glow that photographers call magic light. But Parris was in the shade now and an even deeper darkness lay ahead of him.

When he looked back at the librarian he saw Arthur Best's face streaked with tears. There were dark spots on the concrete where other tears had fallen. Parris asked very softly, "What have you decided?"

Arthur Best looked up at him. "I want a chance," he said.

Parris nodded. He pushed himself forward then and stood away from the car. His spine felt as stiff as a metal rod, as brittle as a dead stick. "That darn Old Testament," Parris told him, "it'll get you every time." He grabbed the librarian by the ankles and dragged him toward the car.

▪ ▪ ▪

It was a long drive home in another man's car. Extended by the uncertainty of what best to do. Neither one is Spangler, he kept reminding himself. Together they aren't Spangler. So keep Spangler out of it and try to see this thing clearly for what it is and who they are.

But he was who he was because of Spangler. Parris was Parris because of him. Spangler was a part of it whether he knew it or not. He would always be a part of Parris's life, like a piece of broken glass stepped on when barefoot, left in too long until it became encysted and is now felt with every step. Sometimes you can forget about it momentarily and you go from here to there without a thought of it, so used to the pain. But usually each stride brings another twinge, another grimace, and sometimes you limp like an amputee, sometimes you would rather remain in bed than let your foot ever touch the floor again.

Parris waited for darkness, then drove the whole way home in the printer's Lincoln—so many miles, yet still he could not reach a conclusion as to the disposition of his cargo. They were crammed into the trunk together, no doubt gnawing at their duct tape. Or maybe just gnawing at each other.

The town of Ormsby seemed unusually quiet to him that evening, almost idyllic. The streets unusually wide and clean and welcoming. He pulled into his driveway feeling the same sense of homecoming as when he returned from a long, difficult shoot. But this time there was a lot more work to do before he could rest.

At the attached garage he backed his pickup truck into the driveway and moved Diana's car to the side, two wheels in the grass. He then drove the Lincoln into the garage and lowered the door. Afterward he stood there in his garage for a minute, just looking around, taking it in as if he had been gone much longer than a few days. The familiar scents and shadows now all seemed new to him.

In the house it was different too. The kitchen was brighter than he remembered it. There was more food than he expected in the refrigerator. The very darkness and the light of the house seemed altered somehow. Its walls stood farther apart.

But Parris knew that it was not the place returned to that had changed. The house was not different, but he was different in it. He knew too that with time and routine that sense of difference would fade, but for a few sweet hours anyway he was determined to languish in it, to know how new wine feels when the sediment begins to settle. To know the quiet exuberance of grass which, once heavily trod upon, has now sprung back to full height.

He drank a glass of water from his kitchen tap. You're a long way from Jamestown now, he told himself. A long way from Brazelton. You're in a whole different state now. You can rest for tonight, but the journey isn't over yet.

After a while he returned to the garage and popped open the trunk on the Lincoln. As he expected, Best and Diffenbaugh had worked themselves partially free, tearing through the tethers that bound their wrists to their ankles. It was what any trapped animal would have done. They had also managed to peel the tape from their mouths. Diffenbaugh kicked at him with both feet the moment the trunk lid sprung up, but Parris merely stepped aside and then showed him his sawed-off shotgun.

"You can keep doing that," Parris told him, "in which case I will have to shoot you and you will spend the night right there where you are, imitating a Jackson Pollock print. Or you can behave yourselves and crawl out of there and move to someplace a little more comfortable."

"Where the hell are we?" Diffenbaugh asked, and blinked in the dim light.

"In the land of the living. But that can be changed."

Arthur Best said, "What are you going to do to us?"

"That hasn't been decided yet."

"I can get you anything you want, any amount of money—"

"Can you get me a time machine?" Parris asked.

"A what?"

"Nobody can get me what I want," Parris told him. "Come on, get out of there. And don't waste your energy trying to do anything stupid."

"You promised to give me a chance," Best said as he squirmed toward the rim of the trunk.

"You're still alive, aren't you?"

In the corner of the garage was a narrow stairwell that led into the basement. Parris herded them down the steps with Diffenbaugh in the front. They hopped down the steps one at a time, then across the concrete floor to a steel I-beam in the center of the room. Here Parris instructed them to sit on opposite sides of the I-beam. Then he removed from his jacket pocket the second item from Best's closet, a pair of handcuffs. He threaded the handcuffs through one of the holes in the I-beam and then snapped one cuff around each man's ankle.

Later he brought them sandwiches and a plastic pitcher full of water. He gave them each a blanket and a pillow. "Just so you know," he told them. "If I hear one sound from either of you, you won't live until morning. I have a freezer too, and lots of sharp knives. And I'll be happy to take Tony's revenge for him."

"What's he to you anyway?" Diffenbaugh asked.

"Maybe a kindred spirit," Parris answered. "Or maybe nothing. Or maybe just a damn good reason to inflict a lot of damage. In any case," he said, and he put his face close to Diffenbaugh's, "it won't be very fruitful to inquire further."

He left them in darkness and went upstairs to his own crepuscular light. He sat for a while in the living room, staring at the blank screen of the TV set. Then he went into his editing room and sat for a while with his equipment, but he could not summon up the energy or the justification to turn anything on and do some work. What did any of the work matter now? What had it ever mattered? Still, he hoped that Henry Carlyle had come up with some good tracks for the wolverine film. But of course he had, Henry never let him down. Parris would like to finish that film at least. He might not be able to make another, but he hated to leave anything unfinished. He wished he could give Henry a call, but he knew it would not be wise just now. He wished he could drop in on Caroline too and maybe watch *Key Largo* with his arm around her shoulders and her body warm against him. But that was not for him now. It hadn't been before and it wasn't now either, but for different reasons. For now the night was an abyss of uncertainty and he was standing on its very edge, leaning ever forward.

He lay atop his bed fully dressed and with no lights on in the house. What it all comes down to is this, he told himself: What do you believe?

Do you believe you can get away with it?

Yes. Absolutely.

But what if you don't?

It doesn't matter.

You're not afraid of prison?

I've been in prison for over thirty years. What about what comes after?

Yes, what about it? Where has it been all this time? Where is its influence?

But what if you're wrong? Can you really fight evil with evil?

Those are just words, Parris told himself. It's just semantics.

You're surrendering your soul to darkness.

To deny the darkness is to deny one side of the soul. And to deny either side, the light or the dark, is to deny the existence of the whole. Can the moon exist without the side we never see? Can there be a coin with only one face? An inside without an outside? There is no such thing as one dimension.

So you've already decided. You have your mind made up.

The trick as I see it is not to deny the darkness but to use it for good purpose. Use it to enhance the light rather than to deepen the darkness. Just as a star will appear brighter if you focus not on the star but on its ambient darkness. See the craters of the moon most vividly by gazing along its darkened cusp.

Two metaphors don't make a reality.

How about three, then? A sudden flash of light against the afternoon sky might go completely unnoticed, but a single Roman candle sent high into the black silence of heaven might make enough of a spectacle to—

To what, man? Get a grip on the language, why don't you. Nobody really talks or thinks like that.

Maybe I'm losing my grip.

Maybe you already have.

And maybe, to paraphrase a friend of mine, I am precisely what the situation calls for.

There are a lot of maybes and mights in your theory, Parris.

"For the good that I would, I do not: but the evil which I would not, that I do. Now if I do that I would not, it is no more I that do it, but sin that dwelleth in me."

The boys in the basement could make the same excuse, couldn't they?

The difference is not in the act but in the motivation behind the act.

And maybe you're just trying to rationalize now. Maybe you're just looking for an excuse.

Maybe you're right, he said.

▪ ▪ ▪

They left the house in the gray light of false dawn. The weather was going to be clear and Parris was grateful for that. He had emptied the back of his pickup truck and made room in it for Best and Diffenbaugh, their wrists and mouths and eyes bound with new layers of duct tape, as were their ankles. In addition, the men were handcuffed together at the ankles. He loaded them into the back of his truck and secured them inside, out of sight beneath the tinted windows of the bed cap. He locked the Lincoln inside the garage with the flight bag full of money inside the trunk. Then he drove four miles to a wide, flat clearing outside of town. There was a single airstrip here and a steel building and two rows of hangars. His Cessna 172 waited behind a chain-link fence near the farthest hangar.

The orange of a rising sun was just beginning to bleed over the horizon when he strolled into the steel building. Frank Harmon was at the desk, asleep, sprawled back in his chair, head thrown back, grizzled mouth hanging open. When the door fell shut behind Parris, Harmon opened his eyes and blinked twice, then sat up and looked toward the door and smiled.

Harmon was in his seventies and was no longer allowed to fly, but he worked the desk seven days a week and probably would have died ten years ago had he been deprived this proximity to the machines he so loved. He was thin and stooped now, half blind, and his hands shook as he pushed the clipboard toward Parris.

"This was always my favorite time for flying," Harmon told him.

"It can't be beat," Parris said. He had telephoned the night before and asked to have his airplane fueled and the floats installed and everything ready for a dawn takeoff.

"Going cruising over the lake, are you?" the old man asked.

Parris nodded and smiled and signed for twenty-five gallons of avgas. He slid the clipboard back across the countertop. "Thought I might head out to Long Point, then swing back and buzz Presque Isle, take advantage of this beautiful sky."

"Something about the light at this time of day," Harmon told him.

"Something magical about the air."

Parris had never been able to speak with the old man without thinking it a crime that he was denied one last flight. Let him take his plane up and push it as high and hard as it would go and then aim it at the middle of deep water and take that long last tumble down through the clouds. If Parris lived that long, that was how he would want to go.

Except that he knew he never would.

"You'll be taking off headed west," Harmon told him. "A little crosswind blowing, but nothing to worry about."

"Thanks," Parris told him. At the door he paused for a moment and looked back.

"I've been meaning to ask you," Parris said. "I don't know if it's carburetor heat or the magnetos, but my engine sounds a little rough above ten thousand feet. How about if you and I go up together later this week and you put it through the paces for me, let me know how it feels to you."

The old man's eyes brightened. "We could do that," he said. " 'Course . . .''

"It's nobody's business but our own," Parris told him. He winked then and stepped outside and the sky was already bluer to the west, the air as clean and quiet and salubrious as any he could remember.

He drove his pickup truck to the lot at the end of the farthest hangar. There was nobody else in sight and in the shadow of the long metal shell the air was still chilled. He backed the pickup's tailgate nearly up against the airplane door and then dragged Best and Diffenbaugh out, one man at a time.

"Put your foot here," he told them, guiding each step until both men lay in the cargo area behind the plane's third seat. He stepped outside again and walked through the preflight check. Then he climbed back into the cockpit and logged his takeoff time. He completed the instrument check and feathered the prop and then he revved the engine until the little plane was trembling on the tarmac. Finally he throttled back and taxied to the eastern edge of the runway and made the turn.

The sun was at his back now, the shadow of his plane lying long and gray and thin before him. The sky was absolutely clear, as empty and beautiful as a child's soap bubble. Parris felt quiveringly alert, an arrow stopped in time, poised to soar, gathering unto itself all the tension and thrust of a taut and trembling past.

He shoved the throttle forward and felt the ground roll away beneath him, the rolling earth, the slow turn of field and grass and the distant trees. Everywhere he looked the world was luminous. And then the earth rolled away and he was in the air. He banked to the right and heard his cargo scrape across the floor. He climbed steadily and listened to the engine's throb and song and he watched out the small side window as the earth diminished below. There was no guilt in the air and no uncertainty. The moisture in the air beaded on the windshield. The small craft trembled like a living, sentient thing, an animal happy to be free again, but loyal, obeying all commands. He leveled out at nine thousand feet and set a new heading of forty degrees. Midway between Buffalo and Rochester he turned due north. For the first time in a long time he was able to close his eyes and smile.

■ ■ ■

He came down steep because of the trees at the near edge of the lake. The crosswind was tricky here, and for a moment when he was close enough to the water to see the white heads of the breeze-riffled waves he considered a flyby, but at the last moment he throttled back to idle and flared and brought it down with a hard bump that sent his heavy cargo bouncing across the floor.

Both men groaned and mumbled and Parris fought hard to hold the Cessna's line as it sluiced across the water, bucking over the riffled surface. But there was plenty of water and he had never really been worried. Any number of things could have happened, but it was bad practice to worry about them until something did.

He revved the engine then and taxied toward the northern shoreline. It was a glacier-gouged lake with gradually sloping sides that allowed him to pull up close to the grassy bank. He cut the engine and popped open his door. The air was sweet and cool and scented with pine. For a while he could hear nothing but the roar of the now-dead engine, until finally this faded too and he heard the waves lapping against the floats and then a loon somewhere off across the lake.

He was in the province of Quebec, approximately two hundred miles west-northwest of Montreal, the same distance northeast of Toronto. According to his maps there were no towns or settlements within a day's brisk walk. There were numerous rivers and lakes and deep forests, and what surprises they contained was anybody's guess.

Along this same shoreline he had watched a wolverine be torn apart by wolves.

Even with death in the air it seemed a beautiful place, serene and restorative. But you didn't come here for your health, he reminded himself. So get on with it.

He removed the handcuffs from around Best's and Diffenbaugh's ankles and slipped them into his belt. He took Best by the arm and dragged him toward the door. "Now, listen to me," he said. "Slide your feet around here," and he dragged the man's legs into position over the edge of the door. "Now sit up. Okay, pay attention. When you hop out you're going to land in about two and a half feet of water. It's going to be cold. If you turn the wrong way, it will only get deeper. So I'm going to jump out behind you and pull you in the right direction. You'd better hop for all you're worth, because if you fight me I'm liable to just push you facedown and leave you there. You understand?"

Best nodded stiffly.

"Then let's go." He pushed Best out the door and jumped out behind him. He dragged him to the bank and told him when to hop up onto the grass. Then he led him well back from the shoreline and told him to lie down in the grass.

"Now I'm going back for your colleague," Parris told him. "You're free to get up and wander off wherever you wish. But I wouldn't advise it."

He returned to the plane for Diffenbaugh. By the time he led the big man to where the librarian was still lying, quivering like a just-dropped fawn, Parris was drenched in perspiration.

"You're going on a diet, whether you like it or not," he said to Diffenbaugh, and pushed him roughly onto the ground.

Next he removed a pocket knife from his trousers and knelt beside the librarian. He cut away the man's clothes and piled them up in the grass until Best was wearing nothing but duct tape. He then did the same for Diffenbaugh, inadvertently nicking the man three times as he rolled and bucked in protest. The fourth nick was not an accident, but it was the one that quieted the printer down.

Then Parris dragged the men back to back. He snapped a handcuff around Best's right wrist, then pulled hard on the empty cuff, forcing the librarian's arm between his own legs until his hand was cupping his own rectum. Parris seized Diffenbaugh's taped wrists and forced them between his legs and then snapped the cuff around the printer's right wrist. Even if they managed somehow to work free of the duct tape they would find themselves in a very awkward position. If they were contortionists they might eventually get their hands out from between their legs, but they would still be shackled wrist to wrist. In any case, that day's walk to civilization was going to take them several extra days. Especially barefoot and naked. There were lots of mosquitoes already and soon there would be more. And when the sun set behind the trees tonight, the temperature would drop into the thirties.

They had better walk fast, Parris thought.

Finished, he knelt not far from the men and gazed out across the lake. He pulled a long blade of grass and stretched it between his thumbs, then cupped his thumbs to his mouth and blew a thin stream of air between them. Depending on the thickness of the grass, the sound it produced could range from high and shrill to a baritone, almost rumbling bleat. Parris blew across the grass and did a fair imitation of a wood duck's broken, rising whistle. With eyes closed he could almost hear the birds coming in over the water, the wing flutter and agile splashdown.

Two minutes later he tore the blade of grass in half and let the pieces fall. "Well," he said aloud, but he did not yet turn to face Diffenbaugh and Best. Another half-minute passed.

And then he chuckled softly. "I'm sitting here trying to think of something brilliant to say to you two, some words of wisdom to help you put your lives into perspective. But I'm drawing a blank, so . . . I guess you're on your own."

He pushed himself to his feet, but continued to face the lake. "Remorse is easy," he said to no one in particular, "but it seldom fixes what has already been broken."

The last thing he did was to peel the strips of duct tape off their eyes. Both men blinked and squinted in the brightness.

"I've brought you to a beautiful place," Parris told them. "I hope you appreciate it."

He picked up their clothing then and went back to the water and waded back to the plane. He climbed inside and started the engines and taxied to the far end of the lake. He made one hard-banking turn from a hundred feet above them, looking out his window at the two curled figures squinting into the sky, their bodies white and fetal against the lush grasses, then small and smaller and finally indistinguishable as the plane climbed above them, disappearing against the sun.

▪ ▪ ▪

Immediately the doubts began, but he could not let them alter his course. He had promised Best a chance, and now he had it. A better chance than Tony had been given. Better than the chances given to the children in the videotapes in Best's closet. Better than the chances given the thousands of lives demeaned and ruined for the insatiable pleasure of others.

So you left them there for Sasquatch to find, he told himself.

No, Sasquatch is a vegetarian.

Then it will be the same cleanup crew that makes sure the Sasquatch's bones are never found. The wolves and wolverines and coyotes and bears and dogs. The lynx and bobcat. The buzzards and crows and flies and mosquitoes. The all-forgiving earth.

He pushed the little plane into a climb so steep that the yoke rattled in his hands. He was surrounded by scalded blue sky, he and his craft less than a thorn against the firmament, less than a splinter. Far below, too small to see, lay the fruit of his morning. It was the biggest thing he had ever done. Maybe the best. Maybe the worst. Probably both extremes at once. Even so, he recognized it as a mere gesture in the overall scheme of things. Not that he was conceding the actual existence of a scheme, a deliberate and conscious formula to this chaos of life. But he would concede that lines had been drawn, sides chosen up. And there he was leveling off at eleven thousand feet with one wingtip on each side, his course anything but straight and sure. What he had done this morning was mere gesture, he admitted this to himself. But in a world without recourse it was something else too. In a world without recourse the gesture *is* the action—the refusal; the affirmation. If a man is conscious he must make such a gesture now and then. He must remind himself that he is more than a stone or a tree or a dog. He must now and then point his finger at the merciless engine of the world, must shake his fist at the target of his discontent, and mutter or shout, if only to himself, with love and murder raging in his heart, I will not be denied.

He had always wondered what he would do to Spangler when he caught him. Whether he would have the resources left after all these years to do anything at all. And now he knew.

And now you've bitched yourself for good, he thought. You've finally started that long, deep fall. From purgatory to hell, one way. Your ticket's punched, there's no turning back. It had to happen sooner or later, Mr. Parris. And now you're on your way.

Still, strangely, he could not escape the way he felt. His regret was vast, as vast as the noon sky, yet just as weightless. His destruction was complete, but he was not afraid. He could put the small plane into a vertical dive if he wished, nose to ground, or he could just as easily continue on and make a picture-perfect touchdown on the tarmac. Any choice made would be the correct one.

■ ■ ■

He refueled near Peterborough, a hundred miles northeast of Toronto, then continued on across Lake Ontario and New York and into Pennsylvania. His sense of exaltation was subdued by his touchdown on the tarmac, by the noise and the smell of all the acccoutrements of man, and he drove home with that same mild disorientation he had when coming out of the wilderness after a long shoot, of having to readjust to the world again, to polite fraternization with all the things he feared or despised.

This time he did not go into his editing room for a few hours of decompression. There was no film to view, no work to process. He sat in his living room with the curtains drawn and a glass of bourbon in his hand and felt a slow gray depression settle into him. He was very tired now and thought perhaps he should take a nap. But it was three in the afternoon and Diana was probably sitting on the edge of her bed in the Jamestown Holiday Inn, staring out the window at the inarticulate river, tapping her fingers on the mattress, nervous for his return.

He dialed the Holiday Inn and gave the room number to the desk clerk. After six rings the desk clerk came back on and asked if he would like to leave a message.

"Just tell her that Mac phoned, and that I'll be waiting at home for her call," he said.

He drank the rest of his bourbon and then a second one. Afterward he took a hot shower and filled the bathroom with steam. He wrapped a towel around himself and lay on his bed and stared at the ceiling.

Waiting isn't your strong suit, he told himself. But for now he had no choice. As soon as Diana returned they would discuss what to do with Diffenbaugh's car. He thought he would probably drive it to Cleveland or Pittsburgh, with Diana following in the Jeep. They would leave the car on an appropriate street, a street where the vehicle was likely to disappear within twenty-four hours, either part by part or all at once. He would put the bag of money in Diana's hands and leave its disposition to her. She was better equipped intuitively to track Miranda down than he was. As for himself, he would file this week away in his memory as if it had never happened. He might summon it up from time to time in the darkest hours of his despair, might glance at it for some kind of sustenance as if it were a magazine review of work well done, but for the most part he was glad to have it over with. Glad to get back to his life again, such as it was. Back to the routine.

But first Diana had to return. Why wasn't she waiting in the hotel room as he had requested? Had she gone out for a walk, for something to eat, for diversion from her own frantic thoughts? What if she had had a change of conscience? What if she had gone to the police? What if she disappeared and he never saw or heard from her again?

Parris sat up on his bed. He could see himself in the mirror on his dresser. He looked old and tired and maybe a little bit crazy. "Your mind is a roomful of idiots," he told his reflection, "all having hysterical conversations with their imaginary friends."

He telephoned the hotel again, but Diana was still not in. "Did she pick up my last message?" he asked. No, she hadn't returned yet. It was just after five and she hadn't returned yet. Parris instructed the desk clerk to cancel the message and to tell Diana that he would see her at the hotel around seven.

"Tell her to wait there until I arrive. With extra emphasis on the word *wait*."

He dressed quickly and went back outside. He popped the hood on Diana's car and pulled the distributor cap and tossed it onto the seat of his truck as he climbed in behind the wheel. Just in case, he told himself.

In case of what?

He could not answer that, so he tuned the radio to an oldies station and turned it up loud and drowned out everything except his sneering and wordless doubts.

▪ ▪ ▪

She had not checked out but her bags were gone and she had already settled the room bill, paying in cash for one additional night. She had left no message for Parris and no indication that she intended to return. He stood at the window looking out on the darkening city and asked himself where she had gone.

She had taken everything that belonged to her, but nothing of his. Then he looked for the keys to the Jeep but they were not in the room. All right, she took the Jeep, he thought. Also the videotape. She had taken the Jeep and the videotape.

Again he went to the window and looked out. Now the lights from the traffic crossing the bridge were reflected on the river, the yellow of headlights and the red of taillights. The lights were fluid and alive on the surface of the dirty water, wiggling eels of illumination, slender squirming threads of fire.

And then he knew where she had gone.

▪ ▪ ▪

He saw the scorched sky from two miles outside Brazelton, a soft red glow, a blush against the black. All streets within a block of Arthur Best's former home were blocked by firetrucks and police vehicles and by people crowding for a look. He stayed there only long enough to confirm what he already knew, to watch a shower of sparks swirl into the sky in a miniature tornado only to scatter at the top of the gyre, disperse, drift apart, and wink out one by one. Even from a block away, with the window down in his truck he could feel the heat of the fire on his face. He wondered if Diana was out there somewhere, feeling it too. It was a cleansing heat, cauterizing. He thought of the Senecas and of the fires they had built around their cemetery when it was being relocated. The purifying uses of smoke and flame. The evacuation of evil spirits, evil thoughts, and evil deeds. Everything carried away on the rising heat. Everything dispersed into the vastness of the heavens.

He drove back to the hotel room with the windows down and the sweet scent of smoke riding with him all the way.

■ ■ ■

He went into the hotel bar and there she was, sitting alone in a booth near the dance floor. The bandstand was empty and the only other customers were four men in business suits at the bar. Karaoke was playing loudly on the big-screen TV, but nobody was singing along with it. Parris walked to the booth and slid in across from her.

"Can't I leave you alone for a minute?" he asked.

She lifted her drink off the table and held it toward him, something clear with a greenish tint in a tall frosted glass. "This is so good," she said. "Taste?"

He shook his head. "How many of those have you had?"

"Not as many as I'm going to."

He nodded and smiled. She could have whatever she needed.

"I was worried about you," she told him.

"I'm still worried about you."

"You want to be my big brother?" she asked.

He waited too long to answer.

"We could have an incestuous relationship," she said.

"I think I'd better get a drink and join you."

"I think you'd better."

Two minutes later he settled in across from her again. He sipped his bourbon and let the warmth in his throat emanate out in all directions.

"Why did you take your bags and pay for the room in advance?" he asked.

"In case I screwed up somehow. Got caught. Trapped inside. Whatever."

"You're too clever for that," he told her.

She smiled. "I'm a lot like you."

"Too much. It's scary."

"We make a good team."

"Don't even think it," he said.

Again she smiled. She looked at him with soft, sparkling eyes. After a while her smile faded. "Should you tell me what happened?"

"Nothing happened."

"Where did you go for so long?"

"I just went home for a while. Took a little ride in my plane."

"Where to?" She was trying very hard for an air of nonchalance.

"North," he told her. "Out and beyond the Gitche Gummee. Up where the wild things are."

"You'll have to take me up sometime."

"There are lots of places to go. We don't have to go there."

"No," she said. "I wouldn't want to go there."

They smiled at each other and sipped their drinks.

Finally she asked, "And what of our friends?"

"We're not the kind of people who have friends," he said.

"That's right, we don't. We just have each other."

He flinched and looked away. "Let's try not to talk like that."

She kicked the side of his leg. "Oh, grow up," she told him.

They sipped their drinks then and sat there smiling in the neon-shattered darkness. After a while a song he knew came on the karaoke, and he turned toward the TV as if toward someone who had whispered to him from the past, and he listened to Hoagy Carmichael's "Star Dust" and he watched the words to the song as they moved across the screen, ghostwords, pale and white and flickering, and he felt the great deep hollowness come over him again because nothing he could ever do could take him back to where he wished to be.

"I forgot to tell you," Diana said, and she brought her purse up to the table. When he looked at her she seemed somehow farther away in the darkness.

"I finally have a picture of Tony," she said, and she handed him a photograph in a small metal frame.

"Yes," said Parris as he tried to see it in the insufficient light. "And doesn't he look fine."